The Explorers

GW01445257

The Explorers

Marion Smisson

Hornby Publishing

Copyright © 2014 by Marion Smisson

All rights reserved. No part of this publication may be reproduced or transmitted in any form or by any means, electronic or mechanical including photocopying, recording or any information storage or retrieval system, without prior permission in writing from the publisher.

The right of Marion Smisson to be identified as the author of this work has been asserted by her in accordance with the Copyright, Designs and Patents Act 1988

First published in the United Kingdom in 2014
by Hornby Publishing

All the characters in this book are fictitious and any resemblance to real persons, living or dead, is entirely coincidental.

The moral right of the author has been asserted

ISBN 978-0-9553267-2-1

Produced by The Choir Press

PART ONE

The young man and woman stood on the summit of the mountain in the early morning sunshine. They were tall, fair-haired, fit and wealthy. Dressed in expensive ski suits with the best skis, and had never known poverty. Wealthy parents, expensive homes and schools. Lucrative career and a full rich life. Lucky people, who frequented Kitzbühel in winter and the Mediterranean in summer. Happy, with no cares in the world. What the glossy magazines would describe as 'the Beautiful People', with secure lives ahead of them. The man was talking and laughing, but the woman turned and skied elegantly down to a dip in the mountainside, blonde hair flowing behind her. Her companion followed and slid to a well-executed halt, his skis spraying snow around him. The couple talked animatedly, their ski tips close. Then he fell.

Jemima watched his body turn and tumble onto the snow below. Hearing his screams she covered her ears; she felt only relief when the screams stopped. She gazed down as the pure white snow turned crimson round his twisted leg.

Eventually she turned her back on the black cliffs and gracefully skied down the steep slope, deciding to avoid the black run and take the longer way down the mountain so the silent beauty of the high precipitous peaks could claim her thoughts: the white glistening slopes in the early morning sun and the majesty of the Alps.

How peaceful the haven of her beautiful home would be for her and her children without the repressed anger and tension of her husband. No longer would there be the sense of fear, wondering what Rupert's mood might be. Would he come through the door acting the charming, smiling, manipulative master of the house, or angry and ready to shout at his family? Now no more, thank God. Rupert was about the most unsuitable name with which he could have been christened. It was a cuddly teddy bear name, not suited to his aggressive, spoilt child personality.

There were no other skiers on the slopes from whom she could ask for help, and all too soon the bottom of the ski lift came into view and she came to a stop in a flurry of snow beside the lift attendant.

'Can you speak English?' she asked, the anxiety clear in her voice.

The Austrian official casually clipping ski passes nodded.

'My husband has fallen off the cliff. I think it's above the North Col. Please, please can you send help?'

His casual manner vanished and he was on the telephone. Calmly he asked her to come into the office and wait. A few minutes later she heard the helicopter take off and watched as it sped towards the North Col, the stretcher hanging below the fuselage.

A taxi took her to the hospital. She was anxious about the children, but their nanny would have taken them to the nursery slopes and they would not be worried. The hospital was in a neighbouring town twenty minutes away and there she had to wait in sterile surroundings until a white-coated doctor came to tell her in fragmented English what she already knew. Rupert was dead.

The doctor was very sorry. 'Do you wish to view the body? No, I mean do you want to see your husband? He is at peace.'

'Yes. Though I would prefer to remember him alive and skiing. But I need to identify him.'

Fortunately tears came readily. The doctor took her gently by the arm and guided her to a white-shrouded bed. She hastily glanced at the battered head; it was disfigured by blood-red cuts, but the fair hair was unmistakable. 'Yes. That's my husband, Rupert.'

A nurse gently led her away and in halting English explained, 'The police and the British Consul will visit you to arrange what you wish to do with his body. Take a statement and funeral arrangements. You understand?'

'Yes, of course.'

After a few more formalities the taxi took her back to her suite at the hotel. Her thoughts, which so far had been mainly of relief, now became full of dread. Firstly she had to tell the children. And the nanny; how would she react? Then there was the hotel. Would the staff know? News travelled fast in a small town. Her booking ran out in two days, along with the tickets for the plane flight. Could the family escape to a peaceful, quiet home in two days?

The marble steps up to the glass doors of the five-star hotel were a daunting prospect but Jemima held her head high and swept into the foyer, past the tall Christmas trees decorated with golden baubles, and up to the reception desk. The expression on the manager's face said that he knew. He gave his condolences in his usual greasy manner and offered any help he could. Jemima thanked him and turned away, paused and turned back to the desk. 'Do you think you could retrieve my skis and poles from the ski lift? And then bring sandwiches to our suite?'

'Of course, Madam. Cheese or ham?'

'My husband has just died; I don't care.'

'Sorry, Madam.'

And she marched away to the lift.

William and Charlotte looked up with worried expressions on their faces when she entered the suite.

'Where have you been?' William asked.

'I had to go to the hospital, darlings. Where's Nanny?'

'In her bedroom.'

'Good. There's something awful I have to tell you and I'd rather she wasn't here. I can tell her later.' So Jemima told the children what had happened above the North Col.

They were stunned, on the verge of tears, and she ruffled their blond hair and held them close. Together they felt comfort from each other. Then William, the elder at eight years, pulled away.

'I won't be hit again?'

'No. You will never be hit again.'

'And no one will shout at us?' asked Charlotte.

'Well, I might.'

'That's different,' and their comforting hug continued.

William's blue eyes looked up enquiringly. 'Will I have to go back to that awful school?'

Jemima wondered about the prep school on which Rupert's superior parents had insisted. She remembered her mother-in-law simpering, 'Rupert was so happy there. Head Boy and Captain of Rugby.' But William wasn't Rupert. Maybe now she could assert her authority.

'I'll think about that, Will.'

4

There was an obsequious knock at the door and a waiter glided in with their sandwiches. The children tucked into these. Hunger seemed to be more important to them than their father's death, thought Jemima. Perhaps reaction would set in later. She helped herself to a whisky from the minibar. Now to tackle the nanny.

Nanny was good at her job, but no Mary Poppins. Her talents lay in other directions, as Jemima had realised when she had pointed out to Rupert there was no need of her services with both children at school, but Rupert had insisted. Jemima didn't have to wonder why his half of the double bed was empty most nights. She hadn't bothered to confront him about his liaison; she was too used to the situation. The first time it had happened he had spent a weekend with Michaela Jenkins-Smythe, the wife of his best friend. Jemima had demanded to know what had happened and Rupert had totally lost it and she had ended up with a black eye. By then he had her where he wanted her; she was too frightened to question him again.

'Kids, Tina's in her bedroom?' asked Jemima.

'Yes, and crying,' replied Charlotte with her mouth full of ham sandwich.

Tina couldn't have known about the accident as she had been on the nursery slopes in the morning and the hotel staff wouldn't have mentioned it in front of the children.

Jemima politely knocked on the nanny's door and went in. It was not surprising that Rupert had fancied her. Tina's young nubile figure was shown off very well as she sprawled on the bed in tight jeans and T-shirt, her long blonde hair in disarray. Sitting beside her on the bed Jemima asked, 'Why are you crying, Tina?'

Tina pulled some tissues from a box by the bed and sat

up, wiping her eyes. She looked a little shame-faced, but came straight to the point.

'You know all about me and Rupert. Well, he's ditched me for some old rich cow. How could he?' The tears started to flow again.

Jemima patted her on the shoulder, and said gently. 'Yes I know,' then got up from the bed and went to the window to watch the gently falling snow. 'Unusually for him he asked me to go skiing with him very early this morning. He wanted to show off about his latest conquest. Why he thought I would be interested after all this time, I don't know. Probably wanted to make me feel inadequate. He was good at that. He enjoyed it. But I wouldn't call Susannah Wellington an old cow. Rich, maybe, but she can't be more than thirty. Her husband's in banking and Rupert wanted to get his foot in the door,' and she smiled. 'But that may be the wrong way to phrase it.' She turned back to the dishevelled girl on the bed. 'I'm afraid I have some very bad news. Rupert is dead. He fell off a cliff above the North Col. I'm sorry,' and she left the room. Probably Tina would care more than anyone else, except Rupert's adoring parents, and that would have to be her next hurdle.

Felicity and Gerald Somerville-Thomas were wealthy and liked to make everyone aware of it. The wealth had started with Gerald's grandfather, who had been a gifted craftsman making expensive boots and shoes for the gentry. Then the name had been plain Thomas. The Thomas boot and shoe shop soon became two shops, then three in local market towns, until there was a string of them all over the south-west. His son married well to the daughter of a local farming landowner and her name,

Somerville, was added to the Thomas. There was also the addition of a son, Gerald. With the hyphened name and son at public school, Gerald's father felt his family had raised their station in life, and in due course Gerald married Felicity, whose father was the local Member of Parliament. Now with more of an eye on status and money than on making good shoes, Gerald sold out to a nation-wide chain and retired to the country to enjoy pretending to be a farmer, whilst others did the work.

Rupert was their only child. He was a strong healthy boy, intelligent and sporty. Tall, fair-haired, blue-eyed, he could be charming when he wanted to be and soon realised he could get exactly what he wanted by this means. His parents revelled in his progress, doted on him until their lives revolved about him. No one had ever said 'no' to him. After public school and inevitably Oxford, Rupert went to work in the City and became an expert in 'investments'. At the same time he met Jemima, who had recently left school and worked in a same firm as a dogsbody. They first fell into conversation when they realised they had grown up in the same town, Bristol. Jemima, enjoying her first taste of freedom from home, fell for Rupert's charms and they were soon married.

Jemima had soon realised that no wife would be good enough for Felicity and Gerald Somerville-Thomas's only son, and she had now to contact this couple and tell them the light of their life was now dead.

'Can we go skiing again, Mummy?' asked William.

'In a while, kids. First I have to telephone Granny and Grandpa to tell them about Daddy's accident. It will make them very unhappy. You two be quiet for a bit, watch TV or something, then we'll go out.'

'Is Daddy really not coming back?' asked Charlotte.

'No, I'm afraid he isn't.'

'Did it hurt when he fell off the cliff?'

'No,' lied her mother. 'It would have been like the time you fell off your bike and knocked yourself out.'

'That's all right, then.'

Perhaps Charlotte, at five, was too young to understand, Jemima thought as she went into her bedroom. Now for the phone call.

This was traumatic, as she had known it would be. Mrs Somerville-Thomas – Jemima could never think of her as Felicity – became hysterical and Jemima was handed over to Mr Somerville-Thomas, who listened with chilling attention. 'I'll ring you back when I've dealt with Felicity,' was his only comment. She tried to put herself in their position, think how they would feel, how she would feel if it were William or Charlotte, but it was impossible after the way they had treated her. If her father-in-law rang back and she was out with the children, too bad. And the same went for the police and the British Consul.

The trio spent a happy two hours on the nursery slopes, then took the cable car up the mountain and had hot chocolate and cream cakes in the café, looking at the view and picking out places they recognised. The three of them would now have time to get to know each other without tension and fear in the background. They played snowballs along the Christmas-illuminated streets of the old town, but Jemima quickly came down to earth when they had left the skis in the basement of the hotel and entered the foyer. The manager, grim-faced, told her the police were waiting in the bar and the Consul had been on the phone. The manager didn't like policemen in his hotel; it gave them a bad name. Jemima told the children not to worry, that this was what happened when there had been an accident, and sent them upstairs to Tina.

After fortifying herself with another whisky she joined the policemen and made a statement about her husband's fall. They seemed satisfied and told her there would be an inquest, then the body would be released for burial. This would take several days. When they had gone Jemima approached the manager and with her most charming smile asked if they would be able to stay until the inquest. The manager consulted his computer, discovered the suite would be vacant and became charming in turn, realising he would make some extra money. Anything she needed, please let him know. Would she be taking dinner in the dining room or prefer something in her room? Jemima didn't think she could cope with other guests' sympathetic comments and said she would ring room service later. Then the manager gave her a telephone message from the British Consul, who would visit her in the morning.

The phone was ringing as she returned to her suite. It was her father-in-law and where had she been all afternoon? Suddenly very tired, she replied she had been out with the children. Mr Somerville-Thomas found this very difficult to understand. Surely the children were too upset to go out. *I think not*, she thought.

Her mother-in-law came on the phone, hysterics over, and insisted on organising Rupert's funeral at their village church. She would arrange everything and Jemima felt, as she often did with Mrs Somerville-Thomas, that her own presence and feelings were irrelevant. As they were the true mourners it was perhaps appropriate. She said 'yes' and 'no' in the right places, wished them a comfortable 'good night' and rang off.

She found the children bathed and ready for bed, their

golden curls damp on their foreheads. The remains of boiled eggs from tea were on the table and Tina was now in control of herself. Jemima told Tina she was staying in for the evening and suggested Tina should go out and enjoy the nightlife, even if she didn't feel like it. Tina, looking relieved, collected her woolly hat, scarf, coat and left. Now Jemima relaxed, selected *Winnie-the-Pooh* from the bedside table and together the three of them enjoyed the old-fashioned comfortable stories. Charlotte was soon asleep but William was more restless. He wanted to talk about his father and was trying to remember things he had done with Rupert.

'I remember he took you to the zoo, once,' Jemima reminded him. 'I was in bed with flu.'

'Yes, that was great. The seals and penguins swimming. Then I got lost and went to the ticket office and he got very cross.'

'Oh dear.' Then she suggested, 'He took you to London on the train.'

'The train was good, but we spent most of the time in boring offices seeing people he wanted to see. But he did take me to the Tower of London to see the Crown Jewels.'

'You must have enjoyed that.'

'Yes, except he forgot to give me any lunch and I was so hungry.'

'Dads forget that kind of thing. At least you have some nice memories. The holidays we have had. Remember the good times,' and she kissed him goodnight.

Later she curled up in her solitary bed trying to remember the good times.

'Damn this machine,' Jemima cursed. *'The paper's jammed.'*

'Allow me to help you,' said a smooth cultured voice behind her. The young man bent down, opened up the machine and retrieved the ink-smeared tattered A4 paper.

'I was trying to do it double-sided, but this can't be the right way.'

'Try pressing this button.' He demonstrated and gave her several perfectly copied double-sided prints. He was tall, blond with intense blue eyes and wearing a well-tailored grey suit.

'Thanks,' she said with a smile. 'I'm finding all these machines so new. Even the word processor. At school we used electric typewriters. Now it's all WordPerfect.'

'Yes, computers have made a difference to the world. You've just started here?'

'I've been in London two months. It's very different to Bristol.'

'You're telling me. I'm from round there too. See you around.' And he wandered off down the office corridor. Even his broad back looked smart. He made her feel very young and naïve, although he was probably no more than five years older than she. Regaining her composure she proudly went back to her office with the perfect double-sided copies.

In the evening back at her new home in South Kensington she told her housemates of the gorgeous young man. It was her turn to cook, so it was spaghetti Bolognese, this being the only meal Jemima could make. The three of them, hungry after a day's work, had given up trying to be polite twiddling spaghetti round their forks and were shovelling it on their spoons.

The Three Furies, as they called themselves, had all been at school together. They hadn't the brains to go to university so had opted for the bright lights of London.

Jemima's father had bought the house as a good investment. Jemima had never been away from home before and
he felt happier filling the place with girls she knew. He
didn't want her sharing a house with just anybody and it
made collecting the rent easier.

'Tall and blond, you said, Jem?' asked Liz. 'What I
do is hang around the coffee machine and when a good-
looking man turns up pretend I don't know how to use
it. The pathetic act makes them feel manly and protective.'

'Like him helping with the photocopier.'

'You're getting the idea.' Even at their exclusive girls'
school, with no boys on tap as there would be at a
comprehensive, Liz had always had boyfriends and knew
how to handle them. Liz's mother had made sure she was
on the pill at sixteen. Jemima always ignored what went
on in Liz's bedroom at night.

Jemima had longed for boyfriends to show off about at
school, but as her interests were with the pony club and
show jumping not many boys were on the scene. She had
walked home from the bus stop a few times with a boy who
lived down the road and he had asked her out once. They
had gone to the cinema and then to a pub, but he had got
over-amorous for a first date and, after Jemima had pushed
him away, called her a 'stuck-up bitch'. She had avoided
him on the bus after that. Then there was a handsome
distant cousin she had fallen in love with at first sight. They
had met on sailing holidays in South Devon but he had
turned out to be very boring. She could only stand so much
talk of the sailing races he had won, and of tacking, jibing
and spinnakers. So she was patiently waiting for the right
man to come along.

The third housemate, Gwendolyn, was a mousy, quiet

girl and had a job at the British Museum. She spent her evenings reading Catherine Cookson novels, listening to Mozart and Beethoven. It had been some time before Jemima had realised Gwendolyn was stoned out of her mind on cannabis almost every evening. Despite their very different personalities the three girls got on well and enjoyed their meals together, swapping stories of their new experiences in the Big City.

Jemima tried Liz's technique with the coffee machine but it was always middle-aged men who came to her rescue, thinking that this attractive girl with long blonde hair could be their own daughter. Usually at lunchtime she went to the local sandwich bar to buy a snack. On this particular day she was debating between egg and cress or tuna and mayonnaise when a man behind her suggested, 'Have you tried the prawn cocktail?'

Jemima recognised the voice and turned to stare into his very blue eyes. 'I used to love having that as a starter when I was a kid. Yes, I'll order that. Take me back to childhood.' She watched as the assistant slapped butter on bread, prawns in Thousand Island dressing and salad on top.

She was lost as to what to say to the young man from the office, knowing this chance might not come again, and was about to stutter, 'Thanks,' but he smiled and said, 'It's a beautiful day. Let's take our sarnies down to the river and refresh your childhood memories.'

Clutching their lunches in brown paper bags, they walked down City alleyways to the Thames, found a bench on the Embankment, opposite the redundant Bankside Power Station, and exchanged childhood memories. They had both been to the restaurant that served prawn cocktails and the café with wicker chairs to eat ice cream sodas. They both knew the centre of Bristol and Clifton.

13

'Did you ever go to the museum?' he asked.

'Yes. I always had to see the giant elk that was stuck in an Irish bog thousands of years ago.'

'Me too. And I liked all the crystals and fossils.'

'Bet you went to the zoo.'

'The gorillas. The old silverback looking cross.' They laughed at their shared past.

'It's Saturday tomorrow,' he said. 'If you're not busy let's check out Regent's Park Zoo.'

'Oh, I'd love to,' Jemima said with enthusiasm. She couldn't believe her luck, or wait to tell Liz. 'By the way, what's your name?'

'Rupert Somerville-Thomas – rather a mouthful. And yours?'

'Jemima.'

Next morning in her sexiest jeans and shirt she met Rupert outside the zoo in Regent's Park. The zoo impressed them. So much to see, not only the animals but the 1930s curved concrete architecture of the penguins' home and Lord Snowdon's aviary. Later Rupert took her to an Italian restaurant in Hampstead, then produced tickets for an open-air concert beside the lake at Kenwood. In the moonlight they walked back, hand in hand, over the heath to Hampstead and the tube train. Jemima had never had such an exciting and romantic day in her life.

'You never told me your full name, yesterday. I think of you as Jemima Puddle-duck.'

Jemima giggled. 'It's quite appropriate. My surname is Poole.'

'Jemima Puddle-duck floating on her pool. Jemima Puddle-duck you'll remain.'

*

On Monday a dozen red roses were delivered to her home. 'Jemima Puddle-duck' was the name on the envelope. Liz and Gwendolyn were impressed and Jemima overexcited.

So the romance continued. Visits to the theatre, art galleries, candlelit dinners for two, picnics with his friends in Kew Gardens. Jemima was overwhelmed. Rupert was so charming, so funny. After two months he moved into the house in South Kensington. Jemima had never been happier. It was like a dream. Home, school and the pony club of her youth seemed a lifetime away. Although she had no men with whom she could compare Rupert, he was a good lover and she looked forward to evenings where 'bed' now had a different meaning.

Jemima stirred in her daydreaming, halfway between sleep and waking. Yes, there had been happy times, but had she been more attracted by the places to which he had taken her, the camaraderie with his friends? With the heady atmosphere of a summer in London she had been unable to take in Rupert's own character. He had always seemed happy, charming, desirable, but no one and nothing had thwarted life to make it difficult. That had all come later.

Now she had to cope with today, with the British Consul, and find out when she could take her children home. That was fine. What was different was Rupert's body. Should he be buried in Austria, or at expense be flown to Britain? Jemima was quite happy for him to be buried in Austria, as he had loved it there, but Felicity wanted him buried in the family churchyard. Having been told by the Consul that the price would be several thousand pounds, Jemima coldly suggested that the Somerville-Thomases should pay for it.

After consultation with the Consul, who only wanted to

15

get Rupert's body back to the UK along with his family as fast as possible, Jemima made a statement about the accident for the inquest and arrangements were put in hand to transport Rupert in his coffin back to England. This took time and Jemima with Tina amused the children on the ski slopes, both deliberately ignoring Susannah Wellington if she should ski past in an ungainly fashion. Jemima spent a few cherished hours skiing from the top of the mountain on black runs, enjoying the speed, the silence and the mountain heights. This might never happen again.

After a few days everything had been arranged. Jemima was relieved she and Rupert had had separate bank accounts. Rupert had given her a mean allowance for housekeeping and clothes so she wouldn't pry into his affairs. On his death his account had been closed, but she had had enough money in her account to pay for several extra nights on the hotel bill, though she was surprised at the cost. She had little idea of money matters as Rupert controlled the finances. Despite her protests he had made sure she knew nothing about them. Her only suspicions lurking at the back of her mind were about the lack of money after her father's death. Where was her father's money? Fear of Rupert had stopped her asking further.

She, Tina and the children were glad to be leaving Austria as the aeroplane rose over the snowy Alps. Death had taken away the image of winter sporting being a happy holiday. The children were subdued, and Tina was coming to terms with her lover's death. Jemima just felt empty.

The grey skies of England did little to relieve their feelings, but as the taxi dropped them outside their spacious home in the best part of Bristol Jemima felt her spirits rise. Here there would be peace, comfort, centrally heated warmth and no anger.

William wanted to collect the dog from the kennels, but it was too late; it would be an event for the morning. Tina helped the children unpack their bags, the TV was on, and Jemima heated up a pizza from the deep freeze. Life was returning to normal. Then the telephone rang. It was Rupert's parents. Jemima realised if she said she was so grief-stricken she couldn't cope with the funeral her parents-in-law would deal with everything, and she was content to let them get on with it. The pizza cooked and a comedy on TV, the four of them sat down to supper.

In the morning they collected Buster, the spaniel, from the kennels and gave him a good walk. The weekend intervened, then school loomed on Monday morning. The dreaded prep school for William.

Jemima rang the school secretary to explain the situation. She was very sympathetic but did mention that Mr Somerville-Thomas's cheque had bounced when he had paid the fees for the coming term. Given the circumstances Jemima suggested she would keep William at home until after the funeral and then money could be sorted out. William gave a great cheer and jumped up and down on the sofa when he was told.

The same thing happened when Jemima rang Charlotte's school. The cheque had bounced. So Charlotte was also home for the week. Jemima began to worry about money, then put it down to Rupert's bank account being frozen, as he was dead. Everything would turn out all right after the funeral on the Wednesday. That was the next hurdle.

Although mid-January, Wednesday was as bright as a spring day and a mockery to those who mourned. Snowdrops nodded in the churchyard and catkins hung on the hazel bushes. Jemima, dressed in long black coat and a sable fur hat, felt very alone as she stood in the front pew next to her in-laws who clung together in their grief. If only her own parents could have been there as support, but her father had died the previous year and her mother was in an old people's home. The service used old traditional words and the hymns, as she had expected, were Victorian. An old school friend of Rupert's gave a pompous address about his virtues, then came the interment, before tea back at the Somerville-Thomas manor house.

Other mourners uttered the usual sympathetic clichés to her and asked after the children. She replied in the same vein, still feeling empty, behaving like an automaton. Liz, her former housemate, was there with her second husband and their supportive comments kept her going. Gwendolyn, her other housemate, was also a comfort. Her rather butch female partner, inappropriately called Cissy, accompanied her. Fascinated, Jemima realised lesbians were something with which she had yet to come to terms.

Her best friend, Carrie, who would really have helped her through this ordeal, was away holidaying in the Caribbean, and knew nothing of Rupert's death. Carrie lived a few houses away in their avenue of homes designed by a prestigious architect, and had helped her through the crises of the last years. Carrie had been the one to take her to hospital for Charlotte's birth, and had shouted 'push' at the right times. Carrie had been the one to put steak on Jemima's black eye when Rupert had beaten her up. Carrie seemed to understand.

Something that surprised her was how few of Rupert's business friends were present. The two girls from the office were there looking sad, and the solicitor – an elderly man with a gentle voice, called Mr Dawes – but none of the smooth grey-suited men and their svelte wives to whom she had had to be charming since she and Rupert had settled back in Bristol eight years ago.

The ordeal of tea over, Jemima kissed her parents-in-law goodbye and promised to bring William and Charlotte to see them soon.

'How is poor Olive?' asked Felicity in a condescending manner.

This touched an open nerve with Jemima. Partly guilt as she hadn't been to see her mother, and partly because Felicity felt Alzheimer's disease was akin to madness and not talked about in polite society. Jemima hadn't been to see her mother or tell her about Rupert's death, as an elderly woman with dementia wouldn't understand. Maybe she should delay the peace and comfort of her own home to visit the old people's home.

As she was leaving through the metal-studded oak front door Mr Dawes touched her on the arm.

'I need to talk to you. Firstly about Rupert's will, and also about his business affairs. Could you come and see me tomorrow morning?'

Jemima's mind was elsewhere thinking about her mother, but realising she needed to know about the will, she agreed.

'Rivendell' – how inappropriate, thought Jemima – was a nursing home for the retired. It was an old Victorian house looking out over the Clifton Downs. A view the residents didn't seem to appreciate, just staring into space. There was every facility from lifts to bath hoists, so the residents were well cared for. In Olive's comfortable room she was watching *Neighbours* without comprehension.

It took Olive some time to remember that Jemima was her daughter. The daughter she had once cared for so devotedly. Then she brightened and Jemima talked about the children, about their holiday and lastly of Rupert's death, knowing it would mean nothing.

'Who's Rupert?' her mother asked.

Looking back, Jemima realised her mother's illness had started many years ago. Her lack of interest in the wedding; letting Felicity take over. She had always been pleased to see her grandchildren, smiled at them, and enjoyed watching others play with them. Her husband, Henry, had struggled on for two years until he couldn't cope, and here she was at Rivendell. Quiet, still smiling uncomprehendingly. Olive couldn't take in the fact that Henry had died from a heart attack, but occasionally asked where he was, making Jemima wonder how much she remembered.

That had been a terrible time. She had gone round to see her father, lonely living on his own, and found him dead on the kitchen floor. Cold on the chill tiled floor. The doctor had said it was a heart attack, quick and sudden. Had he been stressed? Of course he had, Jemima had thought. His wife had dementia.

Rupert had been very considerate and offered to pay for Olive's care. This had surprised Jemima as she had thought Olive had inherited enough from Henry for all her worldly needs. It wasn't until she was clearing her childhood and parents' home that she came upon business papers and realised Rupert had persuaded her father to sell the South Kensington house and to re-mortgage his own substantial home for Rupert's own selfish investment purposes. These investments seemed to have floundered. No wonder Henry had suffered a heart attack! All his hard work, the ideals in which he believed turned to nothing by Rupert's ruthless smart-talking tactics. As well as the womanising and the violence she had added treachery to Rupert's portfolio.

Having talked to her mother for fifteen minutes, holding her hand, she felt it was time to get back to William and Charlotte. First she had to tell the nursing home's matron of Rupert's death as he had been paying the bill.

The matron looked severe. 'I'm afraid, Mrs Somerville-Thomas, your late husband's last cheque has been returned.'

'I expect the bank account has been frozen. That happens when someone dies.'

'You will have to make other arrangements if the bill cannot be paid.'

The matron was so used to death she didn't care. Just crossed another name off her waiting list. In desperation Jemima wrote out a cheque for a month of her mother's care, on her own account. She could still use her own personal account, which had had money transferred into it every month for her clothes and household expenses. She hoped she was not overdrawn, but it was always difficult after the Christmas extravaganza. No doubt Mr Dawes would sort all the money troubles out tomorrow. Rupert's business had nothing to do with her. She had always been excluded from this, as with all money matters. Then she thought about her father's money and started to worry.

At home she found the children cheerfully playing Snakes and Ladders in front of a log fire with Tina reading a magazine. It was good to be home. The two women had resented each other for months, but with Rupert gone they felt a companionship in bereavement and

Rupert's faithlessness. They both put the children to bed, relaxed by warm baths and stories. Later in the kitchen Jemima thanked Tina for looking after the children whilst she had been at Rupert's funeral.

'Now I have the difficult task of giving you notice. I hate doing this as the children love your company and you have been so helpful over the last few days. Do I owe you a month's salary?'

'Actually it's weekly and Rupert hasn't paid me since early December. I don't mind. At present I have nowhere to go. Could I stay till I find a new post? I'll start looking in the paper.'

'Of course. I shall be glad of you here tomorrow, as I have to see the solicitor and the kids aren't at school. But can I pay the bill? Can I pay you? We've got through the last couple of weeks together – sadness and bitterness put aside. Please stay until you find something. Your references will be glowing.'

This particular problem solved, the next hurdle with Mr Dawes could wait until tomorrow.

With the children in bed and Tina's exit at some stage settled, Jemima poured herself a large whisky and sat gazing into the flames of the fire. Her mind went back to the funeral service that day and the last church occasion at the manor. It had been their wedding day.

'Something old, something new, something borrowed, something blue. Where's that garter, Liz?'

'In the box on the bed. Who gave it to you, Jem?'

'The girls in the office.'

'What a shame. I thought it might be another romantic admirer.'

Liz and Gwendolyn were in aquamarine bridesmaid

dresses and helping Jemima into her ivory satin gown embroidered with pearls.

'You look fantastic,' whispered Gwendolyn, and Jemima felt fantastic. What a day.

It had not bothered her that Felicity Somerville-Thomas had taken over the organisation of the wedding. From the first time Rupert had taken her down to the manor for the weekend to meet his parents she had understood Felicity was in charge. She was made to realise she was very privileged to be her son's fiancée. Gerald also toed the line, and was a genial host. They were insistent that the wedding should be at their local church, and then the reception could be in the manor house and gardens.

The following weekend Rupert had been introduced to Jemima's own parents. Olive and Henry Poole had married in their thirties. They had never expected children, so Jemima had been a wonderful surprise ten years later. She was premature, tiny, might not survive, so she became very precious, cosseted. How else could she be kept alive? She had the best costly education and every whim granted. Ponies and holidays. Fortunately Henry could afford this as he was in charge of business investment for the South-West division of one of the big banks. Henry knew about business. Olive just lived for Jemima.

This visit included a dinner at the manor so the two sets of parents could meet. The two fathers got on well with a common interest in local businesses, and the three men talked of financial matters throughout the meal. Apart from the wedding the three women had little in common, but this did not matter as Felicity gushed over Rupert's glowing past and there was little need of conversation from either Olive or Jemima. Olive had the look of a frightened rabbit caught in the glare of a car's headlights.

She would have been far happier sitting at home by the fire with her embroidery.

The old medieval church, awash with pink and white flowers, was the perfect setting for the well-known phrases of the marriage service. The church bells rang out as the guests in their colourful finery made the short walk to the manor where they mingled, glasses of champagne in their hands, amongst the bright dahlias and Michaelmas daisies of the gardens. Felicity, in flowing silk, decorated with a corsage of poisonous-looking green orchids, and a large feathered hat, played the hostess superbly and was in her element. Olive, in a beige suit, did her best to blend into the background. Her husband was talking to business people he knew, Jemima animatedly talking to her friends, so the mother of the bride sat quietly in the garden enjoying the flowers. Olive found deafness kept her apart from other people, but having always been solitary she didn't care.

Photographs over, the guests moved in on the buffet lunch with quiet madrigal music. There were the speeches with jokes and guffaws of laughter. Later, with more laughter and shouting as Rupert's car was decorated with beer cans and streamers, Jemima and her new husband vanished for two wonderful weeks in Italy. She would never forget the quality of light over Amalfi or the deep blue of the Mediterranean Sea.

What a pity everything went wrong, thought Jemima. Life in London had been so happy. Just the two of them in South Kensington with Liz and Gwendolyn in the background.

But maybe Liz hadn't been so much in the background.

Jemima remembered her looking slightly awkward and guilty on a couple of occasions. She had always had a reputation, to the extent that one of her conquests called her 'The Nymph'. Now it was water under the bridge, and Jemima prepared her mind to see Mr Dawes in the morning.

The solicitor was not alone when his secretary ushered Jemima into the office. Another man sat on a mock Chippendale chair with a pile of folders in front of him on the highly polished table. He was introduced as Mr Wilmott, Rupert's accountant, and he looked angry.

Mr Dawes asked the secretary to get them coffee and then started on the terms of Rupert's will. The terms were quite simple; everything was left to Jemima. She sighed with relief. The accountant glared at his coffee cup.

The gentle elderly solicitor looked apologetic. 'I'm afraid it's not that simple. I'm sorry; you've had enough bad news with Rupert dying. Financially Mr Wilmott has more bad news.'

Mr Wilmott turned his glare on Jemima. 'Your husband was bankrupt, Mrs Somerville-Thomas. Not only that, he has made many other people lose large amounts of money.'

'Obviously you, for one,' answered Jemima, surprised at her own level-headed response.

'Yes. Your husband came back here from London eight years ago worth millions after some great investments he made after leaving his old firm in London. He was greatly respected. Businessmen followed his lead. When he said "invest" they did so. Your father was one of them. People trusted his judgment. A year ago it all went wrong. Investments in companies in South America dipped. There was an earthquake near mining regions, mudslides. Wars

25

between big drug dealers. General unrest. The market collapsed and your husband was deeply involved.

'It then transpired Mr Somerville-Thomas's big investment coup came through insider dealing. If the fraud squad had caught up with him he would be in prison now. No doubt you would rather visit him in prison than have him dead, but many people round here have ill feeling towards him.'

'My husband totally excluded me from his business. I'm sorry if you have been let down, but it has nothing to do with me.'

Mr Dawes quietly intervened. 'Mrs Somerville-Thomas?'

She looked at him in surprise. He always called her Jemima.

'I don't think you quite understand,' he said. 'Your husband didn't run a limited company, where debt is limited to the company. He was the company and all his debts are yours.'

'Mine?'

'I'm sorry, but that's what Rupert has left you.'

She turned to Mr Wilmott. 'You're an accountant. Why didn't you warn him?'

'He didn't listen to advice. He knew he was right.'

'Yes, that sounds like Rupert. That killing on the stock market when we came here went to his head.'

Why was she being so reasonable? Just to conform, keep the stiff upper lip, not let the side down? No, something deep down in her being was taking over. Something in her genes made her stand up for herself.

'So, Mr Wilmott, tell me the worst. Have Rupert's children and I got anything?'

'No,' said Mr Wilmott with relish.

'Have you anything constructive to say, Mr Wilmott?'

'Just deal with the bailiffs politely. They don't like the job.'

'Then they can always get another one. Goodbye, Mr Wilmott. I'd like to talk to Mr Dawes.'

The solicitor, not used to these situations, asked for more coffee from his secretary. Together they came to the conclusion Jemima and the children had nothing. The house would go, and everything that would pay off Rupert's debt. Maybe she would be able to keep her car. Then there were the questions of Olive, schools for the children and, most importantly, somewhere to live.

Jemima, having left the solicitor, had so much to think about. After eight years of financial indulgence there was nothing. Driving home she wondered how she would break this news to the children. Instead of the peaceful return to the normal routine of life in a beautiful home and private schools and all the privileges money could buy, they would be living on the limited money she could earn, or on benefits. What this involved she had no idea, as it was something she had never considered. Women with her lifestyle didn't think of going back to work after they had children. It was a pity she hadn't taken her education more seriously as she had no qualifications, except typing. She decided as she parked the car not to tell the children until she knew more about life on the poverty line. She knew reality and that she was dodging the issue, but she needed space to think. She was glad of Tina's presence and that she had enough cash to suggest Tina take the children to the cinema. This might be the last treat they would get.

Although it was early in the day Jemima poured herself a large whisky. Alcohol was a luxury she would not be able to afford in the future, so she may as well empty the drinks cupboard. Besides, it calmed her down.

With a biro and paper she made a list. What income would she have? Badly paid, boring work or relying on state benefits. Her father had always said state handouts were for 'other people'. His family could look after themselves. This idea, instilled throughout childhood, would have to go. Housing – contact the council. Schools – contact the Education Department. Olive – contact Social Services. She would be entitled to some benefits as a widow – contact the DHSS.

She wandered around her beautiful home with views over the river Avon, terraced gardens where the designer-planned grasses blew in the wind. Her feet felt the smoothness of the polished wooden floors, and her hands stroked the plush fabric of the overstuffed sofas. The expensive paintings on the walls would go, the antique china figures on the mantelpiece. All her beautiful crockery and silver cutlery. The warm, safe comfort that money had brought would be gone. Gone forever. No one would be there to help. For a short while this morning she had stood up for herself, and now she realised she would have to do so for a long time, perhaps the rest of her life, and she cried. She sat at the dining-room table and cried a pool of tears. Oh, that she could be Alice in Wonderland and be washed away in her tears. But life wasn't like that. She would have to pick up the pieces of her shattered life on her own. She laughed at herself and the thoughts she had had skiing down the mountain after Rupert's fall. Her home a peaceful haven, with no anger or violence, for her and the children. What a stupid idea! Now she had to face the future alone and care for William and Charlotte. She would have to behave like a lioness at bay, protecting her young.

She was deep into one of the many phone calls she would be making over the coming weeks when the children and Tina bounced back into the house, full of the film they had seen. William was being a space pilot and Charlotte a small furry alien. She couldn't be dejected with two laughing children full of excitement from their few hours in the world of fantasy. Problems with the future could wait. She joined in the laughter and cooked them all a fry-up instead.

Later as she curled up in bed she wondered about that happiness; what was it? Could that mood happen anywhere? It had nothing to do with money. It had to do with people. Perhaps a change in place and home was not so important.

Two weeks later Jemima was beyond philosophy. Rupert's smart Mercedes had been repossessed by a finance company. The children had been very upset by this as they had enjoyed the smooth fast rides they had had in the car. Those had been special. Something Daddy did. But as Jemima still hadn't worked out how to explain bankruptcy to them she just said Daddy didn't need the car any more.

There had been so many telephone calls and interviews. She was sick of every council and government office she could think of, except the Ministry of Defence and Defra. Her mother had been the stumbling block, or could be their salvation. As Jemima couldn't pay for her mother to stay in a home and no council places were available, it was decided after discussions with Social Services that Olive would have to live with the family. The children would just have to accept this and Jemima would get a carer's allowance, which would help with finances.

A disturbing episode every morning was opening the post. There had been several angry and unpleasant letters from Rupert's clients whose investments had proved to be worthless. The milder letters asked why she couldn't pay them back, but some of the correspondence was more threatening.

'Prison is too good for you.'

'You must be as bad as he was to condone his behaviour.'

She found herself in tears after reading the first one and Tina had to comfort her, but in the end she became hardened and just tore them up.

The two women decided the children had better not play outside on their own in case an angry adult decided to take out their temper on them. Jemima had noticed none of the other children had asked them to play at weekends, and when she had asked one of Charlotte's young school friends to tea the mother had replied, 'Rebecca doesn't mix with the children of criminals,' and slammed down the telephone.

As Tina said, in her matter-of-fact way, Rupert's clients had been opening their bank statements in January and found the expected dividends had not been paid. They were reacting accordingly. Jemima was becoming philosophical, as she had noticed many neighbours had given her the cold shoulder; gossip about Rupert must have spread like cancer. How she longed for Carrie to return from her Caribbean holiday. Carrie was a true friend and had known for years how Rupert had treated her.

The worst situation was when an officious woman from the Education Department knocked on her door. The woman was dressed in a tight black tailored suit. She had an official plastic card showing her rank chained round her neck, which made her look like a member of the secret police. In a clipped voice she said it had been reported that the children were not attending school. For children to play truant was an offence and could carry a prison sentence. Was Mrs Somerville-Thomas aware of this?

Jemima wanted to ask if she or the children would get the prison sentence but knew joking with officials was not a good idea. Humour was not their strong point. Jemima answered that she was waiting for the council to find her accommodation before looking for a school. This cut no ice with the educational secret police, but Jemima, being the lioness defending her young, stood up for her family, saying that the death of their father and their change in financial circumstances was enough for two young children to cope with. Angry, Jemima suggested that the two council departments could liaise, as she was about to lose her home and would like to know when she would be re-housed. Jemima firmly shut the door in the education official's face, hoping attack was the best form of defence.

Who, wondered Jemima, would bother to contact the education authorities to alert them about two young children not being at school? Probably the elderly couple who lived opposite, Grace and Clive Sopworth, whom Rupert had insulted whilst he was drunk one New Year's Eve. 'Neurotic fucking hypochondriacs,' he had called them, and for once Jemima had agreed with him. Whenever she passed the time of day with Grace, she was in for a half-hour soliloquy on ailments, tablets and the shortcomings of the Sopworths' doctor. It was part of the grudge Grace Sopworth had against life, and healthy youngsters she would certainly find offensive.

Her thoughts returned to the Gestapo official from the

Education Department and the problem of where they would live. She got on to Mr Edwards of the Housing Department. They had had so many telephone discussions over the last weeks they were on first-name terms and he had a sympathetic voice.

'Hello, Bill; it's Jemima. I've had the Education Secret Police after me, accusing the kids of truancy and threatening prison. And threats from neighbours and some of Rupert's clients.'

'Hi there, Jem of green pastures. Prison's too good for you.'

'Had a letter saying just that.'

'Perhaps a public flogging instead. Get a good crowd.'

Jemima chuckled, and Bill had a smile in his voice when he spoke again.

'The Education lady is only doing her job,' he said, 'though I have heard she cries in the ladies cloakroom.'

'Crocodile tears. If you could only tell me where we're going I'll find a primary school.'

'I'll see what I can do. I'd be glad to get your file off my desk. You know it's going to be a shock to your kids.'

'Of course I do. The sooner I can tell them, the sooner we can get used to the change.'

Should she tell William and Charlotte they would be moving? What was the point when she didn't know where? They had asked why they weren't at school and she had truthfully answered that Daddy's bank account was shut because he was dead and she didn't have any money. It was also true that the local council schools were all full. The children were happy enough. At Jemima's insistence Tina enjoyed being schoolteacher for an hour a day, then they were all happy to go out walking Buster, ride their bikes or play *Chuckie Egg* on the computer.

32

One afternoon, when the others were out for a walk, something happened that made Jemima think she was not a social pariah. Gwendolyn turned up on her doorstep.

'Come to visit the olds. Mum and Dad are a few roads away, and I thought I would look in on you. After all, it's only a walk round the corner. Bereavement is always difficult,' and she gave Jemima an affectionate kiss on the cheek.

'How's Cissy?'

'Off on some conference on Egyptology. Very dry. Although I love Cissy and working at the Museum very much, Mum's cooking and Dad doing the crossword in the *Times* comes as a welcome change. But I came to ask how you are.'

'Let's have a drink and I'll tell you. It might be the last time I sit in our comfortable lounge.'

Over a bottle of wine Jemima told Gwendolyn all that had happened. Gwendolyn's eyes grew large as the awfulness of the situation dawned on her.

'This is dreadful. You leaving this lovely home. How will the children cope? Could I have a refill?'

Jemima replenished her glass. 'There will be no more wine or whisky in cut glass tumblers in a couple of weeks. Let's make the most of it.' She raised her glass. 'Cheers.'

'I can't imagine it.' Gwendolyn also raised her glass. 'Here's to a different future, and may you find happiness there. I know what Rupert was like. One night when you were out he made a pass at me, before he realised I liked women. Then he became very objectionable. Life alters, though,' she said hesitantly, 'maybe for the better.'

'All I can do is hope so. And convince the children.'

Gwendolyn took Jemima's hands in her own. 'You can do it. Rupert turned you into a submissive woman, but inside you are strong enough to look after yourself. We were taught that at school. You'll survive.'

'You and Cissy must have lived through difficulties, but you came through. I must do the same.'

'When you move, send me your address and telephone number. I come down to see Mum and Dad every month. At least they can look after each other, not like your poor old mum. I can pop over and see you. Whatever hovel you're living in.'

They talked of old times and Jemima asked, 'How're Liz and her second husband?'

'He's a pompous ass. He works for the Foreign Office and is very rich. They go to Ascot and Henley. Needless to say he thinks lesbians are beyond the pale, so we don't get invited to their smart dinner parties, but occasionally Liz asks me round to lunch. They live in Belgravia.'

'Couldn't possibly live anywhere else.'

'Usually we have very tastefully done smoked salmon, strawberries and cream, and champagne.'

'Of course.'

'Sorry. Am I making you feel jealous?'

'No. Hungry and thirsty. Have another drink. What about children? Were there any from her first marriage?'

'No. I don't think they're on the agenda. How could she possibly get to Wimbledon if she had babies?'

'Well, like me, she'd have a nanny. Mind you, that was a problem, as Rupert preferred the nanny to me. Since Rupert's death, which upset her more than me, she's been marvellous, and she's working for nothing until we move. I'm going to find it very difficult without her, as I've never looked after the children all the time.'

'And your mum as well.'

'She just sits and watches telly. She rarely says

anything. What goes on in her head no one knows. But at least she's not incontinent. I couldn't cope with that.'

As Gwendolyn left she said, 'Here's my London telephone number. If you want someone to scream at give me a ring. I won't be full of good advice; the only mummies I know about are Egyptian and long gone, but I have a listening ear. And make sure you give me your new address.'

With that she gave Jemima a large hug and walked away down the drive.

Tina was puzzled by Jemima's giggly mood when they came back home, but on hearing she had been visited by an old school friend was pleased. Both of them had too little adult company.

As Jemima curled up in her bed that night she thought, *It isn't all hurdles. Sometimes something good happens which restores my faith in human nature.*

Bill Edwards rang back.

'I have news. Smoke signals have been seen from the mountain. You will be living in Northfields. Finding a house to accommodate your mother has been the problem. No details in writing as yet, but at least you can sort out the schools and adjust your thinking.'

'Thanks, Bill. Now I have to face the next hurdle and tell the children.'

First she contacted the two primary schools in the area, found there were two vacancies in one and went to visit it. It was friendly with colourful children's pictures adorning the corridors, but she knew it was very different from her own school, or what the children were used to. Their past schools had had space, playing fields, cedar and gracious beech trees in the grounds. Here there was sterile grass

35

and asphalt. Then there were children from different races and cultures. How could she make this school a positive, exciting place for her children when perhaps it wasn't?

Her home – what a contrast to Northfields – was empty on her return. There was a note on the kitchen table from Tina. 'Taken W and C to the Suspension Bridge. Maybe Brunel's bridge will be educational. At least it's free.'

With an empty kitchen and time to spare Jemima decided to make them all a curry. She enjoyed cooking. It was a pleasure that had grown during the last eight years, from planning dinner parties for Rupert's clients down to making well-balanced and inviting meals for the children. Picking spices for the curry, she paused, thinking, *This food is from a different country. We eat pasta from Italy. Chinese food. Cheese from all over Europe. It is foreign. We are becoming used to things from different places, cultures. What if we pretend, yes, what if we pretend that, when we move, we are going to a different country? The houses are different – and they are. The people speak differently – which they do. They probably dress differently. Think of money differently. Think of life differently. What if we pretend to be explorers into the great unknown? A different country and culture. As explorers into the great unknown we would have to keep quiet, listen to other people, find out how they think. The kids could do that. Not show off about where they used to live, the schools they went to, skiing and holidays.*

Turning off the simmering chicken, she sat down at the kitchen table and thought about this. Would this make the adjustment easier? Help them find out how to cope with their new school friends and neighbours? Would they come to terms more easily with their new way of life, before they realised that the pretence was reality, and there was no going back? An adult thought flickered through

36

her mind. Were, in fact, their lives so far built on a sham, a pretext of other people's hard work? During the meal she would have to tell William and Charlotte they were going to live in the unknown land of Northfields, and Grandma was coming as well: part of the culture.

Jemima told Tina of her idea as she heated the naan bread and Tina agreed in an absent-minded way. Then Tina announced her earth-shattering ideas on her own future. She was going to become a teacher. Tomorrow she would start applying to colleges. Meanwhile she would get a job with an agency.

'I've realised, being with Will and Charlie over the last few weeks, I can teach. I don't have to spend the rest of my working life changing nappies and shovelling tinned food into toddlers' mouths.'

'You haven't just done that. You have talked to them, read to them and played with them, because you love children. You'd make a great teacher. I'll give you all the support I can. Now d'you think we can suggest this idea of going to a foreign land over a curry dinner?'

'Let's try,' replied Tina.

As Jemima dished out different mouth-watering tastes the children talked about their afternoon expedition.

'That Brunel had an awful Christian name. He was called "Isambard",' piped up Charlotte.

'His parents came from a different country,' said Tina. 'Many of the cleverest people in the world have come to live in Britain because they have never shut immigrants out.' She winked at Jemima, as if saying 'over to you'.

'Yes, we all benefit from learning about other countries and how people from different parts of the world live. We couldn't have this meal if men like Marco Polo and

Francis Drake hadn't travelled the world and brought back different foods and spices. This curry comes from India.'

'And we wouldn't even have chips if Sir Walter Raleigh hadn't brought potatoes back from America.' Tina warmed to the theme. 'Think of all the places Captain Cook discovered and all the plants he brought back here. Do you know what these people were called?'

'Sailors?' suggested William.

'Some of them were sailors, but they were all *explorers*,' replied Jemima with excitement. 'And that is what we are going to be! I think you both realise, as you haven't been to school, that we haven't got so much money now Daddy isn't here. This means we will have to leave this house.' Looking at their stricken faces she hurried on. 'We are going to be *explorers*. Discover a new place, new friends, live a different kind of life.'

'Do we have to learn a new language?' asked William.

'In a way. Where we're going to live and where you'll go to school is called Northfields. They speak English but it's different. The way Craig the gardener speaks. You always laugh when he says, "Good ideal" instead of "idea". You should try and copy the way they speak.' ('Or they might take the Mickey out of your accent,' she didn't add.) 'We are going to live in a much smaller house and Grandma is coming to live with us. Grandma just sits, so she won't be a problem.'

'Grandma talks stupid,' grumped William.

'And she's got a moustache,' added Charlotte.

'She's old. She can't help it. Her brain is, like, worn out,' interposed Tina. 'You had that computer game that wouldn't work any more because you played it so much. Poor old Gran is the same. So you and your mum'll have to look after her.'

'Can't we throw her in the bin like the computer game?'

'Don't be silly. Of course we can't.' Jemima glared at Tina for making the wrong analogy. 'You wouldn't throw Buster in the bin if he got old, would you?'

'Of course not!' William sounded shocked.

'Well, it's the same with Gran. We'll look after her. And we won't have as much money as we're used to, so the house is small. More like a cottage. With people close by who also won't have much money. It will be difficult getting used to it all – but we'll manage, because we'll be *explorers* discovering new places.'

'When'll we leave here?' asked Charlotte in a small voice, 'and can I take my teddies and my bike?'

'You can take all the toys you have room for, the TV and the computer games. I'm not sure when we will be moving. I haven't seen the house yet. I just thought you ought to get used to the idea that we will have to explore a different place.'

The children ate in silence, digesting this information, whilst Tina and Jemima tried to talk with false brightness about European emigrants sailing to America.

'I'm not going on a boat,' announced William. 'I'd get sea sick.'

'No, no boats,' his mother said gently, but she wondered if emigration might not be an answer.

Next morning, when Jemima hoped they had taken on board the information she and Tina had given them, she told the children about the school where they would be going.

'It's called Northfields Primary. And they wear bright red jerseys and grey or black trousers.'

'I don't have to wear a skirt?' asked Charlotte in surprise.

'Not sure. And no more colourful blazers. You can wear your ordinary anoraks to school; it's within walking distance. It will be quite different. Maybe the schoolwork will be easier. There could be kids from other countries who find English difficult to write. As you are explorers, you will have to find out. But don't talk too much. The other children may laugh at the way you talk. You know how kids can poke fun, so don't be upset.'

'You mean take no notice.'

'Yes. Just keep quiet until you get to know them and make friends. Next week is half term, so we have a week to get equipped for our expedition to explore Northfields and make our new home.'

The following day Bill Edwards rang.

'The new Somerville-Thomas mansion will be situated at 14 Meadowleaze. It's a cul-de-sac, so it may be quiet.'

He went on to explain there were only three-bedroomed houses available, but luckily this house had a large kitchen-cum-dining room, a front living room and a downstairs toilet. The former tenants had been an elderly couple, the wife disabled, so the space under the stairs had been converted into a toilet.

'It should be suitable for your mother and I hope you'll be happy there. I shall miss our little chats. Most tenants aren't as polite as you are. Good luck.'

He went on to tell her where to get the key and pay the rent and she thanked him. She too had enjoyed their conversations. They had brought a little humour into her stressful existence.

Now, she thought, Olive could have the front room and

wouldn't need to use the stairs. Her young family would have space upstairs. The council had wisely decreed her children, being a boy and girl, needed a bedroom each, and she could have the smallest bedroom. The need for a double bed and the possibility of future romance was far from her mind. She hoped the kitchen-diner would be a cosy family room. 'Cosy' was a word Jemima found she was using instead of 'cramped'. She was trying to look on the bright side. What if they lived in Asia and there had been an earthquake? Then they would only have a tent to live in.

Jemima drove to look at the house on her own. It was what she expected. Cold, small, drab and dismal. The February weather didn't help, as it was gloomy as well. A few leafless small trees dripped. The pavements slippery in the damp. She noticed the bay window of the small front room. Rotting, tattered curtains hanging at the windows. This could all be changed, she told herself. All it needed was hard work and strength. She could do it. She would have to do it. They would all have to learn to live with the house and make the best of it.

She couldn't bear to wander further than the front garden and turned back to her shiny black VW Golf. She realised that as much as she loved driving it, it would have to go. A brand new car in this area was asking for trouble. She would exchange her cherished Golf for an older, smaller car. The extra money would be helpful.

Tomorrow she would get the key from the council office. She was negotiating with the now sacked but very sympathetic gardener Craig to move some of their 'stuff', as he referred to it, in his white van before the bailiffs moved in. William and Charlotte didn't really understand, but were relieved that their TV and computer would be included, along with a television and computer for Jemima's use in the kitchen area. Plus a TV for Olive if no one was looking. Four single beds, a sofa, two easy chairs and a third for Olive, a table and four chairs. There would be no room for more. Would she get away with the washing machine, fridge and kitchen appliances, saucepans, crockery and cutlery? What were the bailiffs expecting? Better take what she could before questions were asked.

A ring of the front door bell interrupted her thoughts on planning and the endless lists she kept jotting down. Carrie had returned. Jemima hugged her, overjoyed to have her friend back.

Carrie was bubbling with excitement about her Caribbean holiday. Short and plump with dark curly hair, she was the opposite of her tall, blonde friend. Olive would have said she came from the wrong part of town. Carrie had grown up in poverty, with a drunken mother and an absent father. She knew what it was like to be hungry, living on bread and margarine, dressed in clothes from jumble sales; that had been her life until she had married a scrap metal merchant, Dave, when she was seventeen, and he had done well. Their two burly sons now ran the business. Jemima was very fond of the sons, as they had often played with her children in an avuncular way. William and Charlotte having no uncles or aunts, Dean and Steve filled this place. Last summer there had been water fights before they had all ended up in Carrie's pool.

Carrie had been describing the palms, the mountains, the blue sea and the fishing for some time before she stopped and asked, 'What wrong, Jem? You're not laughing.'

Then Jemima told Carrie about Rupert's death, bankruptcy and their move. She spoke quite practically until Carrie put her hand on Jemima's shoulder, then the tears started and they were both crying.

'Why didn't you tell me? Here I've been rabbiting away about our holiday. Why didn't you ring me?'

'After twenty-eight years of life, I have to learn to stand on my own two feet. No more cosy, comfy stuff with father or husband paying the bills. Nor relying on friends, not that they have been in evidence, except Gwen and Tina. So-called friends have just backed off.'

Carrie gently slapped her on the wrist. 'Don't be silly. You won't get anywhere feeling sorry for yourself. I'm your friend and I'm not backing off. "A friend indeed is a piece of cake", or something. "People in glass houses shouldn't burn candles."'

Jemima felt so low she didn't even smile at Carrie's sayings.

'People with money,' Carrie continued, 'are often like that – two-faced. Shallow, no depth. Only fair-weather friends.'

'I'll have to look after my mother and two children as best I can, on my own.'

'I'm so, so sorry. Yes, life can be tough.' Carrie sighed. She remembered life before Dave. Looking after two younger brothers and an alcoholic mother. 'But it can be easier if you don't shut out your genuine friends. Dave and me are here. We'll always help you. Where are the kids?'

'Out with Tina, walking the dog. I was going to head out to sell the car when they get back. Get a cheaper one.'

'Yeah. On that estate keep a low profile. I'll ring Dave. He'll know the best car dealers. And having a big man with you could get a better price.'

*

Mum's car going was the next impact on William and Charlotte, the next sign that life was changing. Jemima was thankful for Tina still being there. She could give the children tea and watch *Blue Peter* with them.

Dave was a big burly man. In his youth he had learnt to box, finding it an easy way to control yobbish boys of his age in the area where he lived. They were scared of his strength. His family and Carrie were grateful for the protection. The scrap metal industry had added more muscle and financial success. Now he squeezed himself behind the wheel of Jemima's VW.

Jemima and Dave spent the late afternoon wheeling and dealing with second-hand car salesmen. The presence of a strong man made a difference to the way salesmen approached them. They would have walked over Jemima had she been on her own. The result was that she came away with a small red Citroën and several thousand pounds. An extra buffer against poverty. Dave bought them all fish and chips, so Jemima and her family were having another happy evening together with friends.

Jemima went to the local council office in her new red Citroën to collect the key. Carrie insisted on coming with her. Tina was taking the children to the local stables for a last ride, and was paying for this herself as a parting gift. Tomorrow she was leaving for her next job.

As they reached the house, both women experienced the same feeling Jemima had felt the day before; the place looked cold, small, drab and dismal. Behind a low crumbling brick wall were a moth-eaten privet hedge and a front garden full of rubbish – damp cardboard boxes and polythene bags full of newspapers, old clothes and crockery.

'Looks like they cleared their rubbish as far as the garden,' observed Carrie.

'Oh dear,' muttered Jemima. 'The council did say there had been an old couple here. The wife was in a wheel-chair and they went into an old people's home.'

'Yes, there's a concrete ramp to the front door. Might be helpful for your mum. Good thing you have the car. Many journeys to the tip.'

'How do I find that?'

'The ignorance of the wealthy,' chided Carrie with a smile. 'It's down near the sewage works. I'll show you on the map.'

The semi-detached house was red brick with peeling green paint on the front door.

Jemima turned the key and they entered her new home. It smelt damp and dirty. Jemima walked round it, down-stairs and upstairs, speechless.

'It's so small!'

The confidence she had mustered yesterday, standing in the garden, drained away. How could she cope with all this?

Carrie, noticing her expression, said nothing but took a bag into the kitchen, checked the water was connected and filled the kettle she had brought. She produced tea and milk, then handed the still-stunned Jemima standing in the hall a comforting steaming mug.

'Half the families in the country live in houses this size. You've only got two children, not six,' Carrie said sharply, then more gently, 'You have the strength to turn this into a happy home.'

'But the dirt. The damp. The smell.'

'Nothing a bit of elbow grease won't shift. And it will be different when it's heated. What was it they said at the council about buying electricity and gas with a key? Pay as you go, no more quarterly bills. And you get money from the council for decorating; make sure you keep the receipts.'

With a feeling of despair Jemima sat down on the stairs. Carrie found a discarded milk crate in the detritus of the kitchen, plonked it down, sat on it next to Jemima and held her hand.

'Where are the kids?'

'Tina's taken them horse riding. A last treat.'

'They've got to get used to this as well. How do we set about this, make it less painful?'

'I've told them they will be explorers in a foreign land.'

'What a strange idea! But just like the Jemima I know. You have more imagination than I, and it might seem like a different country.' Carrie thought of the past – the pain and hard work she had gone through – and paused. 'Say, why not, when they come home, bring them over here with Tina and Buster and tell them they have to turn this into an explorer's home? Captain Cook, or was it Scott? Them islands in the South Seas. Captain Bligh. Then go out and buy emulsion paint, brushes, rollers and they can paint it all. Make it their own territory. Kids adapt so quickly. Far quicker than adults, set in their ways. What was that saying? "The tailor adjusted the cloth to suit the milk." You've said they have adjusted to Rupert not being here.'

'I don't think adjustment was needed. They were just relieved. No more fear.'

Jemima's mind went back to the end of William's summer term.

The school had a sports day and prize giving. Proud parents parked their shiny Volvos and four-by-fours, then stood about in their best clothes looking smug as their darling sons won races and collected prizes. William was not among the star pupils; Jemima knew this, but Rupert had assumed he would be, having neglected to take an interest in his son's progress. His disgust was apparent as he drove home in silent rage, making his passengers shrink into their seats.

Back in his study Rupert read William's report and called loudly for his son to join him. Jemima heard shouting. '"Lack of concentration", "slow in understanding", "doesn't mix with others", why? What's wrong with you?'

Then she heard Rupert's hand meet William's skin and terms of abuse she associated with the rugby field, words that shouldn't be hurled at an eight-year-old child, especially if he was his son. William yelled and she went into the study, forbidden territory to her, and saw Rupert thrashing William's bare bottom with a ruler.

Jemima grabbed the ruler.

'How dare you treat our son like that?'

She protectively hugged William, pulling up his trousers, and the boy fled from the room.

'This isn't the first time you've beaten William.'

'You're too soft!'

'Beating achieves nothing. He is frightened. You want him to be like you. Big sportsman. But he's not. He's an ordinary kid.'

'You should have pushed him.'

'I'm not the pushy type.'

Jemima passed a hand over her eyes.

'Are you all right?' asked Carrie, looking concerned.

'Yes, fine. Just thinking. Designing their own rooms might be an important part of getting away from the past.'

Carrie, wanting to keep the mood light, added, 'I'll do

my bit, hire a carpet shampooer and clean the carpets. The curtains are grotty but you have the curtain rails.'

Jemima stared into her mug of tea for some time, shrugged and said, 'You're right. Right about everything.' She smiled. 'Even the curtains. Thanks for being here. I couldn't do this on my own.'

In the gloom of the late afternoon, the children eyed the house with suspicion, the contrast with their former life even more apparent in the light of an enjoyable session of horse riding.

'Not all that house is ours, is it?' asked Charlotte, used to houses with gardens around them. Buster was running about, barking happily; he didn't care.

'No. Only half of it,' said Jemima quietly. 'It's called a semi-detached house. But you will each have your own bedroom and there is a garden at the back. It's like a cottage in a fishing village – everything will be small and cosy. Do you remember that cottage we stayed in at Port Isaac, in Cornwall a couple of years ago?'

'Oh yes,' answered William, 'white bumpy walls and squashed stairs. But the harbour was outside.'

'Bristol is one big harbour. It's our job to clean this house up and make it our home. Come inside and see.'

The look of dismay didn't leave William and Charlotte's faces as Tina, making no comment, ushered them into the minute hall.

'I couldn't ask Dominic here to play,' said William.

'Probably not,' murmured Jemima, then with determination, 'When you start school here in a few days you'll make new friends and can ask them round. And it'll be nice having Charlotte at the same school. You can look after each other.'

Tina butted in to relieve the tension. 'You're lucky to have carpets and curtains. These places are supposed to be empty.'

How do you know that? wondered Jemima, beginning to realise she knew nothing of Tina's background.

'They're awful carpets,' announced Charlotte.

'But better than nothing and getting splinters in your feet,' retorted Tina.

During the night, in the smartest district in town, Buster was barking wildly, then came a tremendous crash and the sound of breaking glass. Jemima, terrified, but being the lioness defending her cubs, crept down the stairs and found the poker by the unused fireplace in the lounge. Seeing no figures in the streetlights, she turned to switch on the lights and yelled as she cut her foot on a piece of broken glass. By that time Tina had joined her and switched on the lights. There was a brick denting the polished wooden floor, surrounded by shattered glass.

Gingerly Tina, in her slippered feet, helped Jemima into the kitchen. The children were standing on the stairs looking frightened. Jemima, realising they had to be included, called from the kitchen.

'Be careful of the window glass as you come down the stairs. There's some hot chocolate down here that will be soothing.'

Tina put the kettle on.

'Go and comfort Buster,' Jemima ordered the children. 'He's hiding by the washing machine.'

The children, cuddling Buster, watched Tina bandage their mother's foot. It was a very small cut. Warmed by the chocolate drink, Jemima told them some stupid drunken lout had thrown a brick through the window.

'You two drink up your chocolate and take Buster upstairs with you. Tina and I will clear up the mess.'

'It's not much fun living here any more,' William said to Charlotte, taking her hand in alliance, as they climbed to their bedrooms. Buster followed closely at their heels.

'Perhaps exploring won't be so bad,' answered Charlotte.

'Let's hope they're right,' said Jemima, standing up. 'Where are some shoes and the brushes?'

Ten minutes later, when they had swept most of the shards into black plastic bags, Tina stooped down to pick up an A4 sheet of paper.

'Bloody hell. This must have been around the brick. Listen: "Get out, you evil crooks. You've ruined honest people. You should be dead like your husband."'

Jemima gasped, then took a deep breath and said, 'Thank goodness we're going.'

She sank down in one of the deep armchairs, thinking of the parting in the morning, and looked up at Tina. 'I'm so glad you've been here. You've been a tower of strength. It's odd. I ought to hate you for being my husband's lover, but you've been such a help.'

'And you've always been so upbeat and humorous. Presumably because you no longer cared for him. Would life have been different if you had?'

'How could I care for a man who was so selfish and cruel?'

Tina countered, 'But not when you first met him? You said he was so pleasant and charming.'

'I now know that charm is a form of dishonesty. I read it somewhere.'

'Remember that when you next meet Craig.'

'Yes, Tina. You're such a good example.' They both laughed, realising their own shortcomings.

50

The events of the night had given all of them the feeling it was time to move on. The morning was depressing. The sky was grey with drizzle. Even the cereal didn't snap, crackle or pop. The mood continued when they waved goodbye to Tina as the train rumbled its way out of Temple Meads Station. Charlotte was in tears, so Jemima hurried the children off to Broadmead to buy new school uniforms.

The rain drenched shops in the 1950s-dated precinct; drooping leafless trees in large tubs on greasy pavements added to their mood of depression. The children clamoured to buy hot dogs from the fast food carts, but their mother was strong-willed and refused. They all had to get used to not frittering money away. They went to the cheapest shops.

A long-forgotten memory came to Jemima's mind of her mother taking her to the school outfitters in White-ladies Road – the school tunic, tie, hat, blazer and sports shorts. Even then the expense had made her feel uncomfortable. This was much easier: British Home Stores and Woolworths to buy cheerful red jerseys, black trousers, skirts and white shirts as the school had advised them. Jemima looked wistfully at Miss Selfridge and Richard Shops, but those days were gone. Next it was to a DIY shop to get white emulsion and rollers so the children could try to make their bedrooms their own. There was a second reason: keeping them occupied took William and Charlotte's minds off Tina's departure.

Carrie was at the house in Northfields when they arrived. True to her word she had hired a carpet shampooer and cleaned the drab carpets downstairs. They looked brighter.

'A few rugs from Oxfam would cheer this up no end,'

she exclaimed as Jemima thanked her for her hard work. 'I left upstairs as I knew you wanted to paint up there. We can clean them when you've painted the walls. Dean and Steve said they'd come over and help this evening.'

There was some argument about bedrooms decided by William wanting more plug sockets for his computer, so he had the big bedroom looking out onto the street.

Carrie was taking control as Jemima was still stunned by the whole experience. Newspapers had been put on the carpet in what was to be Charlotte's room. Carrie prised open the paint tin and poured white paint into a tray, then showed the children how to use the rollers. The children were unimpressed, so Carrie found a paintbrush and painted stick figures on the walls to make them laugh.

'Look, this is Buster running after a cat. And this is a policeman trying to catch the dog. Then this is an elephant trying to catch the policeman.'

The children giggled.

'Your mum and I are going to start cleaning the kitchen, and when I come back all those funny pictures will have vanished under your white paint.' Carrie had obviously been thinking hard because old worn-out shirts were produced as overalls and William and Charlotte settled to their task.

Carrie ran back downstairs to cope with Jemima.

'Let's tackle the kitchen,' suggested Carrie quietly. 'If we wash out the cupboards, drawers and shelves you can bring food, plates, saucepans before anyone knows.'

Later, pausing as she closed a cupboard door, she asked Jemima, 'Have you thought about your surname in this area?'

'Not really.'

'Somerville-Thomas,' Carrie said, mimicking an upper-class voice.

'You're right. A bit posh.'

'Just drop the Somerville. Tell your friend at the council you're plain Mrs Thomas. The same at the school. One less thing to be made fun of, or worse, bullied about.'

'It doesn't cost much to get it changed by deed poll, and I might just call myself Jem; that's easier. William and Charlotte could be Will and Charlie. They're used to Tina calling them that. Part of their role as explorers.'

Carrie changed the subject. 'Isn't it odd your parents-in-law haven't contacted you over the past few weeks?'

'You mean Felicity and Gerald Somerville-Thomas, those toffee-nosed double-barrelled people?' They both laughed. 'Perhaps they're grieving too much. Maybe they're embarrassed about their son's financial problems. I had thought they might fork out for the prep school fees, considering Rupert was such a star there.'

'Could Rupert have conned them into investing in his imaginative schemes as well? They might have money worries.'

'If he did it would have hit them very hard. Their darling son letting them down. But would that stop them wanting to support their grandchildren, if only in friendship? I always felt I was not good enough for them and that's the way it will stay.'

'Well, Mrs Thomas, what's your next move?'

'My next hurdle is the school.' But it wasn't; it was their new home.

The women had finished cleaning the shabby cupboards. The kitchen was small and it hadn't taken long.

'It won't look so bad after a coat of paint,' assessed Jemima.

'White paint and some stencilled motifs to brighten it up.'

'Good idea. Let's see how Will and Charlie, new names for a new place, are getting on.'

There was no finesse with this painting, but the walls up to five feet were white. Jemima, now Jem, and Carrie took up two more rollers and did the top half of the room. It was dark by now, and they had all been working hard for a couple of hours. Abruptly Charlotte banged down her roller, splattering white paint over the newspaper.

'I hate this. I hate this room. I want to go home.'

'But darling, this is going to be your home. We can't stay in the old house. We haven't got the money. We have to move here.' Jem put her arms around Charlie's angry stiff shoulders. 'There is no choice. It's part of the adventure and being explorers. Sometimes it's exciting. Sometimes it's hard work.'

'Like learning to read,' added Will. 'You don't like that much.'

'When you get your bed in here, and your teddies, it will be like your old room. And we'll stick lots of animal pictures on the walls, then put your dolls' house in that corner.'

Knocking on the door and voices shouting 'Hello!' through the letterbox caused a fortune diversion. Carrie's sons, Dean and Steve, had arrived.

'Hello, sunshine,' Dean greeted Charlie, taking in her tearstained face.

'Hello, squire.' Steve ruffled Will's hair. 'How's the decorating business?'

The children couldn't help laughing.

'Not exactly Michelangelo style, but it'll do,'

54

commented Steve. 'Anyone hungry? Chippy or Chinese? Only just down the road.'

Jem and Carrie had never been so thankful to see anyone.

'You're angels in sheep's clothing,' their mother told them, handing them several notes. 'Your kids like Chinese, Jem?'

'Yes. They like chow mein. What would I do without you all? Thanks.'

An hour later foil trays had been added to the rubbish in the garden and the decorators were refuelled. Steve and Dean then turned their attention to Will's bedroom.

'This wall looks just right for a game of noughts and crosses,' suggested Dean. 'Where's the brushes?'

There was a flurry of activity and soon the adopted uncles and children were laughing away. Carrie and Jem sat on the stairs, there being nowhere else to sit, feeling more relaxed than they had felt for several days. Yes, thought Jem, happiness was about people, not places.

Decorating continued the next day, Friday, but the children were soon bored – it was really too much for little Charlie – so they went back to Broadmead to choose new curtains for the children's bedrooms. Jem was regretting having got rid of her mother's old black Singer sewing machine with the gold scroll decoration. She could have made curtains for far less money.

She packed one of the TVs in the car for their return, and the children sat in the empty living room and entertained themselves whilst the women continued to clean. Jem was curious to see if any children would come back from school in the afternoon, and at about 3.30 several damp boys and girls trudged along the little cul-de-sac in the rain. Maybe there would be friends for Will and Charlie.

Over a sandwich lunch Jem had told her children it might be better to shorten their names, as she had done with her own. She was now Jem. 'You can be Will and Charlie – like Tina used to call you. They can be your explorers' names.'

Dean and Steve turned up again to help out and by early evening the two rooms had been repainted in emulsion. The gloss on the windows could wait.

After sandwiches and cups of tea, which was all Jem had in the house, the young men were off.

'Out for a night on the town?'

'Yeah. Few beers. Maybe a game of darts. Pub on St Michaels Hill. Then a club down Frogmore Street. Good for picking up birds. Then try to avoid the fights in the centre.'

'Especially if you have the birds. They won't like that. An exciting night.'

Having thanked Dean and Steve again, Carrie and Jem, with mugs of tea, sat on the stairs.

Charlie came out of the living room. 'I didn't know Dean was interested in birds. Does he like tits?'

Jem and Carrie collapsed in laughter. In a voice of contempt Will told her, 'Birds means girls. They're looking for girlfriends. That's what you have to do when you get older.'

Jemima, still sitting on the stairs, aided and abetted by the kids, made a list of what they would like in their rooms. She walked to the main road to find a telephone box to ring Craig, hoping he would be free over the weekend with his white van. He was and would bring his mate Wayne.

Saturday morning Jem opened the post back at her smart house for the last time and she was so glad of Craig and his van. The courts would take possession of the house next Wednesday morning. All goods were the property of the Crown and should not be removed. Would Mrs Somerville-Thomas be present to hand over the keys? They had four days.

Jem was relieved to see Grace and Clive Sopworth, the nosy neighbours, had gone out in the car. They couldn't spy on what was being taken. Craig and Wayne cheerfully removed four single beds and mattresses. Jemima piled bedding into her car. Carrie opted out, as her back was aching with all the shampooing, but took Will and Charlie for the day. It wouldn't help if they saw what was being left behind. Perhaps they would go to the museum; it would be quite restful.

Craig and Wayne returned and packed a gate-legged table and four kitchen chairs and easy chairs from Rupert's study. Jemima filled her car with crockery and kitchen utensils. The microwave wouldn't be noticed, or the electric kettle.

The last load was of two chests of drawers and Craig, mindful of his work in the garden, took the gardening tools. He said he would be back on Sunday for the kids' stuff and computers, adding, 'I'm not taking the cooker or the washing machine. You need plumbers and electricians for that and the bailiffs might notice. The council will give you money to get those.'

Jem was relieved when it was the children's bedtime and there was laughter when they realised there were no beds in their rooms. The children had to sleep in the spare room and Jem curled up on the sofa.

Sunday was a difficult day. There was no problem packing the computers. Will took the one in his bedroom and Jem took Rupert's, though she had little idea of how to use it. The problem lay in which toys to take to their smaller home, and then there were the books. Jem and the children had to battle with nostalgia, looking through books she had read to the children so many times but now had to leave behind.

'I need to take *The Tiger Who Came to Tea*,' demanded Charlie.

'You haven't looked at it for ages,' retorted Will.

'We're definitely taking *Winnie-the-Pooh*,' said Jem, because she enjoyed it herself, and it stopped the argument. She did pack a dictionary, encyclopaedias, an atlas, the Bible and her less exotic cookery books.

Jem felt relief as Carrie turned up and took the children off for lunch. The leaving situation was becoming upsetting to all of them. Alone in the house, memories of happier times washed over Jem. All the photo albums were put in boxes along with some ornaments she liked, mostly because her parents had given them to her. They would help change Meadowleaze into a home. She rolled up a couple of Turkish rugs. They would add colour to the drab beige carpets.

She found she was crying at the thought of leaving so many things behind, and the happier moments of the last eight years. Shaking away this mood, she rang Craig to come with his van.

Carrie and her husband helped with the loading, but no other neighbours came to say 'goodbye' or 'where are you going?' The air seemed to breathe hostility and isolation.

'Our bikes,' shouted Will, as Craig was about to slam the van doors.

The garage, empty of smart cars, was opened and their three bikes were wheeled to the van. Jemima's mountain bike and the children's BMX cycles were top of the range. Thinking of the low profile she wanted to keep in Northfields, Jem said, 'These bikes are going to single us out. Make us look like we have money. We should leave them here.'

The children looked horrified but Craig just laughed. 'Don't be stupid. It'll give you street cred.'

Jem was so glad of this diversion. The actual last closing of the front door brought tears to her eyes – eight years of their lives now gone. The click of the lock was very final. She would have to look forward to a different world.

With this view in mind they set off for their new home, leaving the smart houses, well-tended gardens and tree-lined avenues behind them. Jem felt regrets leaving the beautiful house, but relief as well. She felt no remorse in taking the furniture that would have belonged to the bailiffs in three days' time.

It was getting dark as Jem and Craig unloaded the van whilst the children cycled round and round the end of the cul-de-sac. No one was about, but the blue light of televisions glowed through drawn curtains. The children weren't used to the freedom of playing out in the road. The dead end of a cul-de-sac was a novelty for them. Watching them, Jem thought, *Maybe this is the beginning of their exploration.*

Jem thanked Craig profusely and gave him some beer money. As she made up three beds she wondered, from the look in his eye, if he would be back, probably with the offer of gardening but with an ulterior motive. Being a single woman would be a new situation for her, with a different kind of exploration.

With Craig's help she had turned on the central heating. He had made her feel so ignorant as it was so different from the system in the old house, which had worked with the touch of a switch. Next they had carried into the living room a smart electric fire taken from her old dining room. This should keep Jem's mother warm if she could afford to run it. Maybe there were allowances for the elderly. Now that the room was heating up she called the children in from the street. She had hired a special video she knew they would enjoy and produced sandwiches, crisps and Coke. They all cuddled up on what would be Gran's bed, under a duvet with Buster. Charlie was asleep before the film ended and was carried to her new bedroom.

Will was finishing his crisps as his mother returned to the living room. He was looking thoughtful.

'You called this the living room. But at home you called it the lounge.'

'This is home now. It is part of the change, exploration; we call it by a different name. Some people round here would call it the front room, because it is at the front of the house.'

'But when Gran is here it won't be a room for living in.'

'No, I suppose not. The kitchen and dining area will be our living room. I've put another TV in there, and there's the table and chairs. We'll make it comfortable. I should have got more chairs but there wasn't room in the van. Tomorrow we'll sort out the cooker, fridge and washing machine. The council will give us some money for these.'

'When will school start?'

'It's half term now, so in a week's time. We'll have seven days to settle in and do more exploring. We can take Buster for walks and short bike rides. Charlie can't cope if they're too long.'

60

'There was a boy looking out of the window when we were cycling about, but he didn't come out.'

'Well, if you see him tomorrow, say hello. He might go to your school.'

William seemed more relaxed after this gentle chat and they went upstairs together. Jem tucked him under his duvet and opened the top window to let in fresh air rather than new paint. She let Buster out into the garden to relieve himself, then, totally worn out, found her own small box room. She said to herself, 'Jem Thomas, this is your new life. Tomorrow buy hot water bottles.'

Monday was hell. Jem had to go to the housing office to do battle with officials to get a new oven, fridge and washing machine. Perhaps Charlie's whinging, which changed to tantrums, made the negotiations quicker. Jem had no idea what electrical equipment she had chosen but insisted it be delivered as soon as possible, because she had a sick mother to look after. As Charlie's screams got louder the housing assistant, to keep her own sanity, relented and promised delivery would be in the next few days.

Their new home, now becoming warm, seemed a refuge. Then the TV went off and the lights went dark. The electric key had run out. Where did Jem go to top up the key? She would have to ask a neighbour.

She knocked on the door of the other half of the house. She could hear shuffling and an elderly woman opened the door on a chain.

'What d'ya want?' The TV was blaring.

Jem introduced herself and told the old lady of the problem. She was directed to the local shops and stuttered her thanks. Her neighbour, dressed in drab over-washed cardigans, a sagging skirt and slippers, said, 'Don't you go making too much noise or I'll call the police,' and slammed the door.

The children not wanting to be left in a dark house, the three of them drove to the local shops. There was a long rank of shops with two storeys above. Some of them were just closing, with metal shutters being dragged down over the windows, but a shop owner cheerfully directed them to the appropriate machine.

Back at their new home the light and heat returned and they ate a microwaved meal and watched TV.

Solemnly Will said, 'This must be one of the days exploring is difficult.'

'You've hit the nail on the head,' affirmed his mother. At least, now she had been fed, Charlie had stopped grizzling.

Jem rose early. It was still dark. She made herself a mug of tea, then put Buster on his lead to take him for a walk in his new surroundings. She would just have to trust the children wouldn't wake up.

Dawn brought light and a pastel blue sky streaked with orange, signalling strong winds. Jem had gained some knowledge about winds from the sailing holidays she remembered. No one was about, a few lights on in upstairs windows. She noticed small front gardens like her own filled with dustbins and rubbish, older cars parked in the road. But as the morning brightened, there was something missing. No bird song. It was silent. Despite hedges and gardens no sparrows were chattering, no starlings twittering from TV aerials, no blackbirds cheerfully announcing their territory.

After a couple of roads she realised there was a green space that might be a park and Buster was let off his lead for a while. Eventually, worried about leaving the children, she called him back and returned home, where she set out breakfast for when they woke up.

They would all have to stay in until the fridge and washing machine were delivered. Meanwhile, with Buster weaving in and out between her feet, Jem explored the garden. The house, having been built just after the war, had a good-sized garden. There were a few shrubs that might flower if they were pruned, but no daffodils or crocuses to welcome in the spring. The grass needed cutting but Craig might help. She imagined spending time out here once the children hopefully had been settled at school and her mother installed. Gardening was supposed to be therapeutic. There was even room for vegetables. But for now it would be good to get some colour. Perhaps Craig had brought some pots. She looked round the side of the house; yes, beside the utensils, in the wheelbarrow, were some terracotta pots. Maybe at the shops there would be some plants she could buy. This would give her a practical aim through the spring and summer, though expense would come into it.

Will cheerfully ate his Coco Pops and went out on his bike into the cul-de-sac. Charlotte was tearful. She wanted Tina.

'Tina and me always did things after breakfast, and I always had a boiled egg. She would read a story, then we did something.'

Jem was aghast she hadn't known this. 'Well, I could try to boil you an egg in the kettle. And we have a toaster. Let's try and hope the egg doesn't break. You see, we won't have a cooker until tomorrow, so I can't use the saucepans.'

Trying to boil an egg in the kettle fascinated Charlie

and she soon forgot her tears. The first egg cracked, making a white and yellow mess inside the kettle. They both laughed as Jem tried to clean out the kettle. With the aid of a bit of salt the second egg boiled. Jem told Charlie to count, but she got lost at ten, so her mother consulted her watch. Why hadn't she remembered to bring the kitchen clock?

Charlotte was satisfied with her egg and went to find a book. It was *The Very Hungry Caterpillar*. Jem realised this book was young for her daughter but remembered reading in some magazine that children reverted to a younger age if they were ill or insecure, so she went along with this and pointed out some of the words Charlie would be able to read. After all, she hadn't been to school for two months.

'Now I shall paint a picture,' Charlie told her mother.

'What a good idea,' answered Jem, frantically looking through boxes for paper and paints. 'Then we can stick it up in the kitchen to brighten up the place.'

Jem smiled to herself as she washed up the breakfast crockery. She hadn't realised how bossy her little daughter was, as Tina had taken the brunt of this and educated her at the same time. Although so young, Charlie wanted to have power – the power her older brother had. Yes, Jem always listened to Will because, being older, he made more sense. Now she would have to listen to both, treat them the same, and be in control. Maybe in an ideal world!

There was laughter coming from the front garden. Will was pushing open the front door with his bike, followed by a slightly smaller boy, Afro-Caribbean from his colouring, hugging a football.

'Can Tom come in for a drink?' called Will.

'Of course. Hello, Tom.'

Both boys were laughing about something they thought very funny.

'I'm William Thomas,' bubbled William, 'and he's Thomas Williams.'

Jem joined in their giggles and explained it to Charlie, who smiled but looked puzzled.

Making up some drinks of orange squash and finding biscuits, Jem asked Tom, 'Have you got any brothers or sisters?'

'There's Luke who's eleven and goes to the comp, Matthew who's nine, then me and Martha who's nearly five.'

'You must make a lovely family,' said Jem.

'It's OK. But Martha gets a room on her own, and we boys have to sleep in the same room. I don't call that fair.'

'I bet you get a lot of fun, though,' said Jem, not wanting to make waves.

When the boys had gone outside again Charlie asked, 'Is that boy an explorer too?'

'Why?'

'He's a different colour. He can't belong here.'

Jem paused, thinking hard. 'Maybe you're right and he is an explorer, but I expect we will find his mum and dad were explorers, or his grandparents. He sounds very local to me. I'm going to tell you a story, a bit of history,' and she drew Charlie onto her lap.

'There's a place thousands of miles over the sea called the West Indies. Many of the people there have dark skins. But they have little money, so they come over to this country to seek their fortunes.'

'Like Dick Whittington going to London. Tina read me that story.'

'Yes, but they don't have a clever cat, and not many make a fortune, so they live here now just like you and me. There's a saying, "The streets of London are paved with gold". But it's not true.'

'That would be silly,' said Charlie in a matter-of-fact way. 'Grandpa used to have gold teeth, but that's not like whole streets.'

Should she continue with the distant past? Maybe now was the time as Charlie was in a receptive mood.

'Hundreds of years ago, wicked men took these people from a continent called Africa to the West Indies and America in ships.' What a pity she hadn't brought the globe from their old home. 'Thousands of miles over the sea. Then the wicked men sold these African people to other cruel people who made them work very hard and didn't pay them.'

'That's terrible.'

'That's all over now, but they are very poor. So that's why they come here. I expect Thomas was born here, probably in the same hospital where you were born.'

'I still think he's an explorer.'

Charlie had given her judgment and Jem hoped it would be with some understanding.

Soon after this a lorry turned up. The family, with Tom looking on curiously, watched the delivery man lower the back flap with their new fridge and washing machine. With the aid of a trolley the man manoeuvred the machines into spaces in the kitchen units, making cheerful comments to the children.

'Do you know why brides always get married in white?'

Jem, enjoying his banter, had to reply, 'No. Why do brides wear white?'

'All kitchen appliances come in white.'

Jem couldn't help laughing. 'That's true.'

'This washing machine. You've got a plumber lined up? I'm only the delivery boy.'

'Oh. Right.' She signed his delivery note. 'I'll sort something. Thanks.' And he was gone, giving a cheerful hoot as he turned his lorry at the end of the cul-de-sac.

I can't afford a plumber, thought Jem. *What do I do? Carrie's boys. They're probably used to unplumbing machines for scrap. Surely they'll know how to plumb them in?*

This meant another journey to the phone box with Charlie in tow. Getting a phone would be a priority. Perhaps having a disabled mother would speed up the process. She gave Carrie a ring. Carrie promised Dean and Steve would be over that evening.

It was now time to think about shopping and something to eat, so Jem said to Tom, 'We have to go out now. Isn't it time for your lunch?'

'Don't have lunch. Mum's out working. We make sandwiches if we're hungry.'

'Oh. Well, I've got a good idea. We need to get to the shops. We don't know how to walk there. You come with us to show us the way, and we can take the dog.'

'Great,' Tom said.

'Just go and tell your brothers where you're going. Is Martha there?'

'No. She's with Grandma.'

So the four of them set off for the shops, passing houses similar to their own, many with dejected hedges, over-filled wheelie bins, gardens strewn with black bin bags, soggy cardboard and old rugs. There was a feeling that life was hard, then Jem remembered she still had to clear her garden – perhaps next week. There weren't any garages and cars were parked in front gardens or on the road. The cars were older than Jem was used to seeing, some quite rusty. A few gardens had snowdrops and early bulbs in pots bringing colour on this sunny morning.

'We cross straight over here,' said Tom, sounding important as he knew the way.

Now it was daylight Jem was pleasantly surprised to see about a dozen shops providing everyday things. There was also a library, a church and a youth club.

The Co-op had all Jem needed. It would be microwaved bacon and beans for lunch, followed by bananas. There was also a small bar of chocolate for the children to eat on the way home. Pausing at the cut flower stand she bought a bunch of daffodils for the lady next door; perhaps these would mollify her grumpy attitude of the previous evening.

Tom pointed out the road to the school as they walked, saying it took ten minutes to walk there.

'That's easier than using the car,' commented Jem, 'and cheaper.'

'We *always* used the car at our old house,' muttered Charlie. Walking on hard pavements was something she wasn't used to.

Jem suddenly stopped. 'The old house. I've forgotten about the key. I have to hand it over tomorrow.' She didn't want to return there; it would be too much. Anyway, the washing machine was being delivered. She worried about this for the rest of the walk home.

Maybe Mr Dawes the solicitor could be her representative. She popped into the telephone box again and rang him. His voice had its usual calming effect. Of course he would represent her. In fact he would come round this evening and collect the key.

As Jem heated up the lunch she realised Tom was still with Will, so it was bacon and beans for four. Then there was a knock at the door and Tom's older brothers were asking where he was. Now it was food for six. Jem knew it was no coincidence Luke and Matthew had turned up when they had, but she wanted the children to be friends.

The bright sky of the morning clouded over and it started to rain. Jem insisted the children wash up, which, with no dishwasher, was a new experience for Will and Charlie. Charlie spent ten minutes drying a mug but at least nothing was broken.

With rain pouring steadily and no chance of playing outside Will found a box of board games, so the boys settled down on the front room floor. Charlie watched timidly from the mattress of Gran's future bed, having found a much-loved teddy to keep her company. Four larger boys were too much for her and she happily went with her mother and the bunch of daffodils to visit the old lady next door.

Again they heard shuffling feet and the old lady opened the front door. Her clothes looked even shabbier in daylight, despite the rain, but her face brightened at the sight of Charlie and the flowers.

'What a lovely little girl. What's your name?'

'Charlotte or Charlie.'

'And daffodils. Please come in.'

She ushered them into the front room where there stood an old battered settee and two chairs shiny with use. The old lady turned off the television set, her arthritic fingers finding the buttons difficult. Jem made her introductions.

'I'm Jem Thomas and this is Charlotte or Charlie, as she's told you.'

'And how old are you, Charlotte?'

'Five,' Charlotte said, shyly.

'I've a son called William or Will and he's next door playing with the boys from over the road. If they're too noisy you must tell me. We also have a dog, Buster, so I hope his barking won't disturb you.'

'No. It was just the noise last week.'

'I'm sorry. It was my friend shampooing the carpets. I expect the couple before were very quiet.'

'Don't you believe it! He liked opera and played it very loud. I was glad to see the back of 'em. I'll find a vase for these daffs and put the kettle on.' The old woman, using the furniture as a crutch, walked out into the kitchen. Jem followed her to mention that her mother would be living with them as well.

'No man, then. Children with different fathers? Happens all the time round here.'

'No, no,' said Jem, quite taken aback. 'My husband died in an accident in January. There wasn't any money so we've had to move house.'

'Oh. I'm sorry.' The old lady paused, apparently having difficulty finding two clean mugs. 'Put me foot in it. But it's what you expect round here, what with her at No. 5, with children of three different colours, and taxis coming at all hours with different men. Best keep out of her way with kiddies about. By the way, my name's Vera.'

'Thanks for the warning, Vera.'

Charlie was peeping round the corner of the kitchen door, taking in the chaos of the sink and the rubbish beside the swing bin. Jem was eyeing up the whisky bottles beside the back door, wondering what the situation really was.

'And do you live on your own?' she asked.

'No. Bert's down the betting shop. If he wins he will come home happy with a bottle of whisky. If not ...' Vera shrugged. 'Could never cope with this retirement lark. Gets bored, and the horses is his answer.'

'Not easy for you.'

'No, it ain't. But he was a good husband for forty years, so I put up with it, and the family keeps me going. We've got two daughters and a son, and there are five grandchildren.'

'They must give you a lot of pleasure.'

'Yes. The youngest is the same age as your Charlotte.'

Jem stayed listening about the grandchildren and the shortcomings of Vera's family whilst her mug of tea lasted, Charlotte getting increasingly restless, then said with some relief that they had to check on Will and the other boys. At least now they were on a friendly footing with Vera and Bert, who literally lived only feet away from them.

The four boys, bored with games, were playing with Buster on the stairs. This wasn't a good idea in such a small home, so Jem suggested it was time Tom and his brothers went home.

'That was mean,' said Will, sulkily heading upstairs to watch TV.

'You can see them again tomorrow. Dean and Steve will be here later and I'm expecting Mr Dawes, the solicitor, so please behave.'

Charlie, taking her teddy, joined her brother in his room – siblings silently giving support to each other.

Mr Dawes knocked on the door whilst Jem was making cheese sandwiches for the children's tea. She showed him into the kitchen and he refused a glass of sherry, saying, 'I've seen too many problems over the years caused by drink driving. I'll wait until I'm within the comfort of my own home, but I'll have a cup of coffee. Oh dear, how tactless; I'm sure you'll make the house a home in time. How are you settling in?'

Jem filled the kettle and answered, 'We've only been here two nights, but we're managing. William seems to have found a family of boys to play with, and some old friends are coming to plumb in the washing machine this evening. It's all very different and I'm finding it claustrophobic, but I shall adapt in time.'

'Is your mother here?'

'Not for another two weeks. I made some money selling the VW and used it to pay for extra time in the home. I think the children should be started at school before she arrives.'

'Yes, it's important they settle.'

Mr Dawes's own children were now at university, having been to independent schools, and he was out of his depth, having made the mistake of mixing supportive, friendly feelings with his work. But he had promised to deliver the keys to the bailiffs, and this he would now do. In fact a law that turned people out of their houses in this manner disgusted him. He finished his coffee quickly and asked for the keys.

At the front door he turned and said he would always be at the office if she needed help. Maybe it was Jem's blonde vulnerable looks that made him say this – so like his own daughter. He knew he would hate to live here. He was used to spacious surroundings, beautiful paintings on the walls, shelves full of books, and a comfortable wife. Jem was aware of his thoughts, but grateful for his help, and gave him a kiss on the cheek as he left, hopefully meaning they could be friends at a time of need.

*

Will, munching his cheese sandwich, opened the door to Steve.

'Hello, mate. Come to plumb in the washing machine.'

'Hello, mate,' said Will, liking the thought of being a 'mate'.

Steve settled down by the washing machine with various tools and plastic tubes, saying, 'Dean's girlfriend has made him take her out for a meal with her mum and dad. It's their wedding anniversary. Sure I can do this on me own. Hold this, Will.'

Will firmly held a spanner.

Steve tightened some hoses and between them he and Jem pushed the heavy machine back into a space under the work surface. It was run through several washing programmes and Steve left, saying he was taking his dad to a football match at the City Ground. 'City versus Milwall. Oh, I forgot Mum's made you a shepherd's pie you can heat in the microwave and a cake. I'll get them out of the car. She was going to ask you all to lunch but realised going back would upset you. You need time to adjust.'

'You've said it,' Jem said. 'We've just got to get used to it. The lady next door has a husband who drinks when he wins on the horses, and there's a woman of easy virtue over the road.'

'Wonder if I've met her?' They both laughed.

'Take care, then,' said Steve, giving her a hug.

Next morning Jem took Buster for an early walk. There had been a frost after the rain and the hedges sparkled in the weak sunlight. Jem thought that after the cooker had been delivered they could all come to this open space, kids with their bikes and the dog. Then they could find the way to the school.

By mid-morning the sky became dark and snow started to fall. The children, delighted, went out into the garden and met Tom in the road. They were happy running around as the snow turned everything a pure white, from dirty rubbish to the rooftops, if only for a few hours. From the radio Jem knew there was chaos on the roads.

There were several children out in the cul-de-sac, trying to make a snowman, when the van with the cooker arrived. Two burly men dragged the cooker up the snowy path and soon had it wired in.

As they left Jem said, 'Please don't run over their snowman.'

The men laughed, and one tried to make a snowball to throw at the kids. 'No. We'll back out. Wish I was that young again.'

As they reversed down the cul-de-sac a young man on a motorbike roared round the corner, slid to a halt and the driver landed up on the tarmac. Some interesting language between the two drivers made the children look up. The young man, still cursing, wheeled his bike round the back of the first house in the road, the studs on his black leather jacket showing up under the streetlights.

'That's Darren Sparks,' said Tom to the others in whispered awe.

Jem was watching from the kerb with Luke, the oldest of the Williams children, who said in a warning tone, 'Darren's trouble. Never works but has money. Probably a drug dealer, see him near the school occasionally. Best to keep out of his way.'

'Thanks for the information. I'll warn Will and Charlie. They're enjoying having friends to play with.'

The gentle snow soon turned to rain and the children

trooped indoors dejected. Quickly Jem put on the kettle and made mugs of soup and invited in the other children. She wanted her children to have companions and was deliberately being hospitable, bribing the other children to be friends. There were the three Williams children and two younger girls from somewhere in the cul-de-sac. They were called Kim and Sasha. Charlotte proudly took them upstairs to play with her dolls' house.

Jem went to bed that night feeling more at ease. Her children had made friends.

'It's great playing out in the road,' Will had said as she had tucked him into his duvet. 'Even Charlie likes Sasha.'

'Will they be at the same school?'

'Dunno.'

'Well, it's a start. Our exploring has brought you friends and the snow.' With that Jem kissed him goodnight.

During the next few days the explorers explored. Jem realised that after her mother arrived there would be little time for this, so they went on their bikes with Buster in tow. They found the beginnings of a stream trickling through an open grassy space. The murky water was full of debris and supermarket trolleys, but they could follow its course towards more houses and Buster enjoyed the trail.

Friday evening there was a knock on the door. A dark-skinned woman stood in the doorway. She was in her thirties, black crinkly hair held back in clips, and she wore a grey tracksuit.

'Hello, I'm Ruth,' and she held out a slim hand.

'Come in,' said Jem. 'You must be Tom's mother.'

Ruth laughed. 'One of the bonuses of being black. You know who my kids are.' And Jem laughed too, as it was a statement of fact, not a criticism.

As they walked through to the kitchen Ruth said, 'I want to thank you for giving my boys lunch the other day.'

'It was no problem. They were all getting on so well, and we don't know anyone round here. It's good for the children to make friends. Tom showed us the way to the shops and the school.' There was a pause, then Jem asked, 'Would you like a cup of tea, or as it's Friday evening a glass of wine?'

'I'd love a cup of coffee. I'm afraid we're wet blankets over alcohol as we're Baptists. We go to a chapel just off the shopping precinct. But if you would like a glass of wine, carry on.'

As Jem busied herself making coffee and opening a bottle of wine for her own use – she felt she deserved it after the past week – she asked Ruth, 'Where do you work?'

'I'm a nurse at the local hospital. In fact I'm a midwife in the maternity unit.'

'I had my babies there. The staff were marvellous. You must find it a rewarding job.'

'Yes. When you are there in the quiet of the still night and see the joy on the parents' faces. That is the best time. As in any job there is drudgery – giving mothers enemas, clearing up the mess – but the end result is good. My mum lives round the corner. She looks after the kids so I can do this. Joel works at the aircraft factory and his hours are varied, depending on when they are testing aircraft. He's very proud of the Concorde. You'll hear it go over every day at eleven o'clock.'

'I wondered what the noise was. You're so lucky having

a mum who can help. My mother's coming to live here in ten days. There were no spaces in any old people's homes and I haven't any money, so we'll have to look after her.'

With a glass of wine inside her and a willing listener, Jem told Ruth about her husband's death, the bankruptcy and their total change of life.

Ruth was silent for some time. 'Perhaps the kids ...' She paused. 'What did you say they were called?'

'William and Charlotte, but I think their names should be shorted to Will and Charlie.'

'Maybe, God willing, they will adjust. Especially if they make friends, and like the school. It's a good school. But for you?' Ruth laughed, not unkindly. 'It must be tough. Having to think about every penny when you're not used to it.'

'No more bottles of wine, and I'll have to stop putting caviar on the smoked salmon.'

'I think you'll live.' They both laughed. If the two of them could make a joke out of most things they could be friends.

Charlie, teddy in hand, shyly came round the door.

'I got bored with *Coronation Street*. Those old women always sound so cross.' She sat on Jem's lap and, looking at Ruth, asked, 'Are you another explorer?'

Ruth looked mystified, and Jem quietly explained.

Not quite grasping the point, Ruth said, 'I have explored and discovered a land of beautiful gardens, but it is only in my mind. One day I might go there. It's called Heaven.'

'Yes. I remember that from my last school. But if you are an explorer, where did you come from? Over the sea?'

'I don't think you have a convert there,' muttered Jem, and Ruth laughed.

'I'm not bothered about that. My mother came from

over the sea when I was a tiny baby. I don't remember that, but I do remember discovering this place. It was a great adventure – new houses, new people, a school where I could learn. New smells, new sounds, new weather. The cold and the rain. That was the worst. Having to buy so many clothes from jumble sales to just keep warm.' Ruth continued on her theme. 'What do you find different?'

Charlie thought, cuddling her teddy at the same time. 'It's so small. No room. But I like children around to play with, like Sasha, and going out in the road. At our old house we always had to ask grown-ups if children could come and play.'

'They would come in four-by-fours and Mercedes,' whispered Jem.

Clicking her fingers, Ruth smiled. 'Sod it. Mine's stuck in the car pound.'

'The embarrassment! How can you ever live it down?'

Charlie was pleased to see her mother looking happy but couldn't understand the exchange in conversation.

Ruth stopped laughing. 'Sorry. We were having a private joke. I'm glad you like playing with the children round here. Would you like to come and say hello to Martha tomorrow morning?'

'Yes, please,' answered Charlie.

Hoping she had made a friend, Jem bade Ruth goodnight.

Nobody woke up early on Saturday. Jem looked at the empty wine bottle and thought, why not? She had very little pleasure in life.

She took Charlie over to the Williams's house to play with Martha, where they kept each other entertained for an hour with brightly coloured plastic toys. Ruth said to Jem she was pleased to see Martha and Charlie playing doctors and nurses. 'Usually Martha only has boys to play with.'

'Were you the doctor or the nurse?' Jem asked Charlie as they walked home.

'I was the nurse, but I had the gun. Matt gave it me. It was a toy gun. We didn't tell Mrs. I mean Ruth.'

'Good idea.'

Will enjoyed the joke as well.

After lunch the three of them and Buster walked to find the local school.

'It's not very big,' said Charlie, sticking her face through the railings. 'Where are the gardens to play in?'

'As explorers we have to accept there are new places to play. You've never played in the road before. It's all different.'

They walked on to the main road and, feeling adventurous, continued down a winding road to the old village of Eastham. There were cottages and a small river, perhaps the stream they had encountered in the open grassy place. An elderly man was leaning over a stone wall, gazing at the water. He commented on the good weather after the snow and Will told him seriously they were explorers.

'Oh, then you'll be interested in this.' He pointed at a narrow cottage on a corner. 'That's called Dial Cottage. See the clock painted on it? They say that time on the dial was the very moment the lady who lived in that house was jilted by her sweetheart. And she died of a broken heart.'

'How sad,' whispered Charlie.

As they wandered on towards an ancient church she asked, 'What does "jilted" mean?'

'Her boyfriend ran off with another girl he fancied. Dad was always doing that,' replied Will, trying to sound like a man of the world. Jem was too surprised to say anything.

Dial Cottage had provided enough history for one day and the children were not interested in the church, so they made their way to the centre of the village with shops set about a war memorial. There was a bakery with a coffee shop. The children's eyes lit up at the sight of iced buns and doughnuts, and as they were all tired Jem relented. Will and Charlie enjoyed fizzy drinks and doughnuts, leaving the shop with sugary lips.

They had come too far to walk back, so Jem popped back in to ask the shop assistant which bus would take them back to Northfields.

They stood at the bus stop for a long time, and as they waited Jem had time to work out she had just enough money for meals, school lunches and electricity until she collected her benefits on Tuesday. She was thankful her mother had taught her how to make stews out of nothing but a few scraps of meat and cheap vegetables.

The bus, Number 94, trundled them back to the main road near their home.

'That was great!' said Will. 'I've never been on a bus before. And we went upstairs. Sat in the front so we could see out.'

'I like cars better,' said Charlie peevishly.

'You have to take the rough with the smooth when you're explorers,' said Jem as she guided them back to Meadowleaze, and then she added more firmly, 'But don't mention, when you're at school, that you've never been on a bus before. Or talk about cars.'

'You talked to Ruth about Mercedes the other night,' admonished Charlie.

'That was a joke. Ruth understands our other life.

Children at school won't know about where we used to live. Just think before you speak. You are explorers.'

When they got home from their exploration the children were happy to ask their friends back to play, for which Jem was thankful, as Monday loomed.

The alarm was set early so Jem could have the kids' uniforms ready and breakfast on the table. Neither of the children wanted to get out of bed, let alone go to school, now the day had arrived. They hadn't been to school for nearly three months. Will put his black trousers and new red sweater on with bad grace, and Jem had to help Charlie pull up her socks and knot her trainers in between whimpering sobs. Little breakfast cereal was eaten, but their faces brightened with the production of new lunch boxes.

The three of them trudged past red brick houses, overgrown privet hedges and rubbish to the school. Tom and Luke caught up with them near the gate, which made Will and Charlie feel they were not alone in an alien place. The playground was full of children and noise. Charlie clung to Jem's arm. She was frightened, not used to such large numbers of children. Jem, too, felt she would just like to run away and hide, but trying to sound confident she said, 'Let's go and find the office. The staff need to know who you are.'

'Grown-ups aren't allowed in the classrooms in the morning,' Tom told her.

She noticed all the mothers standing outside the gates, gossiping to each other. 'Thanks, Tom. But we need to find out which classes Will and Charlie are in.'

'Don't want to go,' wailed Charlie, going stiff. Jem had no choice but to pick her up and march to the office, aware of the other mothers' eyes following her.

The school secretary was welcoming and went off to find the class teachers. Miss Thompson soon calmed Charlie down and took her off to the classroom, saying, 'Come and help me sort out the paints.' Will, looking philosophical, followed his teacher across the playground. Jem stayed in the office to give the secretary their address details, then she blindly left the building, tears in her eyes. Could her children survive? It was so different.

A bell was rung and she was engulfed in a tide of children swarming into the building. As the tide subsided she had time to pull herself together and make her way back to the road. The mothers were moving away, so she could leave quietly. She was aware that women were staring at her – a new face, with hair that had recently seen an expensive hairdresser, and a smart anorak. They were bound to be curious, but she just wanted to be left alone to recover her composure.

Some physical exercise would keep her occupied and her mind off worrying about what Will and Charlie were going through. She found her way to the tip at Avonmouth with black bags full of rubbish, and repeated this trip several times. The port of Avonmouth, though important for the wealth of Bristol, was an ugly area with factories and chimneys pouring out white steam or smoke. Meadowleaze seemed quite welcoming at her fourth return, and she felt that by driving round the area she had been exploring on her own.

The sun had come out and, finding the shears, Jem set to cutting the privet hedge so the garden looked tidier. Maybe in the summer, if she could afford it, there would be paving slabs as the grass had died long ago.

Feeling sweaty and dirty – there hadn't even been time to scrub her grimy nails – she set off with Buster to the school, dreading the feelings her son and daughter might have after their first day there. She may have said they were all explorers, but today they had done the real exploring.

As she walked along the streets, Buster sniffing at all the rubbish, she wondered why others didn't clear it away and clip their hedges. In the months to come, when tiredness, poverty and monotony had set in, she would regret her thoughts and lack of understanding. She would be appalled by the patronising attitude she had had when she had first arrived in Northfields. She would learn in time to know the resignation that came with living with less money. How ignorant she had been in her affluent suburb.

Joining the mothers chatting at the school gate, she smiled and said, 'Hi.'

One older lady patted Buster on the head and asked his name. 'I comes here every day to collect my grandchildren. I gives them their tea. Makes life so much easier for my daughter. You just moved here?'

'Yes. My husband died recently, so we had to get a new house. My mother's coming to live with us in a few weeks.' Jem smiled gratefully at the grandmother and the fact someone had talked to her. Perhaps it wouldn't be as bad as she had thought in the morning.

Charlie, clutching a painting, came out first with Sasha from over the road. That was a relief. Buster jumped up full of affection, pleased to see his younger mistress, and Jem started looking for William. Why was it that all the children looked the same? There he was, still looking philosophical.

Jem turned away from the crowd before she asked them how their day had gone.

'Can Sasha come with us?' asked Charlie with no sign of her morning fears.

'No,' called Sasha. 'I have to wait for my sister.'

Sasha was a mousy little girl with her hair in a thin ponytail. Kim, her older sister, soon came out. She had a stubborn look, said nothing and, taking Sasha's hand, dragged her off down the road.

Now Jem had the chance to ask, 'How did it go?'

'I did this painting of a snowman.'

'Well done, Charlie, and Will?'

'It was boring. But at least they don't do Latin. I liked the football. I could join the practices after school.'

'Good idea. Now let's get home.'

'Back to our proper home?' asked Charlie.

Jem sighed. 'No, darling. Our new home up the road. You like it really. And after tea you can ask Sasha round to play. You couldn't do that in your old home. I've got sausages for tea.'

The next few days were similar. Jem had to help the children get ready for school (something Tina had done before), get their sandwich lunches made (no more expensive cooked dinners added on to the school fees) and remember their PE kit. She smiled at the other mothers, but said little, listening to their conversations.

'See you at bingo.'

'I says to Ma if you go on interfering in our marriage Ted'll be round. And you knows what that means.'

'That's a nice cardie.'

'Bought it at the church jumble.'

And one remark that made her prick up her ears.

'You've no right, Mavis Cotton, to be claiming benefits and free school dinners. Your Bob's been moonlighting for years. Disabled indeed.'

Of course, free meals if you were claiming benefits.

84

She would have to ask about that when she went to collect her widow's benefit. So far it had been paid into the bank, but when they had moved to Northfields that had changed.

On Wednesday after school as a treat they drove to Broadmead and bought Will some football boots. So Charlie wasn't left out she had some new trainers, then they stopped at McDonald's for a beef burger on the way home.

That morning Jem had collected her allowances for the week from the post office, which gave her the opportunity to apply for free school dinners. Once she got home, working from the two weeks they had been in Meadowleaze, she tried desperately to put the cash in orderly envelopes marked 'rent', 'electric', 'council tax', 'water', 'food'. She was sure her knowledge of cooking would mean she could feed them all well and cheaply, but was there really enough to pay for a treat like McDonald's? Experience over the next few weeks would tell.

Jem's good resolve came a cropper on Sunday when she took the children ice skating, thinking her mother would join them the next day and outings would be a thing of the past.

The owner of the nursing home, arms akimbo under her ample chest, smugly greeted Jem, knowing she could now put up the fees on Olive's room. Olive, looking bewildered, took Jem's hand as she was led out to the car. An assistant carried the old lady's possessions in a black polythene bag, and a nurse gave Jem some tablets for her mother with instructions. Other residents gazed out with forlorn non-understanding eyes as Olive made her departure.

Olive just accepted her new room, sat down in her chair

and asked if there was a television. Jem turned this on and brought in two mugs of tea. They sat together, neither having anything to say, looking at two unknown celebrities telling them how to make pancakes.

'I need the lav,' announced Olive. She would never have said that in years gone by.

Jem guided her to the lavatory, which her mother could manage on her own. When Olive shuffled back with her Zimmer frame to the front room, now her room, Jem adjusted her mother's skirt, which was tucked into the back of her knickers.

'Where's Rupert?' Olive asked.

'He's not here, Mum. I told you. He died in a skiing accident. It's just you, me, William and Charlotte.'

'Oh.' She paused, then stuttered, 'He, he fr-frightened me. He was so, so thr-threatening about m-money.'

Jem hadn't heard such a long sentence from her mother for a long time. Had she been really fearful of Rupert? What had he said to her parents before he took their wealth and gave her father a heart attack?

'Well, you're safe here. He isn't coming back. As I said, it's just me, William and Charlotte. I'll make us a snack for lunch, then we'll have a proper meal when the kids come home from school.'

A few minutes later, Jem was bending down to search for beans in the cupboard and jumped when she found her mother standing silently behind her. She sat Olive down at the table, turned on the TV and finished getting the meal, wondering whether her mother would follow her every-where like some faithful dog.

The afternoon followed peacefully, Jem chatting to her mother in a one-sided conversation whilst she emptied the contents of the black polythene bag into a chest of drawers.

Then it was time to fetch the children. Taking Buster, Jem put the catch down on the front door Yale lock, locked the back door with a key and marched off to school, hoping Olive would understand where she had gone. This might be a problem, leaving her on her own for twenty minutes, but the only way to find out was to actually do it and assess Olive's reaction.

The three of them breathed a sigh of relief on their return as Olive was happily sitting in her chair watching *Countdown*. Her face lit up with delight on seeing the children and she appeared to be listening as Charlie said, 'I got a gold star for my news. I wrote about going to the ice rink, and Miss Thompson said it was very good. Did you know I can skate backwards? None of the other kids have been skating or skiing.' Then she showed her grandmother her new exercise book.

'I hope you didn't show off about it,' warned her mother. 'Remember what I said about being explorers.'

William, still looking philosophical, said, 'I got kicked by an older boy. But I didn't mind. I just ignored it. His name is Dan Sparks. From what the other boys said I think he is a cousin of that man down the road with the motorbike. They said keep out of his way. Can I go and play football with Tom?'

'Of course, but stay in the cul-de-sac. Tea'll be about five o'clock.'

They ate their beef casserole to the background noise of *Blue Peter* with little conversation. Charlie read her reading book to her grandmother, who might not have understood but enjoyed the girl's company, and William raced through his sums saying, 'Far too easy.'

At seven o'clock *Coronation Street* came on. Jem was about to turn it off when Olive suddenly said, 'Oh,

Coronation Street. I love that.' Jem sat back, surprised, and realised her TV viewing habits would have to change. At least her mother had spoken again.

Soon the children went upstairs to play so that Jem could get her mother into bed. Olive was used to the 'early to bed' regime of the nursing home. Would she be all right in the night, or wet the bed? Jem left the light on in the hall and her door open. At least she had got over the hurdle of the first day. Will and Charlie had been marvellous – especially after their comments about Grandma. Tomorrow a health visitor was coming who might give her more help in coping with her mum.

Twice in the night there were calls from Olive not knowing where she was and needing the lav. It was like looking after a three-year-old again. Not that Jem had done much of that, as there had always been a nanny. It was new for both of them.

Olive was up by six o'clock but happy to go back to her room with a bowl of cereal and some toast. She was content with her breakfast and TV. The children were hurried through their cereal and packing their bags. Was it PE today? Again the catch was put down on the front door and the back door locked with a key. They hurried down the road with the other children from the cul-de-sac trailing behind them. Was she being too careful? Should she let them walk to school on their own? Maybe when they were more settled. The journey did give her time away from the television.

The health visitor, Mrs Hoskins, arrived looking reassuringly comfortable. She arranged for a district nurse to give Olive a bath once a week, if she could manage the stairs. There was a day centre for the elderly Olive could go to for a day. Would she like that? Olive didn't appear to understand.

'We can try it,' murmured Jem doubtfully. 'All Mum wants to do is watch television'.

'You need time for yourself,' said Mrs Hoskins. 'We'll have to see how you both get on. After all, Mrs Thomas, Olive has only been here one day. This is my telephone number. Call if you have any problems.'

During Wednesday and Thursday a routine fell into place, but on Friday afternoon Jem realised she hadn't collected her allowances and Olive's pension. There was nothing for tea, or the weekend. Would Olive notice if she went out twenty minutes early? Would it be quicker to take the car? Probably not. She ran to the post office and queued, remembering the past times when bank managers had smoothly grovelled and called her Mrs Somerville-Thomas. She grabbed two packets of chops and frozen peas from the Co-op, then arrived breathless at the school, where William and Charlotte were the last young ones standing alone. Some older boys were hanging around and one called out jeeringly, 'Your mummy's come.'

As they hurried home William mentioned that the heckler was the boy, Dan Sparks, who had kicked him. Jem hoped her son hadn't been singled out as being different. But this worry vanished as they walked up to the semi and realised the front door was open. Jem had rushed out without putting the catch down!

Olive was not in her room although the TV was still on. She was not in the house as the three of them called frantically. William went back to the main road junction with the cul-de-sac but there was no sign. They looked in the gardens but they were just full of dank dead vegetation.

Charlotte started to cry, feeling her mother's fear. They stood there disconsolate. *I'd better call the police,* thought Jem, then the shabby door opened in the other half of the semi and Vera called in a croaky voice, 'Are you looking for an old lady?'

'Yes. My mother.'

'She's here. I saw her in the road, not too happy on her pins, so I brought her in 'ere.'

'Oh, thank God,' cried Jem.

They walked up the crumbling concrete path to Vera, Jem uttering her relief and thanks.

'How long has she been here?'

'About ten minutes.'

'I forgot to put the catch down on the front door. She can't have understood where I was going. I'm so grateful.'

Vera led them into the front room where Bert in a befuddled way was telling Olive about his win on the horses. Olive looked frightened, but brightened up when she saw her family and Jem gave her a hug – not something she often did.

'I'm sorry,' said Jem, turning to Vera, 'I should have told you more about my mother. She is rather vague and I don't know how much she understands. Sorry, I should've told you she was coming to live with us.'

'I did wonder when I heard the telly on in the day and saw the nurse call on you yesterday. This is Bert. Bert, this is Jem and her kids. As you can see Bert's done well on the horses today.'

'Hello, Bert. What did you win?'

In a slurred voice Bert went into the odds on some stee-plechase. It meant nothing to Jem, but to be friendly she said, 'I expect you're looking forward to the Cheltenham Gold Cup.'

'Flat racing is more reliable,' he replied, and carefully walked into the kitchen to refill his glass.

Jem helped her mother out of the chair and hustled the children out, thanking Vera again for her help.

'I can't offer to look after her when you go out,' said Vera, 'but I'll keep an eye open. If I was you, I'd buy a bolt, or a different lock. You can't never go out because of her.'

As Jem walked her mother home Olive said quite clearly, 'That man was drunk.'

How much did her mother understand?

Once Olive was engrossed in children's television Jem put the chops under the grill and Will wanted to know about Bert next door. So Jem explained.

'You've seen your father drunk and angry. Bert, I think, just gets stupid. People round here are far more friendly and open than they were at our old place, but you have to learn when to avoid them. Like the Sparks boy at school.'

As Jem had never had to learn about DIY – there was always someone you could pay – she rang Carrie later in the evening and asked if her boys could come and put a different lock on the front door. As a result the next evening Carrie and her family came round with a chicken casserole and some wine, and eight people had an entertaining evening.

Dean and Steve screwed in a lock with a key, then played board games of their youth with Will and Charlie, whilst Dave, Carrie's husband, made Olive laugh doing card tricks very badly.

When washing up in the kitchen Jem said to Carrie, 'What happened about our house?'

'Men in grey suits turned up with clipboards. Removal

91

men turned up in big vans, then "for sale" signs went up. None of the neighbours have said a word.'

'I didn't expect they would. That life is over. I've had the post redirected but no one from that life has got in touch, except for you. What would I do without you and your family?'

'Blood is thicker than water.'

'But we're not related.'

'I've seen enough blood on your face after Rupert had a go. Let's get on to more practical matters. Your mum. She would be happier if she could get out more. She can't walk far. How about a wheelchair? Take her to the shops and wheel her about.'

'You're right. I didn't take on board what this would mean. I just thought she would be happy to sit in her chair and watch television as she did in the home, and I could help with Will and Charlie around her. But it's not quite like that.'

'At least the kids seem to accept things and have made friends. You're doing OK,' and she gave Jem a big hug.

Over the weekend Jem was glad she still had a car. She drove to local shops, children crammed in the back with Olive's Zimmer frame. They walked their grandmother slowly up and down outside the shops whilst Jem bought supplies for the coming week. The children looked subdued caring for Olive, but remembered the worry of Friday afternoon. 'Come on, Gran.' 'No, this way, Gran.' 'Look at this shop window, Gran.' So Gran she became to them all.

Once the children were in bed and Gran was sitting in the kitchen watching some dire quiz show, Jem emptied her purse on to the table to sort her money out for the coming week. She filled the envelopes and there was a small amount left over. 'Now I have five pounds left over,' she said to herself.

Gran said, 'Holidays. Save.'

Jem looked up, surprised to hear her mother talk.

'We always saved for holidays. Holidays ...' Her voice trailed away and there were tears in her eyes. 'Holidays. The sea.'

Jem sat beside her mum and comforted her. How much did she remember? What was she thinking? Did the memories cause her sadness, or frustration because the words were no longer there? She too remembered the Devon seaside and sailing holidays and a lump came to her throat.

She had read that old people could recall the past, but couldn't remember yesterday. But surely her mother was just senile, and did that apply? Was her brain locked up somewhere and fighting to get out? Did anyone, even the experts, know?

At least she found another envelope and marked it 'holidays'.

On Sunday, after they had all consumed a small roast chicken, Jem drove her family to Blaise Castle, Buster barking and adding to the scrum in the back. After they had parked, the green grassy space meant they could all let off steam. The dog played football with the children, whilst the ladies found a park bench. Jem noticed an old railway truck converted into a coffee stall in the car park and bought ice creams for everyone, which Gran found difficult to manage. Tissues in Jem's bag were useful, something to remember on future ventures from home. The playground beckoned so they were all happy, Jem and

Gran watching the children in the late-winter sunshine for the afternoon. There were even hot dogs for the kids to munch in the car on the way home.

The weekend: another hurdle overcome, thought Jem as she settled down to sleep.

'I need the lav,' was her last hurdle of the day.

On Monday morning Jem telephoned the health visitor, Mrs Hoskins, from the telephone box. She talked about the problems over the last few days.

'It might take weeks to get a wheelchair from the health authority. But if you go down to the Red Cross depot in central Bristol you may get one. Probably be heavier to push or put in the back of the car, but you could have it straight away. And I'll look into day care. If I were you, rather than standing in the cold in a telephone box, I'd get in touch with the telephone company. With an elderly disabled relative you'd get a phone put in very quickly. And you could try for a "Disabled" sticker for the car.'

Jem thanked her, wondering why Mrs Hoskins couldn't have told her all this last week, then rang the Red Cross and was given directions to the depot. She carefully explained to Gran where they were going and went into 'the going-out routine' – lav, shoes, coat. Gran pointed out of the car window with a gnarled arthritic finger and mumbled things. Perhaps she recognised roads or buildings. A helpful assistant at the depot found them a suitable chair and demonstrated how to fold it up to put in the boot of the car. Jem felt pleased – perhaps she wouldn't be so tied to the house – though Gran's face was a mask of bewilderment.

After their snack lunch Jem said, 'It's a sunny afternoon. You can come with me to fetch William and

Charlotte from school. I'll put a rug over your knees to keep warm.'

Jem couldn't tell whether her mother would prefer to watch *Countdown*, but Gran got in the chair without protest ('but first – lav, shoes, coat'). The ramp from the front door made manoeuvring the chair easy and Olive was no weight to push. Jem, bending over Gran's shoulder, could see her pointing at gardens and houses as she had done during their car journey in the morning. At least going out made her more animated.

Several mothers at the school nodded a greeting, and Jem said, by way of explanation, 'This is my mum.'

Will wandered out of the gates and his philosophical expression gave way to surprise. 'That's a good idea,' he said. 'Hello, Gran.'

'Can I sit on your lap?' asked Charlie.

'I think Gran's knees might snap if you did that. You take Buster's lead, instead. Let's get home.'

Luke Williams, Tom's older brother, had come out with her children. His parents had let him watch *Ben-Hur* on video, as it was about Christ, and he suggested, 'Couldn't Gran take Buster's lead and pretend she was a chariot driver?'

Jem laughed at the vision, remembering the film of the 1950s and the chariot race. This idea was talked over and explained to the children as the four of them walked to Meadowleaze. Will at least understood, and thought Gran should be given a whip.

'Can we borrow Luke's video?' he asked.

'You'd enjoy it, but not Charlie. It is rather violent. The first time I saw it, it made me sick, and I had to rush to the ladies'. Perhaps when you're older.'

Jem was still smiling as they reached home. To her, at

least, the word 'home' was beginning to mean what it should convey. A place where they were beginning to feel comfortable.

The days continued into weeks. Like lumps of coal shaken in a sack they settled down, rubbing the corners off each other so they could live together. February turned to March and the days became less grey. As Jem pushed her mother towards the school Olive pointed at crocuses and snowdrops, though the words eluded her.

One sunny afternoon a large man came out of his high spiked cast-iron gate with his dog. Buster barked but Jem said, 'What a beautiful dog.'

The Alsatian's coat gleamed. His owner beamed with pride.

'She's a good dog. And a very good guard dog. Need it round here. Been broken into three times.'

'Did the police catch the thieves?'

'No. I did once. Teenagers after money for drugs. Needed a bloody good hiding, but if I touched them it would be me in court, not them. Ever since I bought the house from the council I've had trouble. People think you're loaded because you can afford to buy a house. It's like putting up a sign saying, "Please rob me". It's a crazy old world. See yer.'

Whistling to his dog he marched off to the park. Jem looked at the house more closely. There was a burglar alarm and new double-glazed windows. He was asking for trouble. Then laughing she pointed out the name of the house to her mother. It was called 'Dunrentin'.

Maybe it was because she was pushing her mother, plaid blanket over her knees in the chair, but she noticed people often passed the time of day with her. Vera and

Bert would wave from their front window. Even Charlene at No. 5 asked how they were settling in. She was pushing the buggy with her youngest child, a two-year-old with coffee-coloured skin and a mass of thick black curly hair.

'Say "hello" to the ladies, Kylie.'

'How old are your other children?' asked Jem as she introduced herself and Olive.

'There's Willow. She's in the same class as your Charlie. And Wayne who's at nursery. I love 'em all to bits.'

Charlene minced up to her front door in too-tight jeans and a leather jacket that showed off her bust to its best advantage. When Charlene was out of earshot Jem explained to her mother, wondering if she would be shocked.

'Charlene belongs to the oldest profession in the world. That's why cars come and go during the night. I wonder how she gets the kids to sleep through all the comings and goings.'

Olive just smiled. 'Takes all sorts.' That was a good sentence from Gran, and Jem wondered if she was becoming more tolerant with her senility. Maybe even understood more with constant company.

On the way home from school Jem asked Charlie, 'Do you know a girl called Willow? I was talking to her mum today.'

'Yes. She has black straight hair and different eyes. She often falls asleep in lessons. When she doesn't walk home with Sasha another lady picks her up in a big car. Sometimes she stays with this lady overnight.'

'Probably her gran,' commented Jem, wondering whether there was a pimp involved protecting the children.

97

Charlie then shyly said, 'I haven't seen Sasha except in school this week. She says it's because her dad's home, but when I knocked on the door on Monday her mum answered and was crying. Her face didn't look right.'

Her mother, with vague concerns about Sasha and her sister, just said, 'Wait until the dad isn't at home.'

Jem cuddled up in her small warm bed that night. It was never like this in their other home. Maybe because they were further apart, or just snooty. No one ever waved at you as you passed by and apart from 'Good morning', there was no conversation. Nor did you know when neighbours had problems. Before the financial troubles and the angry behaviour with anonymous threats and bricks through windows, neighbours had rarely stopped to chat. Were they frightened of Rupert and his belligerent behaviour? Or had they turned their homes into castles where others could not intrude? Well, except for a polite glass of sherry at Christmas; then neighbours would meet in someone's house, awkwardly twiddle their glasses, remarking how wonderful the canapés were, and try hard to think of small talk.

What was that Oscar Wilde story about the 'Selfish Giant'? The Giant built walls to keep the villagers out? Had her smart neighbours been like that? Maybe she could get the book from the library. The kids might enjoy it.

Now there seemed to be fewer hurdles to jump over. Just one-foot jumps, or, to be school-correct, thirty centimetres, like Will's affrays with the Sparks boy, or Charlie not being able to talk to Sasha.

A few days later Jem pushed her mother to the shopping parade, her shoulders beginning to ache with this continuous exercise. As it made such a difference to Olive she couldn't complain. She was missing tennis, her old form of physical exercise. In what she felt was her previous life she had played a couple of times a week all through the year at a club in Clifton. She missed the company too, and had been pleased to receive a note through the post that morning from the secretary, Janet, a good friend of hers, saying sorry about Rupert but why wasn't Jemima at the club? Well, next week Olive was going to a day centre. Mrs Hoskins, the health visitor, had arranged for her to go from ten until three on Tuesday. Jem thought, *I'll use that day to go to the tennis club and see my old friends. Not Rupert's friends, but mine.*

On Monday Jem made sure her tracksuit was clean, her racket ready and her tennis shoes white. She explained several times to Gran that she would meet new people at the day centre, do interesting things, have a different meal, but Gran seemed to close up like a tortoise going into its shell.

'Mrs Hoskins says it will do us both good to have a break from each other.' But Gran didn't respond. Determined to try and get some of her old life back, Jem said, 'Well, you're going anyway.'

The children, at teatime on the Monday, were aware of tension. Will pushing Gran's wheelchair around the house on the two back wheels, which usually made Gran laugh, had no effect.

Even the routine of 'lav, shoes and coat', which usually registered a smile, had no effect on Tuesday. Gran was left at the day centre with a cheery nurse. There were other elderly people drinking coffee, playing card games or doing jigsaw puzzles. There was even an exercise class with music, but Olive remained rigid and mute.

'See you later, Mum,' said Jem, giving her a kiss on the cheek. On the way out she gave the nurse the tennis club telephone number and drove away quickly. *I have a right to my own life,* Jem thought, as she jammed the brakes on at a traffic light.

She enjoyed her welcome at the tennis club.

'How nice to see you, darling.'

'Sorry about poor Rupert.'

'Jemima, you're looking fit.'

'How are the children? Haven't seen William at school this term.'

Jem played a doubles set with Janet, the secretary, against the local vicar's wife and a part-time estate agent. Jem and Janet won, Jem pleased she hadn't lost her skill. The group stopped for a cup of coffee and then curiosity was aroused. Jem felt she was still playing tennis, lobbing a question here, smashing a comment there. She was grateful to get back on the court and enjoyed winning another set against two young smart women from the past whom she didn't recollect, but should have done. They kept saying 'Yeow!' for no reason.

There were delicate sandwiches for the lunch break set out on wrought-iron tables between relaxing chairs.

'Darling, what a fantastic spread!'

Yes, smoked salmon sandwiches with the crusts cut off, a few lettuce leaves and crisps on the side. Adequate, but not fantastic. The other women were talking of holidays they were planning for the summer, what independent schools their children would attend in the autumn, and Jem realised she no longer lived in this world. Did she feel regret or did it seem superficial, away from the need to just survive until the next benefit was paid out? Would there be another inquisition trying to find out her new circumstances?

One of the young 'yeow' players she had just beaten lounged elegantly in a chair beside her. She must have learnt that posture at a finishing school, thought Jem. The yeow turned and lit a cigarette. Puffing smoke into the air, gin and tonic in hand, she asked, 'What will you do about Rupert's problems?'

What was the yeow woman's name? Oh yes, she remembered her from school. Five years younger, and a bully. Delia – that was her name. Her husband was a merchant banker.

Delia went on sarcastically, gloating, 'It must be devastating.'

Jem recollected Delia from school, a fourth-former, being spiteful to a smaller third-form girl and enjoying it. Jem, herself a prefect, had sent her to the headmistress. Maybe this was Delia's revenge.

The club barman came to the table with a telephone message for Mrs Thomas. It was the day centre. Olive was very distressed; could Mrs Thomas collect her mother? The shortened name raised the yeow's eyebrows. Jem had never thought she would welcome such a call, but she did.

'Yes, dear Delia. It is devastating.' She stood up and announced to what she now considered a self-satisfied group of women, living an easy life with no thought for the rest of mankind, 'I'm now going to collect my mother from the day centre. She has dementia and I can't afford a home for her. So she lives with us in a council house in Northfields. I have a drunk as a neighbour, a prostitute over the road next to a drug dealer. But they are real people. Not the superficial drones you've become. I know. I lived with big business for eight miserable years.

'The tennis was good, but goodbye. You've made me realise what I value. It's people, not money.'

101

As she marched back to her car Janet ran after her.

'I understand how you feel. But I would still like to be friends, wherever you live.'

'Sorry, I just lost my cool back there. That Delia's a pain.'

'Look, give me your telephone number. I'll ring later in the week and maybe pop in to see you and your mum.'

'Actually, I haven't got a phone. Here's my address. I'd like to see you. We've been friends for a long time, and it would be nice to talk to another adult. Now I must go and collect my mum.'

Olive was waiting, sitting with her coat on and a cheery nurse holding her hand. The old lady's eyes were red and swollen and she clung to Jem as if she had been rescued from certain death. The nurse was pleasant but suggested the day centre was not what Olive needed. With a sigh Jem helped her mother into the car. She would have to find another way of getting some time for herself. Meanwhile she made another of her seemingly endless cups of tea and switched on *Countdown*.

Charlene had offered to walk home with Will and Charlie – perhaps Tuesday was her 'day off', Jem thought – so mother and daughter sat down to watch telly together. The kids, when they arrived, were relieved to find the tension gone.

'Did you have a nice time?' asked Will.

'No,' answered Gran. Then she said for no reason, 'Jigsaws.'

'Do you like jigsaws?' asked Charlie. Gran nodded. The little girl rushed upstairs to find one, and grandmother and granddaughter spent half an hour before tea doing a puzzle for five-year-olds. Charlie admitted later to her mother she had done most of the work, but it was some kind of communication.

Jem asked herself whether Gran had fabricated the stress, but having seen her fear and distress at the centre realised her mother was beyond such behaviour.

Later in the week she pushed Olive to the health centre to see the doctor as her medication was running low. They waited for half an hour, the well-thumbed magazines being of little interest. Each time patients left a surgery, eager faces looked up. Would it be their turn next?

A middle-aged doctor, who had been seeing patients at five-minute intervals for two and a half hours, tiredly asked them to sit down, looked at the notes from the previous nursing home doctor and had nothing to add. He signed a new prescription with an expensive fountain pen and told them to get repeat tablets from the receptionist. Why had they waited around for so long to learn nothing? Jem politely said, 'Thank you,' and pushed her mother back down the corridor.

A notice caught her eye: 'Dementia Care – Care for the Carers'. Someone who would sit with her mother so she could go out for a couple of hours. She took a note of the telephone number. A game of tennis with Janet, a lunch date with Gwendolyn, a drink with Carrie. Her imagination whirled for a moment. *Calm down,* she thought. She didn't want to see her mother so scared again, but maybe she was not alone; there were others, carers like herself, out there.

That was her first revelation of the day. The next was in the housing office where she paid the rent every week. She parked her mother out of the way and was waiting her turn when a well-known voice said, 'If it isn't Mrs

Thomas of green pastures. What a pleasant surprise. And how are the woods and pastures new?'

'Bill! I recognised the voice. What are you doing here?'

'It may have escaped your notice, but I work for the Housing Department. I was here for a meeting and I happened to overhear you speaking to your mother; I recognised your voice too. I imagined you as a Wagnerian blonde warrior in a winged helmet. You're blonde but more human.'

Jem laughed. 'I imagined you as a poetic type. Lord Byron or Robert Browning.'

'Sorry. No flowing dark locks and sardonic expression. Plain mousy, with a beard and dandruff. And I too live with my mother. My meeting is over, so perhaps, once you have paid your pound of flesh to the council, you could introduce me to your mother and I could take you both for a drink at the local hostelry?'

Jem, enjoying his banter, agreed, so once she had paid the rent the three of them made their way to the Queen's Head on the corner near the shops. It was not the Ritz – chewing gum trodden into the turkey carpet, walls stained by nicotine, noisy gaming machines – but to Jem it seemed a delight after many weeks in the house at Meadowleaze. Olive seemed pleased by Bill's introduction and to her daughter's surprise asked for a whisky.

An hour passed whilst Jem told of the move and their new neighbours. Interspersed with Bill's witty comments it all sounded entertaining.

'And what of you, Bill?' asked Jem. 'You have such a way of putting things. You should be a writer or an actor.'

'Yes, stuck in the Housing Department. But the Housing Department is a refuge, and I don't look after my mother; she looks after me. I went to drama school but got lost in the world of drugs. Heroin can give you a lift but only for so long. Mum and Dad nursed me back to health, and I learnt to accept that the dizzy heights of fame were not for me. I had a wife for a few years but that didn't work out either. I do some acting with the local amateur dramatic society and write one-act plays, but I know my limitations now. Useful knowledge, to know yourself.'

'Thanks for telling me. Oh, that Rupert could have learnt that lesson.'

'Your mum's nodding off; time to go.'

'No, I'm not. Come and see . . . see your . . . play.'

'Good idea, Mum. Now we must go and collect the children. Thanks for the drink, Bill, and for getting to know you. No longer a disembodied voice. Perhaps we can meet again. You know our address. Maybe you should, on behalf of the council, call in to inspect the property.'

Jem pushed her mother to the school with vigour in her step. She had enjoyed their sojourn at the Queen's Head with Bill Edwards. Perhaps she could ask him round for a meal.

'I didn't know you liked whisky, Mum.'

'Henry didn't . . .' But words failed her. 'Wonder where he is . . .'

Jem wondered too.

Henry had always expected Olive to be the little woman at home. Maybe her mother wouldn't have been the dull mousy woman Jem felt she'd always known if she had had the opportunity to engage in more interesting pursuits. As a result Jem tried to talk to her mother more often, and to ask her more questions. She borrowed a simple jigsaw of a Devon cottage from the library and the four of them sat around the kitchen table fitting in the straight sides first, saying, 'Gran, where d'you think this bit goes? It's the same blue as the other flowers,' and other such things with some success. One afternoon Vera from next door popped in to see how they were getting on and said, 'Oh, a puzzle,' and happily spent half an hour finishing off the thatched roof of the cottage. Olive sat there enjoying the company; that was what she needed.

As the weather improved Gran would sit in her wheel-chair in the back garden whilst Jem cut back the overgrown bushes. She knew her mother had enjoyed gardening, and could see her frustration as she tried to get out the proper plant words of which her daughter had no knowledge.

One fine Saturday Craig, the gardener-stroke-removal-man, knocked on the door, his trusty lawn mower ready for work. As Jem watched him in the spring sunshine he looked so fit. Blond hair bleached by the sun, muscular arms tanned by the weather. After an hour some kind of lawn appeared from under the long grass and dandelions in the back garden. He sat at the kitchen table with a mug of coffee, making suggestions for a vegetable patch, but Jem knew from the look in his eye and the occasional way he touched her arm to indicate a plant or bush that other suggestions were in the offing. As he left Jem told him she couldn't pay him.

'I know. How about a night out together? Then I'll come back and dig your veg patch.'

'I like the idea of a night out, but I haven't got a babysitter or a gransitter.'

'My sister'll do that. And she's a nurse.'

'Why waste a Saturday night after she's been caring for others all week?'

'She don't mind. Studying for some exam.'

'Well, that's very kind. As long as she gets on with my mum.'

Debbie, Craig's sister, turned up at eight o'clock the next Saturday, armed with books and files. Charlie in her nightie was sitting on the stairs.

'Where's your uniform?' Charlie asked.

'I'm off duty. I work at the hospital up the road.'

'Do you see lots of deaths?'

'Quite the reverse. I'm on the maternity block at the moment, so it's helping people with giving birth.'

'I might be a nurse when I grow up, or a nanny.' Charlie looked thoughtful with her chin resting on her hands.

'You'd cry if there was any blood,' said Will, also ready for bed.

Jem came out of her bedroom in the one smart shirt she had brought from her other life and neat jeans. She hadn't dressed up for anything since their skiing holiday at Christmas time, except for Rupert's funeral, and found it an effort. She had forgotten how to apply make-up and put up her long blonde hair. But obviously she had got it right as the children said, 'Cor,' as she came down the stairs and Debbie said, 'You look great.'

Olive seemed content watching *The Price Is Right*, so Craig took Jem's hand and led her out to his white van. All week Jem had been nervous about the evening. She knew what Craig wanted. Sex. But did she want it? Having lived like a nun for many months she wasn't sure. After years of Rupert's aggressive dominating behaviour perhaps she would enjoy being sexually excited again, or did she feel too damaged? She remembered Rupert, last autumn, watching Craig mow their extensive lawns and suggesting he would make a 'good bit of rough'. In compensation for his affair with Tina? He might have been right. But any suggestion from Rupert, even if he was now dead, seemed a bad idea. If they went to the pub and had a few drinks she would feel more willing. In any case she had found her contraceptive pills, so like a good Girl Guide (which she had never been, as badges sewn on her blouse sleeves had never appealed), she was prepared.

First they went to the Queen's Head and Jem, having been there before, felt, wrongly, she was a local. The twang of the accent made her realise her error. Craig shoved his way to the bar and bought her a large brandy, then they found some of his mates and talked about the afternoon's City football game that they'd lost. The grandstand experts were replaying the match and Jem sipped her drink quietly, but was aware the other men were giving her appreciative glances. Something she was no longer used to.

Craig whispered in her ear, 'Football's not your scene; let's find somewhere quieter.'

He drove the white van to a country pub away from the town and they had a chance to talk and find out more about each other; at least Jem learnt more about Craig. His father had deserted the family when Craig was nine. 'Me mum couldn't cope, so I ran wild. Stole things from supermarkets, but never got caught. Thought I was real clever. Then some older boys at school got me into drugs. Dropped out of school at fourteen. I lost me skill at stealing and got caught. That was a terrible time. Mum hysterical. Sitting around at home doing nothing. But my class teacher, who was aware of my problems and had seen me drifting around, dropping out of school, wif nothing to do, he asked if I would like to work for a friend of 'is who ran a garden centre. He was a great bloke – Fred Tucker. He taught me the basics. Then there was no looking back. I just likes anything to do with plants and the open air. Would love to have my own market garden like my uncle in New Zealand.'

'Have you got your own garden?'

'No. But you'll have to come and see the balcony at the flats where we live.'

'I'd like to. But perhaps one day you might achieve your own plant nursery.'

'The voice of people with money. You ain't got no money and I ain't got no money. Can you find a banker amongst your husband's disillusioned friends?'

Jem felt upset and humiliated. She felt her part of society had let everyone down, but what could she do?

'If we're playing "what ifs",' Craig said, 'what I would really like to do is to emigrate to New Zealand. I could start a market garden over there. The uncle I mentioned, Ben, has a smallholding near Auckland. Looks after it with his son. He grows tomatoes for shops and apples for export. The North Island has a great climate. The plants I could grow there. Let's go for a walk. Too much talk.'

Craig drove to the Severn estuary and they walked along the coast under a starry moonlit sky. They turned off the path and Craig's hands started wandering over her body. She knew what was coming next and as her feelings were aroused looked forward to making love under the stars. Something she had never done before. Craig was gentle and passionate, unlike the lover her dead dominating husband had become. They drove back to Northfields with her body satiated and relaxed. A feeling she had not felt for many years.

It was back to reality at Meadowleaze. Debbie made them a coffee and, judging by the state of Jem's hair, tried not to ask where they had been. Debbie said she had had a quiet evening, studying most of the time, though Gran had been confused. Craig left with his sister, saying he would be in touch, and Jem went to bed wondering and hoping.

Life was beginning to fall into a new routine as spring progressed. It was monotonous through lack of money and the responsibility of looking after Gran and the children. The days were all the same. Get up, take Buster for a short walk, take Will and Charlie to school, get Gran up, clean the house (which she was not used to), washing, ironing, take Gran to the shops, collect children from school, cook a meal, sometimes homework, then bed. The meals, too, became monotonous. Cottage pie (children saying, 'We had this at lunch'), spaghetti Bolognese ('This is better than school'), bacon casserole ('We only had pizza today') – but at least they were all eating well, even Gran. Sometimes the children whined – why couldn't they go to Spain, like the girl at school whose mum and dad ran the fish and chip shop, and why couldn't they have a new toy like so-and-so at school? – but they seemed to accept the reply, 'There is no money, but I'm saving.'

On one occasion Will and Charlie had watched their mother take the allowances she had each week and put them in envelopes for food, rent, electricity and the holiday money, so they understood the situation. Will had said, 'Boys at school steal things like chocolate and Coke.'

'Don't you dare start that!' Jem had exclaimed. 'It'll only lead to trouble. Can you imagine the beating you would have had from your father for something like that?'

Will had been silent after that.

Most of the time Will was happy with football – and he was doing well in the team – or riding his bike around the cul-de-sac and playing with Tom. Charlie enjoyed playing with Sasha, helped Gran with jigsaws and insisted on a story every evening. Some weekends Charlie felt very grown-up and played with Martha, Tom's four-year-old sister.

It was the proximity of people that made life so different. Hearing Bert singing through the walls when he had had one too many. Vera popping in for a cuppa and trying to talk to Gran. Sometimes looking after Charlene's youngest, not yet at school, while she was out 'working'. Sasha and her older sister Kim's situation remained a mystery as their mother rarely left the house, but the children often came to play.

The monotony was broken by times when Carrie would pop in and buy them all a take-away, occasional carnal evenings out with Craig when Debbie could babysit, and the Sunday when Bill Edwards and his mother came to lunch.

Jem had fed the family on the cheapest casseroles and sausages all week to buy a joint of beef. The meal in itself was a treat for the children – roast beef and Yorkshire pudding, followed by trifle, with a bottle of wine for the adults – after which Bill's acting spirit came out and he tried to teach the children charades. Another bottle of wine was produced and Bill's mother, Susan, joined in with gusto, taking Will under her wing and having him act out 'pancake' in three separate acts – two syllables, then the whole word – with the aid of an apron, a frying pan and an empty carton of eggs. Then it was Bill's turn with

Charlie to improvise 'dog collar' with Buster's help, and Bill acting the vicar with a strip of white paper round his neck. There was much laughter from everyone, though Charlie and Gran looked puzzled at times. The last charade was Jem and Olive doing 'Whistler's Mother', with Gran sitting quietly in her wheelchair with a shower cap over her hair. The adults chuckled away and Jem found an art book with the well-known picture so the children too saw the joke.

'Learning the other way,' commented Bill.

Jem smiled. 'In your light-hearted manner you are the teacher.'

'No. You are. You have the understanding. Think of *The Merchant of Venice*.'

'I don't know it, except it's Shakespeare.'

'In time I will enlighten you!'

As Bill and his mother left, with hugs and kisses all round, he promised he would take them all out during the spring to somewhere interesting. Jem was looking forward to this mystery trip. It was what she needed in this monotonous world.

Something that had disappointed Jem was that Janet, her tennis friend, had only visited her once and, though she had said she didn't mind where Jem lived, obviously felt uncomfortable in such a cramped and shabby home. Patted the chair she sat on in the kitchen as though it was dusty, and wiped the table round her coffee cup with a Kleenex tissue in case it was infested with germs. Gran silently sitting there and occasionally putting a piece into a child's jigsaw unnerved her, so she didn't stay long. Janet was happier on the tennis court, free in the open air, as Jem would have been had she had a choice. After waving goodbye to Janet in her sports car she returned to Gran, who was putting the last piece of her jigsaw in place with a satisfactory snap. Yes, Jem thought, the visit was the end of one way of life and the acceptance of the new. Not better, not worse, just different.

Dementia Care were very helpful when Jem contacted them on her newly installed telephone. They hadn't enough volunteers for all demands, but a Mrs Brimble would visit them next week. It was important that the 'carer' and the 'cared for' got on well together.

Mrs Brimble turned out to be a comfortably plump retired schoolteacher whom Olive seemed to accept, so it was arranged that she would come on Thursday from twelve until three. On the day, Jem stayed to see her mother happily take her sandwich lunch from Mrs Brimble and the ex-teacher relax in front of the television with her knitting.

Given three hours' freedom, Jem's mind had gone blank; she had no idea how to fill the time. She couldn't pop in and see Ruth as she was at work. There was no point in looking round the shops, as she had no money. Turning up in his white van, Craig came to the rescue as he was visiting a nursery to buy plants and she could give him a hand. They had a laugh when they both realised that perhaps lovemaking in the back of his white van in broad daylight would not be a good idea. 'Though,' commented Craig, 'the bags of compost were quite comfortable to lie on.'

'You make a habit of it?' she countered.

Now Jem had a chance to see a different side to Craig. First of all there was the efficient business side to him as he dealt with the nurserymen, then there was his care and knowledge in choosing the plants. He touched them with a fondness that surprised Jem as he explained where they were all going in his clients' gardens.

113

'Now this is why you have come,' he said as she helped him load the van.

The job had taken less time than expected, so they stopped off at Blaise Castle for a snack at the railway carriage on the way home. Olive seemed content with her new carer, and Mrs Brimble, who now introduced herself as Joan, was happy to come in two weeks' time.

As Jem walked Buster to collect the children she realised how in her old life her day had been clogged up with needless expensive pursuits: tennis, horse riding, shopping for clothes, hairdressers, lunch with the girls. These simple three hours had been so refreshing.

Will was staying for football practice and coming home later with Tom, but Sasha and Kim were with Charlie, so they all walked home together. That morning Jem, having spare eggs and margarine, had made a cake, so she asked if the girls would like to come to tea. They all stopped at the girls' house, No. 7, to tell their mum. Jem rang the bell.

'I'm Jem Thomas from over the road. Is it OK if Kim and Sasha come to tea? Are you all right? Oh dear, I don't even know your name.'

The woman at the door had red-rimmed eyes and was desperately pale and thin. She was still in a grubby dressing gown.

'I'm Jo.' She looked embarrassed. 'Actually I've got a doctor's appointment, so that would be good. I won't have to drag them along.'

'Right, I'll look after the girls. If you like, come and have a cup of tea on your way back. See you later.'

The poor girl looked so wretched, as though she wanted to be left alone, and it had taken the sparkle out of Jem's day.

Whilst Charlie was happily playing dolls with Kim and Sasha upstairs – their mother's sad looks and dressing gown were apparently normal – Jem and Olive were in the kitchen whilst Jem knocked up a quick spaghetti Bolognese. One third of the cake had vanished and she hoped Joan wasn't expecting cake every time. Olive was in no mood to say anything about her afternoon as an inane quiz programme held her limited attention.

The children, including Will, tired and muddy, attacked the meal with relish.

'We only had Marmite sandwiches for lunch. Mum wasn't well so we made the sarnies ourselves,' Kim announced with pride.

'Well done,' said Jem encouragingly. 'Is your dad at home?'

'No. He's away with his lorry. It's a very big lorry.'

'It has sixteen wheels,' Sasha interrupted. 'He might bring us some chocolate when he comes home.' The family seemed a mystery.

The four children were playing Top Trumps upstairs and Gran was in her room watching *Neighbours* when Jo knocked at the door, now dressed in a shabby skirt and worn anorak.

'You look all in,' Jem said soothingly. 'Do you want to come in?'

'Yeah, thanks,' so she was ushered into the warm kitchen. She slumped down by the table. 'I've had a rotten day. Felt so down, couldn't get out of bed this morning.'

'Kim said they had made their own sandwiches. She was pleased they could do it.'

'They're good girls. I had postnatal depression with Sasha and was in Barrow Hospital for a long time. Kim had to be put into care. It's been awful for all of us. Ted doesn't understand. The doctor keeps on changing the tablets. These last ones didn't work, made me feel worse. He's given me different ones today. After five years I should be better, but my mum was in and out of hospital with depression. Is it hereditary?'

'I don't know,' answered Jem, cutting them both a piece of cake. Agony aunt had never been a role Jem had envisaged for herself, but then she thought of Carrie and how helpful she had always been. Perhaps she could be the same.

'I drag myself out of bed every morning. Just about get to the shops for food, cook tea, then I'm exhausted.'

'Perhaps there's another cause the doctors haven't found.'

'I've had loads of tests. Ted says, "Snap out of it." But I can't. Then he gets angry and hits me. We're all frightened of him.'

'I know the feeling,' said Jem, taking Jo's hand. 'I'm a widow, but my husband gave me the odd black eye and he beat Will for not doing well at school. We were scared of him some of the time. You're not the only one.'

'It's nice to have someone to talk to. Ted says I shouldn't talk to Charlene because of what she does, or the Williams because of religion. And I haven't got the energy to get up to school and see the mums there.'

'So you stay home.'

'Yeah. What makes things worse is Ted is friends with Darren from school days. Darren gives him some stuff to keep him awake for driving the lorry. But in the end it makes him too wound up, then he's awful. Darren Sparks has always been trouble.'

Jem could hear the children jumping down the stairs. It sounded like the game 'Who Can Jump Down the Most

116

Stairs Without Falling Over?' It was not a safe game, but caused laughter and noise.

'Let's hope these new pills make you feel better and you can cope. But I'm here with Mum, so if you want me to do any shopping, or look after Kim and Sasha, tell me. Now it's time these children calmed down and went to bed. Before Vera or Bert starts banging on the walls.'

'You don't talk like you come from round here.'

'No,' said Jem, smiling, 'I come from a long way away.' (Four miles at the most, she thought.) 'A different place. A different way of life. Then my husband died in an accident, we had no money, and we ended up here.'

Later Will asked, 'Was Kim and Sasha's mum all right? She seems odd.'

'She's not very well. But she's been to the doctor today and new tablets may make her better.'

Jem didn't really believe this, and hoped she wouldn't get too involved. She would make sure they kept out of the way when Ted was about.

In fact, Thursday afternoons became a routine. Will stayed for football practice and the three girls had tea at Jem's house. Jo would come over to collect them and stay for a chat. Her new pills seemed to be helping. Her eyes were no longer red-rimmed and her hair was cleaner and neat.

Ted had been home for one weekend but there were no bruises or black eyes. Jo had told Jem her husband drove over to Eastern Europe every trip, earned good money and was saving to buy a house. Jem hoped this was true, but she had learnt to have a cynical mind. He could be driving all over Britain and staying with a different woman at every night stop for all Jo knew. And where did he save his money? Did he have a bank account? They weren't so common round here. She hoped Darren Sparks wasn't taking more than his share. Still, Kim had shared out some chocolates from Brussels one teatime, so it might be true. Jem would have to ignore their problems; she had enough to deal with.

Joan Brimble's fortnightly care afternoon with Olive was due. Jem had washed her hair and put on a new woolly jersey from the charity shop, hoping that Craig would turn up in his van, but just as Joan had settled in her chair and taken out her knitting Craig rang to say an important client – that is, one with money – wanted him to replant his garden. Jem banged the phone down.

'All dressed up and nowhere to go?' enquired Joan.

Jem asked herself if Mr Brimble had died from an excess of sarcasm. At least she had only made rock cakes for tea. 'I'll take Buster for a walk. It's a beautiful afternoon.'

'Have you found the wood beyond Woodchester Road? Follow the little stream in the open space.'

'The one full of supermarket trolleys?'

'It gets better. Especially on a spring day. May Day last week. Dancing round the May pole.'

Always the schoolteacher, thought a frustrated Jem as she put the lead on Buster, mentally cursing Craig, Joan, everything.

She walked fast to the open grassy space, trying to ignore the litter, cans of Coke and beer. As she followed the stream it improved and gradually the sound of the water soothed her wound-up feelings. Yes, the sun was shining. It was warm on her face. Buster was bounding around her with an abandoned ball he had found. She threw it for him and enjoyed watching him run, then play with the ball, throwing it for himself. Crossing over the road, Buster on the lead, she was aware of children playing outside at lunchtime. A happy shouting noise.

There was a footpath leading down to a valley and she could hear the stream again. She followed the bubbling sound of the water. The stream was getting bigger now and there were weirs holding back the clear still water over grey pebbles. Bluebells were growing along the banks; catkins hung from the hazel bushes. Overhead cherry trees let white petals float down to the path, and birds sang. She recognised a robin, blackbirds and chaffinches.

Finding a wooden seat where another steam joined the first she sat down, taking in the sun, warmth and sounds of the wood, watching Buster splashing in the water. She let her thoughts drift. Perhaps Joan wasn't so irritating if she could direct you to places like this. How many people knew it was here: a haven, a clear sparkling stream in a green wooded valley, with the houses encroaching on every side? She could bring the kids here on their bikes. They would get wet, but she wouldn't mind. Probably not in the evenings, or on their own. Neighbours had told her of warped-minded men in dirty raincoats, hiding behind bushes in the open spaces. What happened here under the cover of darkness? Love and amorous liaison, underage drinking, drugs? But in the brightness of the sunlight there was peace.

Her thoughts strayed further. She was surprised at her frustration and annoyance that Craig hadn't been able to be there. She had not realised she was so looking forward to another insight into his life. Was he that important to her? Where would it lead?

She glanced at her watch – an hour and a half had gone by in complete solitude. When had she last had that? And

119

when would she get it again, with the half-term holiday in a week? With more vigour in her step she returned to the domesticity of Meadowleaze.

Tea was ready for the girls. Will came in full of himself as he had scored three goals in practice and would be in the team. After beans on toast with cheese and a poached egg on top, Will turned to the rock cakes. Took a bite, turned to the tools drawer and found the hammer.

'Steady on,' said his mother whilst the girls tried to stop laughing. 'They're not that bad.' The rock cakes had all gone by the time the children were upstairs playing some card game.

Jo turned up to collect Kim and Sasha. She looked better and happily sat down to a mug of tea and a rock cake Jem had hidden away. Jem, her walk fresh in her mind, told Jo of her afternoon with Buster. 'It's the first three hours I've had on my own for months. The woods were so quiet and peaceful. Oh dear.'

Jo had hung her head between her arms and was sobbing. 'Ordinary people don't understand. Nobody understands. I know the woods where you walked. I often went there with my big brother. I know it is lovely. My brain tells me about the brook and bird song, but I cannot feel it. That's what so awful about depression. Everything is a grey nothing.'

'Everything?' asked Jem. 'Even the children?'

Jo nodded. 'People who mean well say things like, "There's a light at the end of the tunnel." No, there ain't.'

Jem had been about to say, 'Given time, it will pass,' but stopped herself, and just sat there with her arm around Jo's shoulders. She noticed Olive standing in the doorway nodding her head. Did she too understand this bleakness in her demented state?

120

Jem's thoughts went back to her wedding and how Olive had let Mrs Somerville-Thomas take over. Was that depression? She remembered her mother quietly saying after Henry's funeral in a lucid moment, 'I'm here waiting to die.' She had been depressed as well as confused. How fragile normality was. But she had to battle on for Will and Charlie.

It was Bank Holiday Monday. Bill Edwards had promised to take them out in the countryside for the day. They would need two cars because of Gran and her wheelchair. Jem had a plastic bag full of cheese sandwiches and drinks. (The sardine sandwiches she had made the previous evening had gone soggy, but the children had thought they were a great breakfast.)

Gran travelled in state with Bill and his mother, Susan, whilst Jem followed with Will, Charlie and Buster. They drove up Burrington Combe to the Mendip Hills, which Jem vaguely remembered from some school trip, and parked by a Forestry Commission pinewood.

Bill found a grassy space. 'This is our camp,' he explained, and then he set out a folding chair for his mother, and a camping table, before wheeling Olive to a flat stable space beside the table. On this he laid cold chicken, salad, French bread and butter. There was a bottle of wine for the adults, and Jem added her sandwiches and soft drinks.

After satisfyingly stuffing themselves the children wanted to be off exploring the woods.

'Here's a whistle each,' said Bill, 'if you lose each other, or break a leg.'

'Were you a Boy Scout?' enquired Jem when the children had vanished.

'No,' answered Susan. 'He should have been a teacher.

121

But the theatre beckoned and you know what happened. All that matters is that he is content, and the amateur dramatics help with that. You must come and see him in *Blithe Spirit*, in a few weeks.'

Bill was wandering off now, calling in a loud voice, 'I'm coming to get you,' and the women could hear the children in the distance squealing and laughing. Jem was soon joining in and the game turned into Kick the Can. Who could be first to get back to Gran and Susan?

When they were tired and in need of a drink, Bill dramatically produced strawberries and cream for 'afters'.

There was a pool of water over the road and, leaving Olive and Susan to enjoy some peace and quiet, the others went to investigate. It seemed an odd place for a pond and Bill told them of the old lead works that had been here.

'In fact there have been lead works here since—'

'Can we paddle, Mum?' asked Will.

'If you take off your socks and shoes, and don't whinge about the stones. Sorry, you were saying?'

'Lead works. The Romans. Doesn't matter. How is life in Meadowleaze?'

'Compared with many of our neighbours we're OK.' Jem went on to tell him about Jo and Charlene, Vera and Bert. Others wary of Ruth and Joel because of their faith.

'Charlene is well known to the council and the police, but we say nothing. The children are well cared for, and it does little harm. All these things – drunkenness, prostitution, drugs, depression – happen everywhere. We're all human, although the richer people try to cover it up. Always has been the case. Now in Northfield racist behaviour comes into the equation. A volatile mix that most people tolerate and they rub along together, as you are doing. Go back four hundred years and think of

Shylock in *The Merchant of Venice*. He was talking about race, which also applies here.' Bill went into Laurence Oliver mode. 'If you prick us, do we not bleed? If you tickle us, do we not laugh? If you poison us, do we not die? And if you wrong us, shall we not revenge? If we are like you in the rest, we will resemble you in that.'

He straightened up. 'Human beings make cages for themselves. Some they make through religion and beliefs. Others are made for them by persecution, ignorance or illness. Neighbours back away from poor Jo with depression and your mum with dementia. Their lack of knowledge makes them scared.'

'You're right,' said Jem. 'People are people wherever they come from. Views are indoctrinated into them from birth in all cultures. Underneath the skin we're all the same.' What he said was true. She didn't want to make fun of him, but he was so earnest, how could she resist? 'Now you can strip off and swim across the lake to prove it.'

'You're nearer the water than I am.'

Jem glanced over her shoulder, yelped, and ran despite wet shoes.

She reached the dry stone wall by the road, breathless and damp.

'All you said is true,' she said, laughing. 'But what'll we do about Will and Charlie? Philosophy apart. They're swimming in the pool.'

Despite the children being wrapped in the hairy dog blanket in the back of the car on the way home, the company decided it had been a good day out.

It was Midsummer's Day and Jem's birthday. At breakfast the children had timidly given her a box of chocolates and cards; Charlotte had drawn pictures in her card of the three of them on bikes. Jem was so pleased they had remembered, as there was no one to tell them.

Today she was having a rest from housework and was relaxing in the garden by planting some seedling nasturtiums Joel Williams had given her, whilst her mother sat in her wheelchair enjoying the sunshine. There were some marigolds in bloom that Bert had passed over the fence earlier in the year. Her shy acquaintance with these men was slowly turning to friendship.

The postman's bike came to a halt outside the gate and, whistling, he thrust envelopes through the letterbox. None of the family usually got letters.

'Maybe there're some cards,' wondered Jem.

'Birthday,' muttered Gran.

Yes, there were cards from Liz and Gwendolyn. Nothing from the Somerville-Thomases. Then there was a redirected envelope from her old address. With curiosity she opened the envelope to find a folded piece of A4 paper. On it were pasted newsprint letters:

REMEMBER
THE NORTH COL
YOU WILL NOT GET AWAY WITH IT

Jem crumpled the paper in fear. Her forehead came out in a cold sweat and with shaking hands she jammed the paper in the bin. Taking a deep breath she pulled herself together. She had had threats and insults before from people who had fallen foul of Rupert's schemes. This was just another one. But why the North Col? She must have mentioned it, probably at the funeral. She had to forget this and remember the cards from her old friends.

She decided to take her mother to the Queen's Head for

a birthday drink. She needed it, despite the fact she couldn't afford it, having saved money for a birthday tea. A walk to the pub and a stiff drink would take her mind off the poison pen letter.

As it turned out Carrie, Craig and Bill turned up during the long summer evening and they sat in the garden with bottles of wine contributed by the guests. Even Vera and Ruth popped in, so in convivial company the letter was forgotten.

PART TWO

The man woke up. His body was a sea of pain. He couldn't see straight, then he passed out again.

The next time he awoke the pain had lessened and his eyes focused. His chest felt strange and his legs hurt. A nurse spoke to him soothingly in a language he couldn't understand, but he was too tired to care.

Days passed and the pain wasn't as bad, but he hadn't the strength to ask where he was or what had happened. After some time – it could have been days or weeks – a nurse who spoke English came to take his temperature and blood pressure.

'You're making good progress, Michael,' and she patted his arm. 'How are you feeling?'

The patient said nothing. His mouth didn't work. Had his brain gone completely? Was his name Michael?

'I'll come and see you again, soon.'

Later in the day two nurses lifted him from his bed to a chair so they could remake his bed. He could feel bandages round his chest and saw one leg in plaster up to his thigh. Gradually some memories came back to him. He had been on holiday with his family. He had spent the night with some sexy woman, then he had been on top of a mountain with his wife and they had had a row. She was always so unreasonable. Stupid and jealous. He felt angry and memories flooded back. Why shouldn't he have any woman he wanted? After that he remembered nothing but a void.

With all of his neck muscles protesting, he turned his head to look at the name above the bed. It read, 'Michael Brooks'. No, that couldn't be it. He wasn't Michael Brooks. His name was ... what was it, yes ... Rupert Somerville-Thomas. He was thirty-two years old, born on 6th July 1957 at Compton Manor, near Bristol. 'I'm not Michael Brooks,' he wanted to shout, but no voice came out.

The next day a doctor came to discuss Michael Brooks's case with the nurse acting as interpreter. Mr Brooks would be transferred to a British hospital in a few days. There he would be given help to rehabilitate with physio and regain his mobility. Later that day Michael Brooks's luggage was delivered from a hotel. It was a standard hold-all and the address tag on the handle was for an apartment in what he presumed was a block of flats called Elliott Mansions in Chelsea. Chelsea was a good address and his taste in clothes wasn't bad.

During the next couple of days he managed to dress himself, apart from his trousers, and feed himself. He was saying 'ja' and 'nein', and 'danke', which made the nurses smile.

His memory was returning and with it the knowledge of his business fiasco. He owed money to everyone. The holiday had been paid for with a credit card, but there was no credit in his various bank accounts. He had been hoping to win the support of Susannah Wellington's banker husband, but that hadn't worked. Probably the fraud squad would be waiting for him when he got back home. Why hadn't Jemima come to visit him, or Tina? Had they all gone home because of his night with the sexy bitch, or did they think that he had died in the accident? Had there been some dreadful mix-up?

He had long dark hours in which to think and started to plot a new life. The future that lay before him looked bleak as Rupert Somerville-Thomas. Why not pretend to be Michael Brooks? No one professing to be Michael Brooks's wife or family had sat round his bedside looking sympathetic or surprised. Was Michael Brooks a man on his own? Until he was given Brooks's passport for his return to Britain he wouldn't know. But it was worth the risk. The fraud squad made it worth the risk. Michael Brooks evidently had very good health insurance as no one had questioned his payment at the hospital.

So Rupert sat back, smiled his charming smile, and was flown by plane to Heathrow. The air stewardess pushed him in a wheelchair, his plastered leg going before him like a battering ram. A passport was handed to him at the airport as he left Austria. He opened this with feelings of both fear and excitement; who would he be? Looking at the photo of Michael Brooks he understood the mistake. They were facially alike, both fair with blue eyes. Michael was older, born on the 5th November 1954. An easy date to remember. He had been born in London, and his profession said 'Writer'. What did that mean? What kind of writer? It was a solitary way of life. Would that mean he lived a lonely life and Rupert could take up his identity? It seemed unlikely. Next of kin was a Mrs J Brooks who lived in Birmingham. There had been no contact. Was she mother, sister-in-law, or uninterested wife? The mystery intrigued him. Could he become Michael Brooks?

Relaxing on the plane and gaining simpering support from the stewardesses, his leg stuck out on the next chair, a couple of free whiskies inside him, he thought he would soon find out more about Michael Brooks.

It was a surprise to him, coming back to London to find spring flowers out and realising that over two months of his life had disappeared. At the London hospital he said little, trying to imagine a new personality – Michael Brooks. His smile still endeared him to the hospital staff, so there was little he needed to do before the plaster was off and replaced with a small cast to the knee, except learn to walk again. His other injuries were slowly healing.

The consultant unnerved him. His chest injuries would leave him with breathing difficulties, and his leg would give him some pain and was shorter, so he would always have a limp. But he was lucky to be alive. This was a shock to him, having always been proud of his health and well-being. All because of his silly bitch of a wife!

Finally the day came for his discharge. The taxi driver, seeing his plight, walking with two crutches, helped him up the five marble steps, through the stained-glass, black-painted front door and into the lift of Elliott Mansions, carrying the hold-all. Flat 8 was on the third floor of an ornate red-brick Victorian block, decorated in Gothic style. Rupert hoped the key he had chosen from several on a key ring fitted the front door. He was in luck. The driver pushed open the door with difficulty, kicking aside over two months of accumulated post, which he helpfully piled on a table in the small hall. Having tipped the taxi man, Rupert closed the front door with relief. For the first time in many weeks he was on his own.

He surveyed the hall. At least there was no nosy

cleaning lady or friendly neighbour keeping an eye on the place, as the post blocking the front door had shown. No one would suddenly appear using a spare key. He hung up his over-warm ski jacket on the elaborate wooden coat stand and noticed an expensive long black coat and a Barbour jacket. The man had good taste, he thought. That being the case, would there be some whisky in a sideboard? He could do with a drink.

Using one crutch he hobbled into the nearest room, which overlooked the street. Michael definitely had good taste. It was a light airy room with two black leather sofas and a large Afghan rug on the polished wood floor. Against one wall was a Chippendale-style sideboard with a tray of bottles. Rupert helped himself to a large Scotch and surveyed the rest of the room. Most of the wall space was taken up with bookshelves, but there were several modern paintings and statuettes, which meant little to him. He sat in a chair by the bay window enjoying his whisky and watching the traffic pass three storeys beneath him. At this height it was a reassuring hum and reminded him of being twenty-one, when he had first come to London after Oxford. This could be very restful. No resentful wife, no loud over-excited children. He could relax in this flat over the next few days, play detective, and discover all he could about Michael Brooks.

There was plenty to drink, but what was there to eat? He suddenly felt hungry. Painfully rising to his feet he limped off to find out about the rest of the flat.

The room next to the living room was a small study with a computer and printer on the desk by the window. There were more shelves of books, files and two filing cabinets. It was all very businesslike. The bedroom, which looked out over the back of the flats to a dull court full of dustbins, was itself comfortable with a king-sized bed and William Morris-style curtains. Off the bedroom was a bathroom, fully tiled in pearly green with an exercise bike in one corner. Kitchen next; would there be food? There were no mouldering dirty dishes in the sink. The fridge held out-of-date eggs, dried-up bacon, cheese and apples, as would be expected, but the margarine was OK. The deep-freeze was full of prepared meals. This guy was too good to be true! He behaved like a housewife. Then a thought. Was he a homosexual? So what? He didn't have to answer the door and he could always put the phone down on anyone he was suspicious about. Was there an answering machine? This might give him useful information, but later. A meal was his main concern.

Rupert selected a frozen dinner and for the first time in his life pressed buttons on a microwave to serve himself up shepherd's pie. Admitted it wasn't as good as Jemima's, but it was food. He could live.

So much exertion, after weeks in bed, understandably left him very tired, so he found the king-sized bed and fell fast asleep.

He awoke as dusk turned the sky a silvery blue. Feeling peckish he browsed the deep freeze again, found a sliced loaf and made toast, then opened a jar of marmalade from the cupboard. Taking these to the living room he poured himself another drink, realising it deadened the pain in his leg and chest, switched on the television and settled down to watch an evening's programmes in peace and quiet. He felt free and tomorrow would begin his research.

After making a pot of black coffee he took the post into the study and went through it. He threw all the junk mail in the bin, put in different piles letters that looked personal, bills, magazines that seemed academic, and bank statements. These statements were very informative and reassuring. There was a sizeable income coming in from investments. If this amount came in every month he could live comfortably. There were the usual standing orders for local urban tax, mortgage, health insurance (for which he was grateful, considering his injuries), and utilities. There was a monthly payment to a Mrs J Brooks. Was she an aged mother for whom he paid the care, or a divorced wife?

The personal letters were more difficult. Two were thank-you letters for Christmas presents, and there were a few belated Christmas cards. Michael Brooks must have started his holiday on Boxing Day as Rupert and his family had done. They may have been on the same plane. Lastly there was an erudite letter from someone in Oxford he could make little of, but it referred to medieval history. This must have something to do with the entry in Brooks's passport saying he was a writer.

Rupert sat back in his chair, wondering about this. If he really did intend to be Michael Brooks he would have to reply to this letter in vague terms using the computer and practise forging Michael's signature. He'd have to use this on cheques as well. No doubt he would find a sample somewhere in the filing system. He was hoping he would find a banker's card PIN code somewhere so he could get cash, but perhaps he could telephone the bank saying he had lost the card.

Rupert needed refreshment after all this thinking and reading. He had not used his brain since January, so he took his crutch and returned to the living room, poured himself a gin and tonic, and started looking at the book-shelves. The books were mostly historical and, typically of Michael judging by his efficient housekeeping, systematically divided up – first the Romans, then Saxons, Normans, Tudors, Stuarts and lastly the Georges and Victoria. The biggest section was on the Normans, which corresponded with the letter from the man in Oxford.

He replenished his glass and scrutinised the spines of the books on Norman times. There were two books here by Michael Brooks. They were on monastic life in Yorkshire and Northumberland. He put them by the chair in the window for later reading. He started surveying the books on the other wall. These were works of fiction, but mostly historical novels. Jemima was an avid reader of these so he knew the names of many of the authors, but here was a whole shelf dedicated to one writer he didn't know.

Michaela Rivers. Rupert laughed. The first time he had done so since the accident, and it hurt his ribs. Was this Michael's pen name? He took the first one from the shelf; it had a Norman castle on the dust cover. It was just entitled *Gwendoline* and was a love story of the daughter of a Norman lord called Fitzhurbert. Gwendoline had fallen in love with a monk. The dust cover didn't reveal what happened, but there was obviously an impact on the next book, which featured a bastard Fitzhurbert son. Reading the synopsis on each dust cover, he found the stories traced the Fitzhurbert family through several generations. There were border skirmishes with the Scots; the Hotspurs came into the story, as did the power of the Church and the Black Death. It had all the elements of a good saga and he could see women getting hooked on the characters and awaiting the next novel, in the same way they liked *The Archers* and soaps. Michael would have the knowledge to make it work, and it would be a good money-spinner. This was how Michael Brooks made his money as 'a writer'. Though not Rupert's scene – he was more a Wilbur Smith fan – he would make these novels his evening reading to get insight into the author.

He dozed through the afternoon, then the scents of spring waved in through the window and he decided to brave the outside world despite the pain in his leg and just walk round the block. Having been shut away from the ordinary world for months he found the noise and speed of the traffic daunting, but with two crutches to help him he managed to walk to a quiet side street. There were attractive three-storey terraced houses with daffodils and tulips in window boxes, and on the corner a Victorian pub. The exterior was decorated with brown and green tiles and engraved windows saying, 'Wines, spirits, lounge bar and public bar,' surrounded by swirls of leaves and grapes.

Rupert used his shoulder to shove open the door of the lounge bar. The two crutches brought a sympathetic smile to the face of the barman, who after Rupert had ordered a double whisky said, 'What happened to you, mate?'

'Skiing accident. Fell off a cliff. I've been in hospital for two months. This is my first outing.'

'Glad you're out and about again, mate. Thought you looked all in when you pushed through the door. 'ave one on the house.'

This exchange made Rupert more confident and the whisky began to revive him.

'I only moved into the area just before Christmas. Now with this' – he pointed to his plastered foot – 'I haven't had a chance to find my way around. Where's the nearest bank with a "hole in the wall" and food shops?'

The barman obligingly fished out an A-to-Z map and

showed Rupert where the nearest bank was and a Spar shop within easy walking distance. Rupert thanked the man profusely and said he would certainly be in for a drink in the near future. With difficulty and some pain he made his way back to the flat – it was not yet home – with a feeling of triumph. Tomorrow he could replenish the deep freeze and the drinks tray – if he could forge Brooks's signature. He turned to the filing cabinets.

His outing the day before had given him confidence. He had a chequebook and, having practised Michael's signature, with the use of the cheque card he could buy what he needed at the local shop. Feeling strength returning he ventured forth, hoping Michael had never visited the shop. He enjoyed being out and about, feeling part of the town's life again, but he soon tired and was glad of the small supermarket's trolley taking some of his weight. He found various frozen dinners, eggs and bacon, cheese, bread, milk and enough alcohol for several days. At the counter he could feel tension rising, but the name and the signature aroused no suspicion as he passed the cheque to the assistant. He then asked if he could telephone for a taxi and, seeing the crutches in the trolley, the assistant kindly found a chair and called for a taxi. The taxi driver was equally as helpful and carried the bags to the lift in the block of flats – hoping for a large tip, which Rupert gave him.

As he jammed the lift open with one of the bags so he could unlock the flat, a lady from the flat opposite opened her door.

'Oh, you poor man,' she exclaimed. 'Let me help you. You must be Mr Brooks. I'm Eunice Gibson from Flat 7. I've been here since November, but I don't think I've ever seen you. Mavis, who cleans the stairs, said,' then in hushed tones, 'you were an academic. I imagine you study much of the time.'

'Yes, I do,' replied Rupert, not wishing to get into conversation that would lead to gossip, but glad to find someone to carry the shopping. She'd probably notice the gin and whisky and tell the cleaner he was a secret drinker.

Eunice Gibson helped carry the bags into his hallway, chattering continuously about other people in the building and where she was going for lunch. Rupert, giving nothing away, thanked his neighbour profusely, but smiled as she left for the lift. She was an attractive blonde, with large blue eyes, in her early forties, who had the look of what he considered 'a woman on the hunt.' She was either divorced, widowed or had been let down by a boyfriend and was looking for a new man. He hoped she wouldn't start being neighbourly. He would have to be wary. At least she had assumed he was Michael Brooks.

Once he had put the groceries away and had a whisky in his hand his confidence returned. He had survived and enjoyed two outings into Chelsea. Now he would more thoroughly examine the study and the filing cabinets. There he would find out more so he could take on the personality of Michael Brooks.

Rupert was reminded of university days at Oxford when he had to do research for essays and delve into relevant books to establish the facts. It was aesthetic, pure – just using your mind. But he wouldn't want to do it for long. Interspersed with frozen dinners, whisky, TV and visits to the pub he enjoyed the research and the intellectual effort. He always had enjoyed research, but it never had the excitement of investments – the chase after money.

After five days he had discovered Michael had been born in Bradford. From his birth certificate he discovered his father was a mechanical engineer. Obviously Father had done well and ended up owning his own firm. When Michael had been twenty-three his father had died in a road accident, leaving his family very well off. His mother had died a couple of years later, so Michael had become wealthy. There were no brothers or sisters.

Michael's CV told Rupert he had been educated at the local grammar school and then Leeds University where he had studied history. He had gone on to do an MA degree and finally two years later he had achieved a PhD, so he could call himself Dr Brooks. It was after this, with no money worries and no necessity to find a job, that he had written the two books on monasteries in Yorkshire.

A marriage certificate told Rupert that during this time Michael had presumably fallen in love and married Jean Robinson – a teacher. The wedding took place in Leeds Registry Office (so he was probably not religious), and by then Michael's job was stated as university lecturer. There was a record of a house purchase on the outskirts of Leeds, and a year later correspondence with a local publisher began. This was when the first historical novel came out.

Life seemed to be going very happily for Michael and Jean. There was a file labelled 'Holidays' with odd brochures and receipts for trips to many European countries and an annual winter sports holiday to Austria. They had once been to the USA. Life must have been good.

Then Rupert came across a file marked 'Fertility Treatment'. It commenced six years ago, covered two years' treatment and was quite thick. It was obviously unsuccessful as after this a 'Divorce Proceedings' file came to light, followed by a 'House Sale' file and the purchase of Michael's London flat. The end of a dream?

Looking through the most recent file of random letters Rupert realised Michael was trying to make the most of a depressing situation and turn his aims around. He had come to London to make use of the British Museum and the Reading Room. He was continuing his work on monasteries and researching the south-eastern counties. The files on the shelves confirmed this with copious notes. Maybe the computer had the beginnings of a book within its hard disc.

Lastly Rupert came to the file marked 'Banking'. Looking carefully through it, he came to a slip of paper with a PIN code on it. He smiled to himself and pocketed the paper. Now he could take out money without having to show himself to anyone at the bank. He felt pleased with himself. He knew the history of Michael Brooks.

Next he listened to the answerphone, hoping to find out how Michael's voice sounded. Did he have an accent? Turning it on he heard a strong Yorkshire voice say, 'Michael Brooks is not available to take your call. Please leave your name and number after the tone.' Yes, he would have to practise that voice. There was no evidence he possessed a car – what was the point in the centre of London? – but he did find a driving licence.

But what of Michael as a person? Oddly in this day and age there were no photos. With no children, family photos didn't happen, and with the divorce perhaps wedding photos had been destroyed, but neither were there pictures of Brooks's parents, school days, or university friends or colleagues. A cold fish, or something of a recluse? Perhaps damaged by the divorce. No one had knocked on the door. No one had telephoned since he had been here. No recent letters. Did no one care for Michael Brooks? Or was he so reserved no one noticed him? Rupert was beginning to think of Michael as an invisible friend. He had spent five days finding out about his life. He wanted to know more about what he was like. Had he no friends? It would be pleasant to think there was a secret mistress, but there were no signs.

The only other items to be investigated were his music collection and his clothes. There was an expensive music centre in the living room and a rack of CDs. Disappointed, he discovered they were all of classical music, mostly Bach, Mozart and Beethoven. Probably conducive to study, but nothing to lighten the mood. Maybe Jean had taken the lighter stuff. The clothes were conventional. Two well-tailored suits, sports jackets, casual trousers and many jerseys in neutral colours. No sign of any sports gear. Both men were of a similar build, so the jerseys and shirts could be useful, but the trousers were all too short and the shoes too tight, as his broken foot had been telling him since he had come back from Austria. Now that he could obtain money from any 'hole in the wall' he'd buy a casual, comfortable jogging suit and some trainers. New trousers and shoes could wait until the plaster came off later in the week. Yes, tomorrow he'd take a taxi to Sloane Square.

Rupert sang cheerfully as he poured cereal into a bowl and put bread in the toaster.

A taxi took him to Peter Jones in Sloane Square. He took out cash and bought two jogging suits, shorts, shirts, swimming trunks and trainers in the sports department. The assistants, seeing his leg in plaster, took pity on him and treated him with kindness, and the purchases were sent down to the door porter. Then Rupert went to the restaurant and ordered the most expensive steak on the menu and a bottle of claret. Feeling very self-satisfied he found the music department and bought CDs of his favourite jazz singers – Johnny Dankworth and Ella Fitzgerald. He felt like a celebrity as the front door porter hailed a taxi and handed the driver all his purchases, then he was driven in state back to his flat. This was the life!

In the evening, wearing a new jogging suit and one trainer, he went to the pub where he got into conversation with a couple of young men, Charles and George, with whom he had exchanged jokes on earlier occasions. They said they would recommend his membership of their sports club. Evenings of squash, tennis and swimming in the future.

Rupert hopped home, his crutches swinging. He was beginning to enjoy being Michael Brooks, and tomorrow his plaster cast would be sawn off.

Rupert gritted his teeth as the tiny circular saw vibrated down his leg and the cast fell away like two halves of a walnut shell. He was speedily wheeled to an examination room and told to lie on the bed as the consultant, suave in his dazzling white coat, swept in followed by his entourage of confused students in their longer white coats. He talked eloquently to his disciples, pointing out on X-rays the several fractures in Rupert's leg held together with pins; he asked them questions that they nervously answered, and then the magnificent man turned to Rupert.

'Considering the severity of these fractures and your other injuries you're lucky to be alive. You will walk again, but bear in mind your left leg is shorter than your right leg. It will be weak for some time and physio will be very important.' He turned to his students and remarked, 'I don't think he'll be going skiing again.' Then he swept away, the students tumbling after, wondering whether the remark was a joke and they were expected to laugh.

Rupert stared at his leg. The self-important consultant had said it was shorter than his good leg but he would walk again in time. He remembered the consultant saying this when he first came back to London, but at that time he hadn't taken it in. To always walk with a limp. His left leg was sickly white, wrinkled and withered. There were long scars from the operations. His right leg was still bronze from last summer's holiday on the island of Rhodes and muscular. The contrast was appalling, especially to Rupert, who was proud of his body and his physical fitness. He lay there, numb with shock, until a nurse brought him an appointment for physiotherapy and summoned a porter to take him down to the hospital entrance.

'I can walk,' Rupert shouted at her as he swung his feet to the floor, but he would have fallen if the porter hadn't held him.

'Use your crutches,' commanded the nurse, handing them to him. 'Just be patient, and remember your appointments.'

The next few hours in Michael Brooks's flat were a nightmare. Rupert could not come to terms with being, as he politically incorrectly termed it, 'a cripple'. One leg shorter than the other. He would limp through the rest of his life. He remembered picking up the ball in rugby and running for the line. Never would he be that speedy again.

(Not that he had been for several years.) He'd never go jogging on the Downs with his friends from Round Table, or ask amiable clients for a game of squash at the Country Club. Those days were gone forever.

He had forgotten it was his own decision to become Michael Brooks to keep out of the clutches of the fraud squad, and he felt sorry for himself. He imagined Jemima and the children still enjoying the luxury of his home, Jemima playing tennis, William scoring tries at rugby and Charlotte having pony-riding lessons. He was jealous first. Why should they be enjoying the good life whilst he was stuck here? Then he became angry. He fuelled his anger with whisky and directed it towards Jemima. It was her fault he was here. He was far too good a skier to have fallen. She must have pushed him. That was the only explanation. She had been annoyed by his dalliance with Susannah Wellington when she had no right to be. It was just business. Rupert had wanted Susannah to influence her husband into investing in his business. Jemima was so stupid, never understood anything. He knew it would be pointless explaining anything to her; she wasn't bright enough to understand. A pretty face upon an empty head. She was being soft with the children. They would end up so silly with no backbone.

By the end of the bottle of whisky Rupert was feeling extremely sorry for himself and, flopping down on the bed, fully clothed, soon asleep with troubled, distorted anxiety dreams.

Rupert was not surprised by his hangover. He had no energy for anything and stayed in bed most of the day. He was totally dysfunctional and didn't care. The following day he had to pull himself together to get to the physiotherapy session.

Most of the physiotherapists he had met in the past, when recovering from rugby injuries, had been young, slim, with athletic figures. He was hoping to meet a young girl he could chat up. Feminine company was something he was beginning to miss. But his luck was out. The physio was over forty, plump, with flabby arms, and reminded him of Matron at his boarding school.

Although he found the exercises painful and tiring, after a few days he felt more hopeful and decided to try walking to the pub. He needed company. His two new sporty friends, George and Charles, gave a cheer as he tried to walk up to the bar. Rupert put up a false front, telling them he would soon be walking properly and looking forward to some sporting activities. Charles, with a wink, suggested they might find some different sporting activities later in the evening at a club he knew, but at the moment he was hungry. So the three of them climbed into Charles's Mercedes and dined at a bistro in South Kensington.

Fuelled with food and alcohol they made their way to a cellar bar in Notting Hill. There was loud throbbing music, subdued lighting illuminating the cigarette smoke, and girls. Rupert had some success chatting up a young blonde called Louise, who took the Central Line to the City every day to work in an office whose purpose she didn't really understand. When Rupert said he was a writer she was really impressed. 'Oh, *really*?' she kept saying, and Rupert enjoyed fabricating his illusionary career. Louise asked him back for coffee at her flat on Camden Hill, saying it was not far. She took pity on him as he limped up the street and suggested he could stay the night. Rupert remembered little of the night except that they satisfied each other, and by the time he awoke in the morning Louise was well on her way, strap-hanging, along the Central Line. There was a note saying, 'Thanks for a great night. Help yourself to cereal. Leave your telephone number, I'll call you.'

Perhaps it was fortunate he couldn't remember his phone number. He left a note saying that he had enjoyed the evening and suggesting she might like to buy some flowers and remember him, along with a five-pound note. As he slammed the door he wondered if he should add condoms to his shopping list.

The evening's activities had encouraged him. Louise hadn't seen the state of his injured leg, so he could still find sex if he wanted it. With that he walked with crutches as far as Kensington High Street and hailed a taxi to Elliott Mansions. *Yes,* he thought, *I can survive this – but why should I, when Jemima and my children are living the life I created for them?*

For a month he endured this life of physiotherapy, Charles, George and their Sloane Rangers lifestyle, but underneath his bitterness grew. A month later his leg was strong enough to take him for a walk to the Thames with the aid of only one crutch. It was the end of May, the bank holiday and half term. Usually he would have been away with the family in Cornwall, staying at Rock and surfing off the coast at Polzeath. But not this year! He was stuck in limbo in a flat in Chelsea, as a non-person. As his anger grew so did his strength and he walked straight back to Elliott Mansions, only stopping to buy a newspaper and glue. Back at his flat he took pleasure in cutting out the letters to compose the anonymous note Jemima would receive several weeks later on her birthday. She deserved it. He hoped it would fill her being with fear and dread.

144

PART THREE

Jem had other problems on her mind, not poison pen letters, as she looked at the broken glass in the back door window. Gran and the kids were staring too.

'Who's been here? Buster, come. If anyone's in there, sort 'em out.'

Buster, released from his lead, bounced into the kitchen but to his disappointment found no one, and came out with his stubby tail wagging.

It was obvious what had happened. A thief who knew what he was looking for. He had gone straight to the drawer in which Jem kept the envelopes with their week's allowances and the holiday money. The empty drawer had been thrown to the floor. Their holiday at Butlins, Minehead, gone.

Jem rang the police and after an hour they turned up in a panda car. There was little they could do other than send round a fingerprint man (who never turned up).

The presence of a panda car alerted the neighbours and it wasn't long before Ruth and Vera were round drinking coffee and giving sympathetic advice, not realising how much money Jem needed to raise for the Butlins holiday.

'You'll have to get some sort of part-time job,' advised Ruth. 'Perhaps in one of the late-night shops on the main road. The off-licence or the chippy? Second thoughts, not the off-licence that changes cheques. That place gets held up quite frequently.'

'Chippy. Get free chips,' mumbled Gran, but she was ignored.

'I don't mind babysitting. Gran and me could watch *EastEnders* together,' said Vera.

'There are loads of office cleaning jobs, too. It would get you out and about a bit more,' added Ruth.

'You're missing the point. If I go out to work I lose my carer's allowance. And if you work more than fifteen hours they take away the other allowances. Even if I didn't declare any wages the benefits office would check my employer's books.'

'What you need is a firm with a dodgy accountant. Plenty of those round here,' commented Vera.

Jem made more coffee to stimulate their brains.

'You reckon the thief knew where to find the money?' asked Ruth.

'Yes. Nothing else was touched. I wouldn't be surprised if Charlie inadvertently let the cat out of the bag. Other kids at school would be talking about holidays and she wouldn't want to be left out. It would be passed on to older children and maybe some teenager needing money for drugs would make use of the information. Charlie's too young to understand when to keep quiet.'

'If you desperately wanted money,' suggested Vera, 'you could always take a leaf out of Charlene's book. She's taking the kids to Disneyland in the holidays.'

They all laughed. Jem countered, 'One Charlene in the road is enough. Besides, the clients would have to put up

146

with Gran looking on. Craig wouldn't like it and I've got quite fond of him.'

It was Carrie who came up with the answer. Jem rang her the next day and like a fairy godmother she came round to see them in the evening.

'I've just had some curtains made. There's this great fabric shop up in Clifton. Just a one-man band called Curtain Care. He has the most wonderful Liberty materials. I asked him if the curtains were made up on the premises. No, he said, the work gets sent out to women who make the curtains in their own homes. You could do that.'

'I haven't got a sewing machine.'

'You can have mine. I rarely use it.'

'What about his accounting? It would show on his records.'

'Let's go and see him. Smile sweetly and perhaps you could be written off as petty cash.'

With a feeling of adventure in the air, leaving Vera reluctantly keeping an eye on Olive but understanding the situation, Jem and Carrie went to see Mr Styles of Curtain Care the next morning. He was delighted at the idea, as his best machinist had just left to have a baby. Two hours and many notes with instructions later, they left loaded down with material and Rufflette tape.

They stopped off at Carrie's home to pick up the sewing machine. This was the first time Jem had been past her old home. She had imagined there would be painful feelings of nostalgia, but she smiled in wry amusement at a couple of four-by-fours in the drive and an ostentatious dovecot on the front lawn. A new couple, Jem thought, telling the world how splendid they were. How long would it take Grace and Clive Sopworth to insult them? But it

147

was good to have a quick lunch in Carrie's comfortable and spacious kitchen with granite work surfaces and Aga, before returning to Gran and the kids.

The next week was a nightmare. Measuring out the material in Gran's room, as it had most floor space, was difficult and tried Jem's patience to the limit.

'Please, Gran, just sit down and watch *Neighbours*. Don't walk on the material.'

'I need the lav,' and so it went on. Maybe Gran was playing up as she had been put in second place after paying work? It took all of Jem's patience to cope. *Now I understand the meaning of the phrase 'sweatshop labour'*, she thought.

Then, after they had collected the kids from school, it was, 'Ouch, I've got a pin in my foot.' And, 'You've taken over the kitchen table. Where am I supposed to do my homework?'

The children's mother had a terse reply. 'You have a bedroom.'

But they all soon settled down. Everyone had to wear shoes or slippers and Will and Charlie were put on 'pin watch'. As soon as they understood what curtain making involved, they helped measure the curtains and make sure the patterns lined up. Will could even cope with the sewing machine and create a straight row of stitching. By the end of four weeks a neat roll of bank notes had been carefully hidden away in Jem's knickers drawer, with everyone sworn to secrecy.

It was at this time the second letter appeared on the doormat. Again it had been redirected. The theme was the same:

THE NORTH COL
YOU ARE GUILTY
YOU CANNOT SLEEP EASY AT NIGHT

Again Jem screwed the paper up and threw it in the bin. There was nothing she could do about it. It was best to forget it, and she was so busy. She looked after the children and Gran, cooked, cleaned, sewed and slept.

Increasingly Craig would turn up in the evenings, because, he said, he enjoyed the company. He would take the children and Buster down to the grassy space by the stream, which they called 'the Green by the Stream', and they would all play football. Then in the soft summer evenings he and Jem would sit in the garden they were creating, drinking cans of beer, and enjoy the dusk and the stars coming out.

One Sunday in mid-July Jem felt she and Craig were getting on so well she asked his mother and sister round to lunch. Craig's mother, Doris, was very down-to-earth. She seemed to know all the gossip of the neighbourhood and had them all laughing with tales of Darren Sparks's tangles with the police. 'He was a devil since the day he was born.'

'And that Charlene.'

'Charlene's OK,' interjected Jem.

'There has been talk that Charlene and Darren are half-related on account of Bert Sparks carrying on with Irene Brown back in the sixties. Now Irene was mother to Ted, who lives at No. 7.'

'Jo's husband.'

'Yes.'

'That means Ted Brown is half-brother to both Darren Sparks and Charlene. Do they know?'

'I expect so. Wouldn't want it leading to incest like that family in Dulverton Crescent. Half of those kids are the oldest daughter's. No wonder they go to a special school for the sub-normal. There was lots of drugs about in those days. I keep an open mind.'

After cups of tea in the garden Craig's mother remarked, 'You're off to Butlins in a few weeks?'

Charlie was sitting with the women, having got tired of football. 'Would you like to come too? You're a lot more fun than Gran and we like Debbie. You could have a cabin next to ours.'

Later Craig took Jem's hand. 'If we could get a booking, would that be a good idea?'

'A cabin next to you, once the children and the grans were asleep, would be pure romance,' Jem said with a smile.

Next day Jem was telephoning.

'Yes, I would like an extra self-catering apartment to sleep three singles for the week before the bank holiday.'

'Great. I'll send you a cheque as a deposit.'

So in five weeks they would all be going away on holiday. She would never have imagined that when they moved in February.

The next day she had the third letter.

YOU ARE SCARED NOW
PROBABLY ON TRANQUILLISERS
THAT IS WHAT YOU USUALLY DO

Instead of anger and the feeling of desperation something went cold inside her. It had to be Rupert. Somewhere he was out there trying to hurt her, as he had done most of their married lives. But he didn't know where she lived.

That was on her side. And he didn't know she had grown. Now she could stand on her own two feet, without him being there to undermine her. Maybe she should keep the letter. If more letters came, as she expected they would, they could be evidence. She put it at the bottom of her underwear drawer and tried to forget about it.

The end of the summer term was a happy time, with a sports day and a school disco. Will won his year's running race and Charlie the egg and spoon. Will came back from the disco saying he fancied Emily in the year below him and might be meeting her down at the Green by the Stream tomorrow evening. Jem realised Will was growing up and hoped he would not turn out like Rupert. Charlie had been very pleased with her denim skirt and lime green T-shirt, which had been the cost of a bag of chips at one of the local charity shops. The shops of Broadmead seemed far away in another life.

Will did meet Emily on the Green the following evening, but half an hour later they both ran into the kitchen looking scared. Dan Sparks had told them they had to buy 'these sweeties', as he called them, or else his gang would get them. Will had just grabbed Emily's hand and run home.

'Will, you stay here and look after Emily,' Jem said. 'I'll sort him.'

She took the dog, as she always felt his barking was protection, but when she got to the Green there was no one there. She rang the police and told them her son had been offered drugs with threats, and gave the names of the boys, but the police said the evidence was only hearsay and were not interested. It was twice now that Jem had contacted the police to no effect. She would be down on their list of interfering, fussing women. But what was in a way worse was that she had lost her faith in the police.

Jem had written again to Felicity and Gerald asking if they would like to see the children over the holiday. She was hoping she might get a break and that the grandparents might take them again down to Rock, near Polzeath. But there was no reply. She was saddened that the grandparents would regret not seeing their grandchildren grow up, but also relieved that Will and Charlie would not have the opportunity to come back complaining about the life they used to lead before Northfields. Anyway, Rupert's parents might be shocked at the change in the children's accents.

As long as she kept up with the curtain making there would be time to take them all out in the car once a week, if she could afford the petrol.

They had a great surprise one week into the school holiday. Charlie had had an argument with Sasha, who had taken home one of Charlie's fluffy toy animals and would only return it under pressure. Charlie had called Sasha a 'thief'. Jem, trying to keep the peace, knowing they all had to live close to each other, had just said Sasha didn't understand. Charlie had retorted, 'You wouldn't say that if I took something,' which was true, and she was now sulking in the kitchen trying to do a jigsaw. Gran was helping, which made the matter worse.

It was raining, so Will and Thomas couldn't play football and were making a noise throwing a tennis ball up and down the stairs. Jem had resorted to paracetamol for her tension headache when there was a knock on the door and there stood Tina with a large haversack on her shoulder.

She was greeted with hugs from the family and, having been settled in the kitchen with a mug of tea, told them of her life since she had left them.

The nanny agency had found her a job with a family in Guildford. The parents were lawyers and commuted into Waterloo five days a week, leaving three children under five in her care for eleven hours a day.

'They were evil. They wouldn't get up without being bribed with chocolate after their Sugar Puffs. So much for the parents' demands that they should be fed healthy food. Then there was the battle to get their shoes on. They were good at that, kicking all the time. The battle continued getting them into their car seats, then they screamed all the way to the nursery school.'

'Then you had peace until three o'clock,' said Jem.

'No. The youngest, Giles, was only eighteen months, so I had him all day. He had a rest mid-day, but I had to keep him happy. He was OK until his sisters came back. They wound him up to make him cry. Alice and Lucy would do anything to make a scene.'

'What awful things did they do?' asked Will, enjoying the thought there were really bad children somewhere else.

'They deliberately spilled their drinks on the carpet and smugly watched me cleaning up the mess. When we went in the garden they would run off down the road, so we never went out. They kicked Giles's toys out of the way. If I sent them to their rooms they would throw all the toys and books about. I tried the "naughty step at the bottom of the stairs" routine, but I would have had to use iron manacles to keep them there.'

'What did the parents say?' Jem asked.

'When the parents came home Alice and Lucy were as

good as gold, but Giles cried, so the parents said it was my fault. I was making the children feel insecure.'

'Manipulative, more like.'

'After a month, with the Easter holidays looming, Alice threw her fish fingers and chips with tomato sauce against the kitchen wall. I could not resist spanking her and sending her to bed. Lucy, Giles and I had a very happy evening until the parents returned. That was interesting.'

'Alice was just spoilt,' commented Charlie.

'She made you two seem like little angels,' and they beamed. 'Before the parents came home I packed my bags. Alice heard them come home and all hell was let loose. I told the parents what I thought of them. How was it possible for a nanny to look after children who had never known parental control? But I was just dismissed. "Alice will need a boot camp when she's fifteen," I shouted from the drive. Then I found a Greenline bus back to London.'

'Good for you,' said Jem, clapping her hands, the children following suit.

Gran had been following all this. 'Where did ... did ... you ... sleep?'

Jem patted her arm. 'Well done, Gran.'

'I had a school friend who took me in.'

'I suppose you couldn't go back to the agency, if you'd spanked a child?'

'Well, I did. They said they could no longer give me references, but the parents had had five nannies in two years, and were no longer on their books.'

'Why have the kids in the first place,' asked Jem, 'if you don't want to look after them?'

'Status symbol?' suggested Tina.

'That mother spent twenty-seven months being pregnant

154

for someone else to enjoy the end result and look after the baby. That's stupid.'

'Each to his own ends,' said Gran.

'What happened next?' asked Jem. They were all enjoying news and talk from a different world.

'I've got a place at a teacher training college in Oxford.'

'Well done!'

'The school friend let me stay in her flat and I got a job waitressing in a café in the West End. I've saved up enough money to go travelling in Europe for a month before I go to college. My first stop is here. I'm so pleased to see you.'

'And it's a fantastic surprise you being here. Now I have to think of where you're going to sleep.'

'With me, me,' shouted Charlie, waving her arms, 'then I can have more stories.'

It was good to see the kids excited, but Jem's mind went to money and a meal. Her allowances weren't due until tomorrow and she literally had no cash in her purse. It would be a packet of soup and the remains of bread and cheese tonight. There weren't even any eggs for eggy bread. They had that last night. Tom and Sasha too often seemed to be here at teatime; that made life difficult. Maybe their mothers were equally as hard up.

Fortunately Tina asked, 'What time does the Indian open? I seem to remember you two liked a curry. We could walk up the shops with Buster now the rain has stopped. I fancy some air.'

Delighted, the children found their bikes and the three of them set off with the dog to the precinct. Jem, relieved to have some breathing space, laid the table, coped with Gran, who didn't understand who Tina was, and tidied Charlie's bedroom, even finding her guest a clean towel.

155

The meal was a very happy time, Will and Charlie telling Tina things about school Jem knew nothing about, like that the head teacher was having an affair with the school secretary. Then they played games including pick-a-stick, which made everyone laugh, and later Tina got into her old role and put the children to bed with several stories.

As the ex-nanny came downstairs looking exhausted, Jem opened the bottle of wine that Tina had bought at the off-licence. The two of them sat at the kitchen table, helping Gran with her jigsaw, and talked about their very different lives during the last five months. Tina admitted that the father of her charges in Guildford had invited her into his bed but she hadn't been there long enough to indulge. They all laughed at this. Jem, with amusement, remembered when Rupert and Tina had done this to her. She in turn told Tina about Craig and their planned holiday at Minehead.

'Yes. I remember Craig,' mused Tina with a distant look in her eye. Jem, in mind of Rupert's attraction to the nanny, turned the conversation to the interesting neighbours she was getting to know.

As they were clearing up the glasses and Jem was getting Gran ready for bed, Tina asked, 'If I paid for the petrol, could we all go for a day out in the car tomorrow? Gran could sit in the front and Charlie on my knee in the back. We could take a picnic.'

'Oh, what a great idea. Just to get out of Northfields. One of the most depressing things about lack of money is life becomes very monotonous. But I'll have to get my allowances first. I've no money at all.'

Tina put a hand on Jem's arm. 'I realise that. You were very good to me when Rupert died, letting me stay and sort myself out. Especially as I'd been his mistress.'

'I'd got very used to mistresses over several years. I'd

ceased to care. We'll ask the kids in the morning where they'd like to go.'

'Butlins,' muttered Gran.

'No, that's later,' explained Jem.

Gran looked at Tina. 'Were . . . were you . . . his pie?'

'She understands more than we realise; try "tart",' whispered her daughter.

Tina grinned at Jem. 'Yes, I was his cherry tart.'

'With cream,' added Jem. Although looking forward to a day out, she now wanted her own quiet bed.

Jem was up early to withdraw her money from the post office and buy food for the picnic. Tina helped get the family breakfast and after much chatter they decided on a trip to Uphill near Weston-super-Mare, where Jem could drive the car onto the beach.

Excitedly they set off, Gran's wheelchair and the food in the boot, along with bathing costumes, bat and balls. Charlie sat on Tina's lap and Buster on Will's knees. After parking the car on the beach they made a camp on rugs around Gran's chair.

'Where's the sea?' asked Will.

'Oh dear, the tide's out, but it might come in soon.' Tina, enjoying the idea of explaining tides to the children, did her best.

'I don't get it,' said a puzzled Will. 'The moon pulls the water in and out?'

'Yes. It has to do with gravity.'

With the children looking baffled Jem whispered, 'Better pitch your explanations for younger children. Good experience for you.'

'Anyway, build sandcastles, play cricket and explore the sand dunes and in a couple of hours the sea might come nearer.'

157

The children were content and the adults settled down, reading magazines and sunbathing, until Will shouted, 'I've lost Charlie.'

Jem panicked. Had Rupert or a paedophile snatched her? Was she drowning in quicksand?

Sensibly Tina asked, 'Where were you?'

'On the sand dunes.'

Both women went searching, crawling through tunnels of the sea buckthorn that grew on the dunes. The thorns scratched their arms, caught in their hair, but once they were at the top and stood up they could see Charlie on the golf course on the landward side of the dunes. Even from a distance they could hear her howls and two elderly golfers trying to calm her down.

Relieved Jem scrambled down to the course and retrieved her daughter from the anxious men.

'I couldn't find anyone,' wailed Charlie.

'It's all right, darling. You just went in the wrong direction. You're quite safe.'

'Better buy her a compass,' joked one of the sportsmen as they pulled their trolleys to the next tee. 'And go through that gate. Save you more scratches.'

'What's a compass?' asked Charlie. Tina was soon into schoolteacher mode again.

As the family demolished the picnic they were soon laughing about the incident, but Jem remained disturbed, thinking of Rupert.

The tide did come in, so the children were excited about getting into sea and put on their swimwear. They ran over the damp sand to the water's edge with Tina keeping a close eye on them. The warm water tickled their toes and they laughed with delight until they saw the colour of the water. Paddling was all right, but swimming in the brown water of the muddy Bristol Channel did not appeal.

'It's not like the sea at Rock,' complained Will.

The sun had disappeared behind clouds and raindrops started plopping into the water, so they ran back to their camp to find Gran already sitting in the car. Jem suggested that as it was turning into a gloomy day it might be interesting to see Cheddar Gorge.

The mysterious deep gorge became dark as the cliffs shut off the daylight. The children were fascinated as they went deeper and deeper, then they were in a pretty village with a tumbling stream and a peaceful pool. They stopped outside the Cosy Café for ice creams and a pot of tea.

'Can we have a cream tea?' asked Will.

'No,' said his mother firmly. 'We're saving for our holiday.'

'We should have a cheese tea, 'cause we're in Cheddar,' announced Charlie.

Jem drove them home with Tina singing songs and the kids joining in, but the day was not over. The evening skies cleared, and Craig came round.

'A client gave me this barbecue kit he didn't want. Wouldn't do on the balcony of our flat, so I brought it round here. And some sausages and beer.'

'You're marvellous, Craig,' and Jem kissed him on the lips. They all crowded round while Craig carried the charred metal basket to the back garden. He set it up on the paved patio he had made and the children watched with interest as he lit the coals.

As he stood back with a burnt match in his hand Jem said, 'I've an extra person here: Tina. You may remember her from my other life.'

Jem was aware as Tina shook hands with Craig that Tina was becoming flirtatious. Her body language changed and there was a sparkle in her eye.

The children bubbled around Craig and Tina, telling them about their day out, then Charlie asked, 'Tina, are you coming to Butlins with us?'

Jem, seeing the way Tina looked at Craig, knew Butlins would be a disaster if she came, so she intervened. 'I have a feeling we may be barbecuing for a lot more than six, with the smell wafting over the gardens. I'll take the car and get more beef burgers and buns.'

As Jem had expected, most of the kids in the cul-de-sac had ended up in the garden by the time she returned. Vera was out weeding her front garden and chatting to Ruth.

'Come on round the back, both of you. Bring Bert and Joel and some drink if you want it. The smells are too much.'

As dusk fell the back garden was filled with her new friends chatting and laughing, but where were Craig and Tina? Jem found them in the shed looking slightly embarrassed, and she realised by their rumpled hair and clothes that she had interrupted some kissing and cuddling.

'We were trying to find some more fuel for the barbecue,' explained Tina.

'There's no fuel in there,' Jem announced, 'but this might quell any fuel you have.'

With that she picked up a bucket full of rainwater and threw it at the couple. They ducked ineffectively.

There was laughter from the neighbours as the pair crept away, slightly damp. Tina ran into the house to gain her composure, but Craig, shaking the water out of his hair, asked with a grin, 'I suppose there no chance of Tina coming to Butlins as well?'

Joel had found the water hose, and turned it on Craig as Jem shouted, 'No! Tina is travelling in Europe from tomorrow. It's part of her education.' She added sarcastically, 'I think she should start at the Bastille in Paris, to find the guillotine.'

Then she went into the house to find a glass of wine, calm her nerves and recover her temper. She found Tina packing her rucksack.

'You'd better stay till tomorrow. You won't get any transport at this time of night.'

'I'm sorry.'

'You just can't resist flirting. You're like my old housemate, Liz. She's on her third husband. It makes you feel powerful. Anyway, it's made me realise Craig's important to me.' Then Jem laughed. 'And you did look funny. So let's forget about it. You can put the kids to bed. Apart from the shed incident it has been a lovely day. Wasn't I complaining about monotony last night?'

Later, when Jem was saying goodnight to Craig, she remarked, 'Don't look so glum. She took my husband – hook, line and sinker. I think she's like that with all men. You were just a minnow in her pond. I'm the old bad-tempered trout waiting in the shallows for a friend to come along, and I hope I've found one.'

'I love you – you old trout. I wish my mum had been here. She'd have laughed herself silly. See you when the piranha has gone away.'

So equilibrium was restored. Tina was dropped again at the station, the children saddened and puzzled by her swift departure, but peace had been made between the adults and they were happily talking of Tina's route around Europe.

As Tina had paid for a tank of petrol Jem had planned afterwards to take her family to Clevedon for the rest of the day. She had memories of going there as a little girl with a school friend and fishing for crabs from the jetty near the pier.

'All you need,' she told the children, 'is meat bones. We've those left over from the barbecue. Use a long length of string for a line and tie the bones to the string. And you'll need to have a bucket of water to put the crabs in.'

'And not throw it, like you did last night,' added Will. 'Why'd you do that?'

'You wouldn't understand,' retorted his mother.

'That means it has to do with sex,' whispered Will to his sister.

The car was parked on the sea front and luckily the tide was coming in, as they had learnt from their trip to Weston. The children rushed off down the concrete jetty. This concrete hid the stone from which the jetty had been built, which was where the crabs lived. Gran was carefully wheeled down the cobbled slope to the beach where the two women could sit in the sun, watching the children and the other holidaymakers. A competition developed between Will, Charlie and some other children as to who could catch the most crabs.

'I thought Charlie mightn't like crabs and their claws, or the muddy water, but she seems to be enjoying this.'

Gran just nodded, smiled and took her daughter's hand. Jem felt Olive was really enjoying this summer. Although verbal communication was minimal, Olive looked happier and seemed more relaxed; she smiled more, even chuckled. Jem reflected on her infrequent visits to the home last summer when there had been no connection at all, and felt how selfish she herself had been – but it had been a selfish way of life. It was different now. Not better, not worse, just different.

Charlie ran back to them. 'Come and see our catch!'

Jem wished she had a camera. The look of delight on the children's faces and the buckets of squirming crabs.

'You've all got a great catch, but it's best to put them back now. Then they can find a place to hide when the tide is out.'

So with shrieks of laughter from everyone, the contents of two buckets of crabs went scuttling down the jetty, back to the safety of water and stones to await being caught the next day.

After a picnic of cold sausage sandwiches from the barbecue the kids climbed on the rocks with their new-made friends, whilst Jem pushed Gran along the promenade, past the bandstand. Realising the amusement arcade was in front of them, and the amount of money the machines would consume, Jem called to the children that it was time to go home. There was some argument about this, which came to a truce with the suggestion of ice creams.

'Can you imagine what it would cost if we'd gone to the pier at Weston-super-Mare?' Jem asked Gran. 'Fish and chips, donkey rides, swings and roundabouts. We just couldn't afford it. Thank goodness at Butlins you pay to be there, then most things are free.'

Gran nodded.

Once the children were in bed Jem had to stay up until two in the morning to catch up with the curtain making. She needed the money, but only another two weeks and she would have enough.

As she finally dragged herself to bed, feeling tired and

drained, she wondered if there would be a letter in the morning. She had managed to hide her fear from everyone, but she dreaded the post.

There were no letters.

Two weeks later with a lighter heart Jem packed the clothes and food, as they were self-catering, in her small red car. Footballs, cricket bat, tennis rackets and Gran's chair were packed in Craig's white van. The family waved goodbye to Thomas and his brothers, who had volunteered to look after Buster, and then together they set off down the M5 to Minehead.

Butlins was an experience that reminded Jem that seven months ago she had told the children they were explorers in a foreign land. Now that no longer mattered. They had adjusted, were happy, and did not think of the adults and children they met as any different from other people they had met in the past. There were no grumbles about not going to Rock, staying with Rupert's parents, sailing in his friends' boats. And the best thing was they were accepted in return. But to Jem, who had lived the smart life for twenty-eight years, this was indeed a strange country. As with the cul-de-sac it was a matter of space. She wasn't used to so many people around her, especially on holiday. It didn't seem to bother the children, but on holiday she had hoped for space where she could relax. She hadn't anticipated the romance of the Mediterranean, the austere beauty of the Alps, or the pastoral tranquillity of Cornwall, but she had expected to be able to get away from people.

She had to keep reminding herself Will and Charlie were enjoying all this. The swimming pool, the adventure playground, go-kart racing, competitions arranged by the Redcoats and the entertainments in the evening.

Olive was happy to watch the young enjoying themselves and to be in the company of Doris and Debbie, Craig's mother and sister. Jem could imagine her mother's snobbish remarks in her former life – comments like, 'These common people are pig-ignorant.' Sometimes no memory was a benefit.

To Craig and his family just being on holiday was great. Craig was enjoying cheap beer. They were all happy to eat fish and chips, Jem's own children regarding these meals every evening as a treat. Jem had to shut out of her mind the fish restaurants of Padstow and the pasta of Italy. *This is the food of this foreign land,* she told herself. Her privileged home, school and social life clashed more here on holiday than it ever had in Northfields.

She kept telling herself, *The children are happy. They are no longer strangers in a new land. It's me that has to unlearn twenty-eight years of life.*

She did her best to join in the singsongs at the bar, the crowded swimming pool with the kids, the sports (and she did teach Will how to play tennis), but she wasn't at ease.

The nights were very different, with French-farce exchanging of rooms so that Craig and Jem could share the same bed. Jem's disillusions of the day melted away in Craig's arms. Nothing else seemed to matter.

Early on Wednesday morning as Craig stroked her long blonde hair and tickled her ears he said, 'You'd like a day away from 'ere. I feel you'd like to see some wide open spaces.'

'Is it that obvious?'

'No. I'm just getting to learn about you. I want to know what you like, and what you don't like.'

Jem was happily astonished. Rupert had never considered her. It had always been what he wanted.

'Thanks. I'm not used to anyone thinking about me. Except Carrie, but that's more in a sisterly way.'

'So I should hope. I think you'd like a day out on Exmoor. My mum could look after Olive, Debbie could cope with Will and Charlie, and we could 'ave a day out. Just you and me.'

'That would be unbelievably marvellous,' murmured Jem as she pulled Craig towards her.

After the two families were fuelled for the day with eggs and bacon, Debbie and the children were going to the adventure playground following by swimming and the two mothers had decided to watch the more elderly at a tea dance. Craig and Jem, reassured everyone was happy, set off for Exmoor to climb Dunkery Beacon.

As, hand in hand, they climbed the stony track with purple heather full of the hum of honey bees, Craig said, 'You like the open air, don't you? I've noticed when we've been out weedin' in the garden you smile more. You enjoy walkin' Buster and playin' tennis. I 'ave this daydream that I've bought a couple of acres and you're helping me turn it into a nursery.'

'No doubt you'd get me to do all the rotivating.'

'Only when it's rainin',' and they both laughed. 'Seriously, you'd be much better with money than I'd be, and charmin' to the customers.'

'Pity it's just a daydream, like the wide-open spaces of New Zealand, but land is so expensive. By the way, how are your uncle Ben and cousin in New Zealand?'

'They're doing OK. They're now growing kiwi fruit for export.'

'So you still have the dream.'

'If you have imagination you can always dream.'

By now they were at the summit of the Beacon and plans for Craig's future were put to one side as they took in the view towards the Bristol Channel spread out below them. There was a patchwork of fields and woods, islands, headlands and towns.

'That's Porlock,' said Craig. 'I went there wif the school when I was eleven. I remember the pebble bank.'

'There's Minehead. You can see the holiday camp, and the funny parasol roofs.'

'Those 'ills are the Quantocks.'

Jem sighed. 'This is so beautiful. You're right; I do like being outside.'

They wandered back down the hill, Jem wondering what Craig meant by including her in his daydream. She was definitely physically attracted to him but their backgrounds were so different she wondered how much they had in common. She had assumed their affair was temporary, but maybe if they both enjoyed gardening and the open air they would grow to have more common interests. He was very good with the children. She wasn't interested in marriage, especially if Rupert had somehow survived. This fear she was keeping to herself.

They found an old pub in a village of thatched cottages, where they sat in the garden bordered by geraniums and snapdragons, drinking lager and eating ham sandwiches. In the heat of the afternoon they wandered by a tumbling stream in the dappled shade of a beech wood. They leaned on the bars of a wooden bridge, watching spotted trout in the clear water, then startled a deer in the bracken, which jumped away into the undergrowth. Jem wanted to keep a picture of this day in her mind. It would keep her going in the grey days of winter that loomed ahead.

When they returned to the holiday camp they found the

five sunbathing in the early evening. The children lay on towels on the grass with bottles of Coke, the adults in deck chairs with glasses of wine.

'Tea's on the table,' announced Doris. 'I've done tinned salmon salad, and Debbie and the kids have made a trifle.'

'This is wonderful,' said Jem. 'You're all spoiling me.'

'We're going to a talent contest later. D'you want to come?'

'That would be a laugh.'

And it was. Some acts were funny when they weren't supposed to be, and others surprisingly talented like Debbie singing, 'Baby love, my baby love,' as Diana Ross and the Supremes.

The last two days were very happy, ending up with a trip to Minehead to paddle in the sea, Craig taking the children on a fishing trip whilst the women looked round the town and bought souvenirs. They all had the promised cream tea, then a final evening in the bar with entertainment before they packed up to travel home.

As she packed Jem thought that she was adapting and could accept a way of life that would never have entered her mind a year ago. She thought of Bill Edwards acting out Shylock in *The Merchant of Venice*, and smiled. It was so true. The children were content, and she was looking forward to returning to No. 14 Meadowleaze and home. She was aware that Will and Charlie were grumbling about going back to school, but what child didn't? She remembered the heavy stone feeling in her stomach that the thought of school had created during the last week of her own summer holidays.

PART FOUR

Rupert's health and strength continued to improve through June. He walked further each day and even enjoyed wandering round the Tate Gallery in Pimlico. He sat in Kensington Gardens and, chatting up a blonde sitting on the same bench eating her lunchtime sandwiches, got himself a dinner date and the chance of an affair. The evenings he spent with Charles and George in the pub, or at the sports club, as he now felt confident enough to swim in order to build up his physique again.

Superficially life was going well, although there had been one scare when his publisher had telephoned. Putting on what he hoped was a convincing Yorkshire accent he had said his skiing accident had left him very weak and he found concentrating on his present work very difficult. The publisher was understanding and suggested a new date for the book to come out. Rupert thought he'd better look at the work on the computer, but monasteries in South-East England were beyond him. Perhaps he should visit the Reading Room at the British Museum for the fun of it – but perhaps not; they might remember Michael Brooks.

The blonde from Kensington Gardens turned out to be

very friendly. She had a flat in King's Road and was called Melanie. Evenings spent in her company became more frequent.

But still inside part of Rupert was angry and bitter, and it became part of his life to keep Jemima in a state of fear. He would build up to a peak of anger and send a message from newspaper cut-outs. It could keep him happy all day thinking of the fear it would bring her in the smart house in fashionable Bristol and how it would destroy her confidence with her upper-class friends at the posh schools and the tennis club. He smiled as he posted the letter saying,

THE NORTH COL.
YOU ARE GUILTY
YOU CANNOT SLEEP EASY AT NIGHT

He imagined the terrified look on her face, but never thought that his children, fear free, might be happy. In fact he never thought about them at all.

He sent the third letter in late June.

YOU ARE SCARED NOW
PROBABLY ON TRANQUILLISERS
THAT IS WHAT YOU USUALLY DO

Melanie had become a major part of his life. The late-night drink often become coffee and toast in the morning. As Michael Brooks's money came easy he suggested a month away in the Caribbean, and whilst away regaining his suntan and satisfying the beautiful Melanie he sent no letters to Jemima. But his mind still festered over his wife and her part in his fall on the North Col. He decided on his return to hire a private detective so he could learn and enjoy second-hand how frightened Jemima was.

Mr Robinson, like his name, could be anyone – average mousy hair, blue bleary eyes, average height, could be anyone in an anonymous jacket, sometimes a false uniform. Which was why he was good at his job. As a gas employee in Jem's old avenue address he found out she had moved to Northfields. And as a water board inspector checking the mains he found 14 Meadowleaze. Thus it was that whilst Jemima was away at the holiday camp and unaware, Mr Robinson came snooping around the cul-de-sac, in the uniform of the water company, and fell into conversation with Darren Sparks. Darren, with the promise of money, was happy to keep the detective in the picture. Jemima and her family would be spied on, and they would be oblivious.

PART FIVE

Jem and her family followed Craig, Doris and Debbie in the white van back to Northfields. The break had done them all good. Made them all more relaxed and cheerful. School might loom in a week's time, but they were all strengthened to cope with school, autumn and troubles that might happen.

Thoughts like this were dispelled from Jem's mind when Buster rushed out of the Williams family home followed by Tom, Matthew and small Martha. They all danced around happy to see each other, then Tom told them the news.

'Guess what. A house burnt down in Lavender Grove, but no one died.' He sounded disappointed. 'But it could be arson.'

Then Matt piped up, 'Concorde keeps on flying over low. They're servicing it. All the houses shook. It was so loud – fantastic.'

'Wish I'd seen that,' said Will.

'It'll be over again,' replied Matt knowledgably.

'Can I get my bike out,' asked Charlie, 'so I can go see Sasha?'

By a few sentences, interrupted by Buster barking and

172

Ruth coming out to give Jem a hug, life returned to normal. But she had the memories in her head.

They had unpacked the car and the van, and had got Gran settled in front of her TV with a cup of tea, when Doris bustled in with a box of unused groceries and said, 'You've given us all such a wonderful week away. Craig's going to take you out for the evening. Me and Debs can look after Gran and put the kiddies to bed. They know us now. So put your glad rags on, something smart, and go out for the evening.'

Jem said, 'Thanks, Doris,' and rushed upstairs to find something good to wear. What a great way to end a holiday, especially with her mother content and Doris's approval. Ten years ago Olive would have regarded Doris as an alien being, but now she happily accepted her. After a week at a holiday camp Jem could accept all human beings as the same – but different.

Craig drove the white van down to the waterfront in Bristol. They walked along the old wharves where ships used to dock, then found a quiet Italian restaurant in an old vaulted cellar, bricks painted white, and talked about their holiday, and more ordinary things like Olive's future, the kids at school, Debbie's nursing career and Doris as if they were an ordinary couple. Craig with a sparkle in his eye even suggested marriage, but Jem had to sidestep that issue. Although she had grown to love him, there was the matter of the anonymous letters; bigamy was not a good idea. They had a wonderful romantic evening, ending up on the road at the Sea Walls, with the white van rocking on its shock absorbers. She could not commit herself. What if Rupert was still alive?

By the end of September her confidence grew. The

children were settled back at school, and a lady from Social Services now came to care for Olive twice a week and give her a bath. This meant Jem could get out more. One Tuesday she had lunch with her tennis friend, Janet, in an anonymous wine bar in Redland; smart Clifton was no longer in her social sphere. On Fridays she met Craig in his van, so their romance continued. Then a letter arrived on her doormat. Yes, all the words were cut out of newspapers as before. But now he had her address, which was frightening, and the words were threatening, conveying menace, malice and revenge.

YES, I KNOW WHERE YOU LIVE.
THOSE CHILDREN ARE MINE.
I WILL TAKE THEM WHEN I CHOOSE.

The children were at school, her mother watching TV, so no one heard her bringing up her breakfast. The children. He could take them. Kidnap them. She had a vision of blankets being thrust over their heads, of them being pushed into cars, driven off at speed and never being seen again. And it would be done in revenge, because he had never loved them. They had been status symbols, made to perform, and the prize would have been his – as a successful father. Now, with no status, she knew care and love were far more important, but she was angry.

To give herself time and space to think she told Olive she was taking Buster for a walk. They walked on the Green by the Stream towards the wood. It was quiet, with only a few hooded boys, who had bunked off school, skulking under some willow trees in the distance. Green was a calming colour and the flow of the water made her more peaceful, so she could think. Her most important aim was to protect the children. But how could she be with them all the time when they weren't at school? Now she was worrying about her mother being left on her own. She couldn't be looking after all of them twenty-four hours a day.

In desperation she rang Carrie. Her friend came to her aid, as she always did. They sat at the kitchen table, Carrie deep in the news Jem had given her. She was trying to cope with the idea that Jem's husband was still living. How could this be?

'If he's alive, he is still a right bastard,' she said accusingly.

'We know that. We also now know he was bankrupt, and many other people wanted him dead. Now he is anonymous. Just what the bastard wants. I assume the hospital must have got two injured men mixed up. I saw a body, at least a face like Rupert's. I can't have looked close enough. Relieved he was gone. Now I'm just aware I've had several anonymous letters. The last one knowing where we live.'

They talked intensely over cups of coffee with Olive listening mystified.

'The children are all I care about. I must make sure they're never left alone. There must always be someone with them. No more walking home from school with just other children, or taking Buster out on their own.'

'How can you do that without worrying them? They'll know something is wrong.'

'I've had other threats from people who lost money. I could say there's a new one.'

'I wonder how he found out where you lived? You'll have to keep your eyes wide open. Tell Craig. Tell him

175

you think Rupert is still alive and out to get you. You two are obviously now an item.'

'I hope so.'

'I know what I've got at home. Dave says, "Why have a cat and bark yourself?" He gave me something to use if I was visiting his scrap yard, or was walking down dark alleyways. Now it sits by our bed. You pull the pin out, and the noise! I'll bring it round.'

They noticed Olive was agitated. 'Is Rup . . . going to, to kill . . .'

'No, Mum. We're all going to be quite safe. I've just had a letter from some nasty person. Don't worry. We'll just have a nice cup of tea and walk to collect the children from school.'

Jem, with Buster (whom she would happily have swapped for a Rottweiler) in tow, pushed her mother in her chair, as she had done since March, but now every passer-by, every unexpected noise made her jump or twist round anxiously. She looked more closely at the mothers waiting round the gate; maybe some weren't mothers, like Charlene's minder or the occasional father who worked nights at the aircraft factory, but there was no one unfamiliar, and Jem relaxed. But only for today. Tomorrow would be the same. Fear every time Will and Charlie left the house.

One evening Jem jumped as the doorbell rang, but it was only Jehovah's Witnesses, whom Buster frightened away with his barking.

Craig asked, 'Why are you so nervy? You've even made Buster bark to guard you? Is it something to do with Darren Sparks? He's been very chatty recently.'

Jem just shrugged. What lover wants to learn about an ex-lover, even though she had come to hate Rupert?

'Someone Rupert cheated,' she lied. 'Keeps on sending threatening letters. It's like the brick I had through the window at the old house.'

Craig seemed reassured at this answer.

There had been fireworks around the neighbourhood for a month before November the fifth. Olive was too deaf to hear the bangs, which was a relief, but the children were excited. Half term was at an end, the clocks turned to wintertime. The pavements covered with sodden leaves.

Will and Charlie's primary school PTA put on a fireworks display on Friday evening, a few days before Bonfire Night itself. It was anticipated it would stop children using fireworks and burning themselves. Several incidents had occurred in the past resulting in kids having burnt hands, and one case of an older child being blinded. Fireworks through letterboxes of immigrants, such as Asians and Africans, had also caused problems.

The PTA hoped the bonfire, a hot dog stall and sparklers would bring all families together, whatever their origin, and all were welcome. Ruth came from over the road to say she was going with Matt, Tom and Martha. Would Jem and Olive like to come with them? Gran shook her head, conveying she didn't like the crowds in the dark, and nodded to say she was happy to stay home watching *Coronation Street*. Jem, thinking how much her mother had improved since coming to live with them, decided she would be all right, but more importantly she didn't want the children on their own. Who would recognise Rupert in the dark? No one.

'Buster will be pleased. You look after him, and he'll look after you. And Vera is next door. You only have to bang on the wall.' *Now,* she thought, *I can protect Will and Charlie.*

The fireworks were a success with 'ooh's and 'ah's. Showers of Roman candles, Catherine wheels and brilliant cascades of stars. Hot dogs all round with extra onions. Jem and Ruth walked home arm in arm talking of the evening, the five children prancing around them.

'Come in for a coffee and talk to Joel?' asked Ruth.

'No. But thanks. Best get in to see to Mum and get the children to bed.'

Jem's gate clanked behind the three of them. Ruth stood outside her own home looking at the stars, thinking how much brighter they used to be in Jamaica with no street lights, sighed and turned to her front door when—

'Ruth, Ruth!' Jem's voice called to her in alarm.

Ruth rushed over the cul-de-sac to the open front door. The three of them, with Buster looking forlorn, were looking at the body of Olive, prone at the bottom of the stairs. Jem was bending over her mother, trying to cuddle her, talk to her and keep her warm. The old lady must have fallen, breaking either her hip or her leg.

'I've dialled 999. An ambulance is on its way. She must have tried to climb the stairs to see the fireworks. She keeps on saying, 'stars, stars'.'

'OK. Will and Charlie, go and find some blankets to keep Gran warm.'

The children rushed off upstairs, eager to have something to do, whilst Ruth held Olive's wrist to find her pulse, and groped for Jem's hand to give her comfort.

'Olive'll be OK. We're so near the hospital. I can hear the sirens now. Don't worry. Go with your mum. I'll stay here with the children.' Ruth gently swept Jem's blonde hair off her sweaty forehead in a motherly way. 'Don't worry. For better or worse, God will support you. To be more practical find a nightie, washing things.'

'Yes. My mind's gone blank. Where are they?'

Jem rushed around frantically whilst the others put blankets over Gran. Ruth thought Olive was indeed cold. The front door didn't fit well. She could feel the chill air, and the old lady must have been lying there for some time.

Two supportive ambulance men arrived at the door and gently lifted the old lady onto a stretcher and wheeled her out to the ambulance.

'Might I suggest you bring your car, Missis, then you can drive home? Might be safer than walking. Can get a bit rowdy this close to Bonfire Night.'

Ruth was left to comfort the two children. Charlie was rather tearful and Will looked solemn.

Vera came and knocked on the door to find out what had happened, having seen the ambulance, and ineffectively joined in the comforting whilst Ruth went home to tell her family where she was and that she might be there all night. She came back saying Tom had hired a video of *ET* and was bringing it over so they could all watch the film to take their minds off Gran.

Eventually the children settled to sleep. Tom went home and Ruth settled on Olive's bed under the blankets. It was hard to sleep with fireworks going off until after midnight.

It was four in the morning when Ruth heard the car return. Jem slumped in a chair, exhausted.

'She's broken her hip. They've made her comfortable and sedated her. But she's going to be so frightened. I've learnt to understand what she means and what she wants, but I can't be with her all the time. I have to be with the children.'

'I'm sure neighbours will help out. You've looked after their children often enough.'

'But you don't understand. How could you? I've had threatening letters. I think they're from my husband, and he isn't dead. He wants to take the children.'

'How awful. Frightening. I've wondered why you've seemed so nervy since you came back from Butlins.'

Jem pulled herself out of the chair, went through to the kitchen and brought back the two letters she assumed came from Rupert to show Ruth.

'Oh no! "I will take them when I choose"?'

'Every time I see a strange car in the cul-de-sac, every time an unknown man passes us in the street, I go all tense. Then I snap at the kids. They get upset. Sometimes you could cut the atmosphere in this house with a knife. It seems worse as we were all settling down so well.'

'Why not go to the police?'

'I went to see them when Will got offered drugs, but they were useless. They'd just think I was a neurotic mother. I've no proof. And when you think of that poor mum at school – have you seen her at the gate with her face all black and blue? Her ex beat her up, although there was an injunction out that he wasn't supposed to go near her. The police aren't going to take any notice of me.'

'You mean they can't do anything until it's too late, so we'll have to look out for you.'

'Yes. Craig's been very helpful. I told him I had been threatened, but not who the person was. Sometimes he picks up the kids from school, and takes Will to his football practice on Saturday. But now, with Mum in hospital, it's going to be so difficult. She'll be scared and the nurses won't understand what she wants. It's something that has been so good about Olive being here since March: learning to communicate with her in a

180

limited way. It's made her much happier, but it takes time. They haven't got that time in hospital.'

Through Saturday and Sunday Jem spent most of her time with her mother in the ward, aware that her mother's temperature was up and she was delirious. The nurse said that lying on the hall floor with draughts through the ill-fitting front door had given Olive a chill and pneumonia had set in. Jem comforted her mother, telling her the tubes in her arms were to help her. In no way was she to pull them out. Liquid was important and Jem tried to get her to sip as much water as possible. She tried to feed her the hospital meals but Olive's appetite had gone. For herself she had to buy sandwiches from the WVS shop. Olive, in her lucid moments, was content with the television; her pain was sedated.

Jem had to put her trust in the Williams family and Craig to look after the kids, feed them and keep them safe. She was so thankful for their help. She thought back to her previous life when her father had died and all she had from neighbours were cool enquiries and murmurs of sympathy. Here there were people who took on the situation as part of life and did what they could to help. They had not been isolated and insulated by wealth.

On Sunday night Jem went home totally exhausted and very worried. From some inner resource she found the strength to thank Ruth and her family, then put Will and Charlie to bed with calm reassurances that Gran was all right, though Jem didn't feel it herself. She slept little, and then was up early again. She didn't dare walk the dog, because that would leave the children on their own, but ironed their uniforms ready for school and with bleary eyes through lack of sleep walked them to school with Buster. They would be safe for six hours.

After a strong black coffee she walked to the hospital and found her mother had deteriorated and was gasping for breath. Now the only thing she could do was sit holding her mother's hand and wait for the end.

Olive had lived her life quietly and left it as she had lived. The gasping ceased. The slight grasp of Jem's hand fell away and her mother had gone. If an afterlife existed Olive was now at peace. Jem would have liked to believe in a Heaven, though she had doubts. But the thought of her mother being whole again in some other world, instead of the confused person she had become, gave her tranquillity.

She went on sitting there, holding Olive's hand as it became cold, until a nurse came in through the curtains.

'Just come to check Olive's temperature. Oh. I'm sorry. I see there's no need. Can I get you a cup of tea?'

'Please. What's the time?'

'One o'clock.'

'Must pick the children up from school at 3.30.'

'OK. I'll let the ward sister know.' The nurse placed a comforting hand on Jem's shoulder. 'I'm glad you were here when she went. She must have been a lovely mum. I'll find the tea.'

It was the consoling remarks that made Jem cry. She sat there crying, her head on the bedcover, wondering how she could have done things better, regretting taking the kids to the fireworks.

The ward sister came back with a cup of tea and biscuits. She gently took Jem's hand. 'Don't distress yourself. She was in no pain. You did all you could for her. Now you have to help your children. Tell them what's happened and give them a meal, but look forward.'

182

'Yes. Yes, you're right. I have to keep going for Will and Charlie. I'll pick them up in the car, so I don't have all the other mothers looking on. Then we'll buy a special tea. Thanks.'

'Come back tomorrow for the death certificate. I can advise you about undertakers, and all the forms the government require. Now go and think about your family.'

Jem walked home the long way round. She was trying to come to terms with her relationship with her mother. They had never been that close. Her father had always dominated their lives. In these last few months the divide of her father had gone, and although verbal communication had been almost nil, there had been different communication – laughter and fun with other people, which had brought her closer to her mother than ever before. If, twelve months ago, Olive had died in the home, Jem and Rupert would have gone through the paces of a formal cremation and never thought more about it.

Yes, now they would go to the cremation, but her thoughts would be different, positive for a woman she had loved, cared for and begun to understand.

Jem met the children in the car with Buster. She took them to the Green by the Stream in the dismal fog of a November day, with Buster bouncing around them, and told them Gran had died.

'Gran wouldn't like you to be unhappy, so let's go to McDonald's and have a beef burger.'

The children just accepted this and enjoyed the comfort food. It was back home, and now they all thought of it as home, that the truth hit them. The front room, clothes everywhere, and the grandma smell. It was the unfinished jigsaw that made Charlie cry.

'Gran wouldn't like us to be unhappy. We'll finish the jigsaw. Gran said life goes on.'

The number of neighbours who came to express their sadness heartened Jem. Charlene even brought a bunch of chrysanthemums. Darren Sparks stopped her in the street to say how sorry he was, and she was puzzled by his curiosity over Gran's fall down the stairs. Why should he be interested?

The next few days were a torment of protecting the children, seeing Mr Dawes the solicitor to find out the terms of will, and speaking to the undertaker for the cremation details. There was a grant from the state for funeral expenses and Jem went for the cheapest option. Apart from herself, who was there to mourn? Then there were Olive's clothes to take to the charity shop, and she had to admit the kids liked to have the living room as their space. They had done their best with Gran, but the young want life, not the dying.

Then there was the change in allowances. Jem would no longer get her carer's allowance. (And her guilty conscience said why should she have it anyway as she had taken the children out to the fireworks, to protect them, and left her mother alone?) Since the last letter from Rupert she had stopped collecting her widow's allowance, and the book lay unused in the drawer. If the authorities ever found out he was alive she would have to pay it back. She didn't want to be accused of fraud. Finding paid work after the funeral would be her priority.

Jem remembered the crematorium from her father's funeral, but that had been a very different occasion with many of his business acquaintances in grey suits and black ties. Today it was just herself, Vera, Carrie, Craig's mum, Joan Brimble and Mr Dawes. Ruth hadn't been able to get off work.

She found her mind wandering as the local vicar, whom she had never met, droned through the fifteen-minute service. She felt grateful that she had been able to look after her mother for a few months and make her last days happier than they would have been if she had stayed in the home on the Downs. She now understood Olive better. A timid, shy woman, dominated by her husband so she never became a person in her own right. As the coffin slid away into the unknown, to the sound of some taped organ music, Jem realised that with Rupert life had been the same for her. Domination by a husband, but a cruel one. Her father's domination had been kindly meant. He had behaved like many men of his generation. The past nine months had taught her to stand on her own two feet.

As Mr Dawes shook her hand in parting he said, 'I've been going through your mother's file and right at the back came across some old share certificates that she bought before she married. She had obviously forgotten about them. I shall do some investigating and see if they are still worth anything. I'll be in touch.'

The five women stood outside the crematorium feeling sad until Carrie said, 'Let's go to the pub. Lunch is on me,' which cheered them.

The following day Jem was looking down the job adverts, wondering if her office skills of eight years ago were out of date. There were several jobs at the hospital that were part-time. What bothered her were the school holidays. How could she keep the children safe? They were too old for a child minder. Could the neighbours help? Vera was home much of the time, and Charlene with her three. If she

185

explained the importance of the situation, and the threat from Rupert, perhaps they would help. It was a pity Tina had fancied Craig, or Jem could have asked her if she would like to stay for college vacations. With determination she rang the hospital to ask for job application forms.

The doorbell rang and there stood a burly man and a young woman who introduced themselves as the police and asked if they could come in and ask her a few questions.

Nervously she took them into the kitchen, and after they had refused a mug of tea the man, the detective sergeant, began.

'We're here to ask you about your mother's accident last week. Can you tell us exactly what happened?'

'Why should the police be interested?'

'Please could you just answer the question?'

'Well, I took my two children to the firework display at their school. I left my mother happily watching television, and when we got back we found her lying at the bottom of the stairs.'

'How long were you out?' asked the policewoman.

'About an hour. I phoned for an ambulance. Went with her to the hospital and was told she had broken her hip.' Jem was thinking, *They're checking up on me for fraud. They think I've been claiming money under false pretences.*

'Then your mother died.'

'Yes. Lying in the hall she got chilled, as there is a draught under the door. It doesn't fit properly. She developed pneumonia and died on the following Monday.'

'We understand,' said the man, 'that your husband died after a fall earlier this year.'

'He had a skiing accident. What has that got to do with this?'

186

'We've had anonymous information that you pushed both these people to their death. What do you have to say to that?'

Jem was nervous no more, but shocked and angry. She pushed back her chair and glared down at the two.

'That's absolute rubbish. Two accidents, and some sick person is accusing me for no reason. And you're happy to believe someone who isn't even honest enough to give their own name!'

'We have to follow up these accusations,' answered the policewoman calmly, 'in case some crime has been committed.'

'Well, it hasn't. My mother tried to climb the stairs to see the fireworks, and fell. My neighbour Ruth Williams was with us all the time at the display, and when we came home saw my mother lying at the bottom of the stairs. She noticed how cold my mum was and said she must have been there for some time. You can check with her. She lives opposite but is out at work most days.'

'We'll call back to see Mrs Williams this evening.' The sergeant paused. 'Tell me, why did you change your name when you moved here? Did you want to hide from something and change your identity?'

'What, you mean from Somerville-Thomas to Thomas? Sergeant, you live in a very suspicious world. Would you want to live in this area with a posh double-barrelled name and have the Mickey taken out of you?'

'Why did you move here?'

'My late husband was in debt. He owed people money, so we had to move.'

'Must have been difficult for you,' he said sarcastically, and the two police officers left.

Angrily Jem slammed the door behind them. Obviously

the police saw some terrible crimes, and the man had a chip on his shoulder, but there was no need to take it out on her.

She went back to the kitchen and did some quiet thinking. Rupert, wherever he lived, was getting more aggressive. This wasn't just a threat to unnerve her; this was an accusation of crimes. Somehow she had to fight back.

Craig turned up just after they got back from school. As winter approached his working day got shorter. A couple of times he had stayed for the night. Jem had suggested he move in, partly as she would feel safer, but he had pointed out she would be thrown out of her council house if he took up permanent residence. If she paid her own rent it would be different. A job was important.

The children were happily eating sausage and chips in front of the television in the front room, so Jem took Craig into the kitchen and told him about the visit from the police. Craig was angry, but Jem put a hand on his arm and said calmly, 'There's more. I didn't want to tell you, but the threats I have had come from my deceased husband. He is alive and threatening. I must have identified the wrong dead man at the hospital.'

'But how? That Rupert, assuming it's 'im, is a right bastard. If 'e's alive 'e should make 'imself known.' Craig was angry and with anger his accent became broader.

'He won't. He conned so many people into investing in some scheme that went wrong. He would end up in prison if he turned up, so he has some false identity.'

'Where would 'e get that from? Get some crook to give 'im a false passport?' Craig was pacing up and down tensely at this new information.

'No. I think it is far simpler than that. Come and sit down and I'll explain.'

Craig got himself a beer from the fridge and slumped at the table.

Jem continued, 'If Rupert is still alive, someone else is in his coffin. That someone must have been at the same hospital in Austria. I think two similar-looking men had accidents around the same time on the same day, and the bodies were mixed up. Maybe they were similar in age and build and both British. The body I identified was this other man. When somebody's dead you just glance at the body because you're upset.'

'If we told the police all this, would they exhume the body?' asked Craig.

'There could be another way. After Rupert's so-called funeral the solicitor, Mr Dawes, made me meet an unpleasant and angry accountant. He told me all about Rupert's financial situation and I'm sure he would love to bring him to account. I'll ask Mr Dawes if I can see him again.'

'Then what?'

'Suggest he get a detective of some kind to inquire into serious injuries at the hospital where Rupert is supposed to have died. If inquiries show a similar person was there that day, Rupert is probably that person. The fraud squad could then take over.' She hesitated. 'I've just thought of something else. How did Rupert, assuming it's him, know my mum was dead? I reckon he has employed some kind of spy. It's probably Darren Sparks. He's been nosy under the guise of sympathy. I'll ignore him in future.'

'You're so clever.'

'I just want Will and Charlie to be safe.'

Jem's view was given strength when a letter arrived the next day.

DO NOT EXPECT YOU LIKED THE VISIT FROM
THE POLICE BUT IT IS WHAT YOU DESERVE.
ARE WILLIAM AND CHARLOTTE MOURNING
DREADFUL OLD OLIVE THAT YOU PUSHED
DOWN THE STAIRS – LIKE YOU PUSHED ME
I AM NOT GOING TO GO AWAY

Jem rang Mr Dawes and asked if she could meet the accountant again. Mr Dawes, surprised, said he would arrange a meeting with Mr Wilmott. This took place three days later in Mr Dawes's office. He was as curious as Mr Wilmott.

The three of them sat round Mr Dawes's conference table as Jem told her tale of anonymous letters, producing the last three, her fears for the children and the final straw – the visit from the police. Then she made the suggestion that Mr Wilmott might be interested in looking into the records of the hospital in Austria to find out about other men injured on that day in January. From her handbag she brought out a photo of Rupert, which had been taken for some business investment brochure.

'This is a good likeness of Rupert,' she said, to which Mr Dawes nodded his agreement. 'If some investigator can find the name of a similar man injured and taken to that Austrian hospital, I would bet the body has been buried in Rupert's grave. The postmark on the letters is W1, London, and I reckon that's where Rupert is hiding. Prison would be his just reward.'

'Even if he were arrested,' warned Mr Dawes, 'he would probably get bail until his fraud trial. It takes time, so you would still have to be on your guard. Maybe move again.'

Mr Wilmott stared at the photo and rubbed his hands in

anticipation. 'If we find him, I shall really enjoy this. He ruined so many people's investments.'

'It killed my father,' added Jem bitterly.

Mr Wilmott looked slightly more human when he wasn't angry. He said he would do his best to pursue this line of inquiry and would let Mrs Thomas know the outcome.

'Please remember,' she said on leaving, 'I am scared stiff about my children. He threatens to kidnap them. He expressed no love for them. It is just revenge.' She could be dramatic when she was angry.

To calm down on her return home she took Buster for a long walk on the Green by the Stream and on into the wood, remembering the walk Joan Brimble had introduced her to in the spring. Perhaps they could do that again now Gran was no longer with them. In fact there were so many things they would be able to do, and Craig would be able to stay occasionally. Life could get better.

She was about to collect the children from school when the phone rang. It was the hospital replying to her application for a job. Could she come for an interview for a typing job tomorrow morning? Jem was delighted. Perhaps she should spend the evening practising on Will's computer. She practically skipped to school but regretted she had no money to buy doughnuts for 'afters'. Bacon, eggs and baked beans would have to do.

After their makeshift tea Will felt very important as Jem tried to get her mind round WordPerfect. Yes, eight years ago she had used it, and occasionally typed letters to friends, though now they did not reply. She had wiped this memory from her mind. Now she was adjusting her mind to 'dot leaders' and 'widows and orphans'? She did some straight copy typing to get back in the swing of things until Charlie got bored from lack of attention and made a fuss. Helping Gran with the jigsaw puzzles had been an important part of her evenings. So Jem gave up on the computer and they played Old Maid until Craig turned up.

'Hello, kids. I've brought a video of *The Karate Kid*, some Coke, crisps and bananas. I need your mum's help with my accounts. I'm hopeless with sums.'

'Mum's going to get a job tomorrow at the hospital.'

'No!'

'Yes. I'm just going to an interview. They'll ask me questions and give me a test to decide if I'm OK.'

'Of course you're OK,' said Craig.

'How do I know? I haven't worked for eight years. We'll have to wait and see. Now, kids, enjoy the video. Craig and I are doing accounts.'

'Bet I could do them,' said Will, still proud of showing his mother how to use the computer.

Jem and Craig sat at the kitchen table whilst the video blared from the living room until a bang on the party wall made Jem tell the children to turn it down.

Jem looked at the accounts Craig wanted to send out – all written out properly. Then she looked at the small amount of bills to be paid. Craig found it difficult to balance the two, and this was where Jem could help. She wrote it all down in a notebook, two columns that balanced in the third column.

'You're fine. Even taking into account the money you've paid yourself, you are in profit to £500. You could buy a new mower or put it towards your dream of a nursery garden. How much is agricultural land?'

'No idea. How do you know these things about money?'

'Partly I've always lived with it. Then when I left school my father made me do a crash course on word processing and bookkeeping. Bookkeeping is logic.'

'I love you.'

'That's not bookkeeping. But I love you too,' and she kissed him on the nose.

'Why? We are so different.'

'You're honest.'

'Now I am, but not in the past.'

'Hard-working. You are good with the kids. Sometimes you're very funny, like the faces you're pulling now.'

Craig smoothed a hand down his face to make it look serious and they both chuckled.

'I like the way you look after plants with such care. Remember that time I had to take splinters out of your fingers? I asked why you didn't wear gloves, and you said, "I can't feel and sense the plants." It shows you love what you're doing, which is important. And you have beautiful fair hair, blue eyes, and you're sexy. Why do you love me? It's certainly not the money.'

'You're just lovely. When do the kids go to bed? Then we can have the rest of the evening to ourselves.'

Next morning, having seen the children safely to school, Jem put her blonde hair in a neat chignon, dressed in her only smart suit, which she had worn to her mother's funeral, found her O-level and typing certificates and walked to the hospital. She now realised how big the place was: so many different departments, like a small town. She needed a map to find the orthopaedic department where her interview took place.

She was interviewed by a woman from personnel, and then given a typing test. The woman returned and offered her the job. She would be working from 9.00 am to 3.00 pm typing letters and reports for the consultants. Could she start next Monday?

Jem was so delighted she wanted to hug the woman. Walking home she tried to work out how much money she would have – enough for the rent, enough for food, enough for the electric and water. She would be paid monthly, so her dormant bank account could be used again. The first month would be a bit tricky, especially with Christmas on the horizon; perhaps Craig would lend her some of his £500 profit. Next Monday would be a new start.

PART SIX

Rupert was whistling as he walked back from Knightsbridge with several Christmas parcels in his hand. Tonight he was going to a smart dinner dance for some charity with 'the love of his life'. He gave a very convincing performance to his present woman that she was the love of his life. That was how he had got away with it so often in the past.

Blonde Melanie had been ditched in October for brunette Joanna Parkinson whom he had met whilst swimming at the sports club. She had a small house overlooking the Thames, which she shared with a large poodle, but had the hindrance of two children when they were not at boarding school. The ex-husband was busy in Dubai dealing in oil. After a couple of romantic candlelit dinners she asked him for the weekend to her country house near the South Downs in Sussex. Rupert thought this really was the good life. Horse riding on the Downs by day, a meal in Brighton followed by the theatre and a nightclub. Now she had asked him to stay for Christmas. The children would be going to Dubai.

Mr Brooks, as he called himself, had enjoyed his meetings with Mr Robinson in a greasy spoon café near Victoria

Station. Now he knew that Jemima no longer lived in the smart house, gone were the private schools and she was living with her demented mother in a council house. What a comedown! The situation gave him much amusement. The skiing accident had forced him out of the scene just in time, before it was discovered the investments had been a fraud. It had been a lucky escape. So he took pleasure in sending the latest anonymous letter to her new address, and when he found out about Olive's fall and death, via Sparks and Robinson, took even more pleasure in informing the police. That should frighten Jemima. It could even be true, then she would be sent to prison and those irritating children would end up in care.

Every so often Michael's publisher would ring, and to keep the money coming in, Rupert agreed, for a considerable sum, to continue the northern historical saga under the name of Michaela Rivers. Having read all the novels and delved into the medieval textbooks he would probably be able to do it. It would keep his mind from stagnating and, if he was supposed to be a woman, it would draw no publicity. It would be a laugh if he got away with it.

So it was with a light heart that he showered, dressed in his dinner jacket and was sampling a gin and tonic before Joanna's charity ball, when the doorbell rang from the street. That must be the taxi to take him, he thought as he picked up the door phone. But it wasn't. It was the police fraud squad. Could they come up and speak to him? The fraud squad! He panicked, slammed the phone down and headed for the fire escape. He dodged round the rubbish bins in the back yard and ran through the rain to Joanna's home. He hoped she would let him stay the night as he expected the police would be watching Elliott Mansions.

Joanna, being on the committee of this charity ball, had hoped Michael would give her some charming support, so she was annoyed to see him arrive late with no taxi, looking damp and dishevelled. She was icy in her manner all evening and informed him at the end of the dance she was going for drinks with some friends. He could make his own way home. Hoping the fire escape door was still open he trudged home in the rain.

Having spent all his money in the bar trying to make the most of a wretched evening, he put his card in the machine outside the bank. He was dismayed. It didn't work! The police must have frozen the account. He needed to get back to the flat and think.

The fire escape door was shut, locked from inside. It was now raining very hard. Descending the metal steps, he thought that by turning up his coat collar, covering his white shirt, he might get away with going through the front door. He was in luck as the young plain-clothes constable sitting in his unmarked Ford Escort had temporarily nodded off. Not daring to turn on any lights he stumbled up to the third floor and, using the touch of his pocket key ring, found the lock and let himself in. After stripping off his wet clothes he found himself a drink by the aid of the streetlights and, looking out of the window as the rain eased, he could just make out the figure of a man sitting in a Ford Escort. No ordinary man sits in a car after midnight. It had to be the police and, yes, the flats were being watched. He made for his bed thinking that tomorrow he would have to get out of here, but he needed to find some money from somewhere.

When it was light he arose, careful not to put on any lights. He made strong coffee, dressed in casual clothes and packed a large hold-all. He looked through drawers and pockets of clothes and came up with fifteen pounds in notes and change. The computer was an expensive portable and could make some money in the King's Road. He found Michael Brooks's passport and stuffed it in the hold-all. With a sigh he realised he had got fond of this flat over the past few months and even turned off the heating before he left via the fire escape. More unfulfilled dreams. Dreams that could have led somewhere, he thought, as he walked through the dustbins. He would have enjoyed trying to write a historical novel, however bad.

It was still raining, so with Michael's winter coat and hat pulled well down over his face he made for the tube station and left his luggage in a locker. Saving his money he walked to Joanna's. But there was no reply to the bell and no barking from the poodle. She might have taken him in, but no, she must have gone to Sussex. That was the end of his Christmas dream. Maybe his friends would be at the pub and if he said he'd lost his bankcard they would lend him some money, but they were not there.

Over a lone pint of beer thoughts of Christmas lingered. He remembered Christmases with his parents at the manor. The big Christmas tree, log fires, old-fashioned roast turkey. Surely if he went back to his childhood home his parents would shelter him. Keep quiet to the police. Even provide him with money or an air ticket. He had a feeling his future was abroad. If he took the ferry to Ireland no one would check on him, then he could catch a plane to the States. He could hide with all the other illegal immigrants from South America. The idea of being cosseted by his doting mother and father appealed. First of all he had to make some money selling the computer, then go to Victoria and find a coach to Bristol. It was cheaper than the train.

*

The coach sped west along the M4. The motion of the windscreen wipers banishing the raindrops lulled him to daydreaming. He imagined the look on his parents' faces when they opened the door. Shock turning to delight: their one and only son still alive. They would welcome him in, sit him by the warm fire, feed him and finally his old boyhood bedroom would be a refuge for the night.

Although he had the reassuring feel of a few hundred pounds in bank notes from the sale of the computer in his wallet, he wanted to save this and caught the bus to the nearest village to the manor. As he walked up the long drive his bag got increasingly heavy and he swore aloud when the house came into sight with no sign of lights. When he rang the bell there was no answer. Where the hell were his parents when he needed them? No longer having a key he would have to break in, as he had done as a teenager, through the ill-fitting window of the downstairs cloakroom.

As he walked into the hall the house had the chill damp air of emptiness. Yes, the furniture was there, but no sign of habitation. A note on the hall table, addressed to the cleaning lady, brought realisation home to him. 'Dear Mrs Mogg, please redirect our mail to our letting agent, who will forward it on to Spain.'

Spain! What were they doing in Spain? Rupert opened the front door and hauled in his damp, heavy hold-all. At least there was whisky in the dining-room sideboard. So much for a happy reunion! Again he would have to do the best he could – on his own. All he had had to eat today was a sandwich in the pub in Chelsea, but he was too tired to care any more. He took the whisky bottle up to his desolate bedroom.

*

He awoke late the next morning to the sound of church bells, which did nothing for his hangover. There was coffee in the kitchen, and food in the freezer, so he defrosted a meal for an early lunch. He turned the central heating on full to warm the house but realised smoke from the chimney, and lights at the windows, would alert any neighbours to his presence. He didn't need that.

Going into his father's study he felt vague curiosity as to where in Spain they had gone, and why. There were some brochures of Spanish properties on the desk, all quite cheap. How about bank statements? His father had always been tidy and these were in the filing cabinet. He was shocked to see how little money was in the bank. Was that the reason for Spain, or was it the fact his mother suffered from arthritis? He found he didn't really care.

Turning on the television in the kitchen for background companionable noise and finding a fresh whisky bottle, he considered his future. First he had to get more money. He laughed at himself for not being a better thief. Perhaps he could sell some of the silver, or jewellery if his mother had left some in the house. He knew some of the pictures were valuable. Rousing himself, he found the keys to the garage and his mother's car. Tomorrow he would drive to Clifton and see what he could sell in the many antique shops. He would enjoy seeing how much he could make; the instinct to make a profit was always there at the back of his mind. Returning to the kitchen he decided that if he had enough for a ferry, a few days in Ireland and the airfare to America, he would leave the country. Anonymity would be easier travelling on the ferry at Christmas time with so many others doing the same.

It was a lonely prospect and as the whisky worked its way into his brain he felt extremely sorry for himself.

Carols were being sung on the television that reminded him of the life he had lost. Bitterness and anger built up inside him. He still wanted revenge but had no desire to come into direct contact with Jemima again. In his imagination he remembered the last time. She must pay! His ideas of taking the children to hurt her would only be a burden to him if he wanted to leave the country. There had to be another way. Of course – the boyfriend. Beat up the boyfriend. Probably a wimp. That was a good idea. Take a kitchen knife, slash it about, and scare him so much Jemima wouldn't have a chance with him. A stab in the right place and watch the blood flow. If he did this just before driving to Fishguard and the Irish ferry, then the police wouldn't have time to catch up with him.

Mr Robinson's spy had told him they had been away on holiday together, and now the mother wasn't there, the boyfriend sometimes spent the night. Now that Rupert had the use of a car he could keep watch on the boyfriend's vehicle, incognito, like the police near Sloane Square had tried to watch him in the flat. He would get to know where lover boy went, somehow try to stop him and get him with the knife. What a cheerful Christmas Jemima would have. He chuckled to himself. Everything was so easy when you were drunk.

The next morning he loaded up the car with what valuables he could find. A Georgian silver tea set, two original Victorian landscapes by known artists; Rupert had always despised his parents' traditional tastes, but they might be worth something. He had found some of his mother's jewellery in the safe that his father had forgotten to lock.

He heard a postman pushing mail, mainly Christmas

cards, through the letterbox. What if Mrs Mogg turned up to redirect the post whilst he was staying here? Even if he were out she would notice the blank unstained patches on the walls. He found her number in his mother's telephone book and, imitating his father's pompous voice, said Mr and Mrs Somerville-Thomas had returned from Spain and would not need her services this week. He was pleased with himself for thinking of this.

Realising he was not unknown in Clifton he put on an old-fashioned raincoat and hat of his father's, hoping this was an adequate disguise, and went out to sell.

With several hundred pounds in his pocket, and the promise of more in a few days after the artistic valuer's assessment, Rupert decided to go and find Meadowleaze, Northfields.

It was dusk and no one noticed him. What a shabby place, he thought, with scruffy boys playing in the street. The boys were kicking a football in the cul-de-sac under the streetlights, their breath a mist in the cold night air, but he didn't recognise a taller, older William out of his prep school uniform.

A white van swung round the corner, stopped outside No. 14. One of the footballers greeted the man and they went into the house. Later Jemima, William, Charlotte and the man all climbed into the van. Rupert noticed the name on the van, 'Jones Garden Improvements', and followed it. The name seemed faintly familiar, but he had lived in Bristol most of his life and many things were familiar.

His patience was tried when the van stopped at a row of shops and Jemima jumped out and disappeared inside a supermarket. Ten minutes later she climbed back in the van with shopping bags and they drove off to a block of rundown flats where they all got out. There seemed little point in staying. It must be where the boyfriend lived and he noted the name. He would be back at the flats tomorrow early and resume his reconnaissance.

PART SEVEN

The alarm went off early. It was still dark on a Monday morning and Jem groaned. Work today. Craig had stayed over the weekend and they had had such a wonderful time, like a proper family. They had watched Will play football on Saturday morning and battled with crowds Christmas shopping, followed by an *Indiana Jones* film at the cinema, a treat from Craig. Then yesterday had been so lazy.

Going back to work was hard, Jem not having worked since she had given birth to children. Getting them to school, taking Buster for his walk, then going to the hospital was another new shock she had to get used to. The medical terms that came over the Dictaphone were new to her and she was continually referring to the medical dictionary. What was a 'Pott's fracture'? The consultants always wanted everything yesterday, but were friendly and helpful when she got things wrong, as were the other typists who happily gossiped about their families whilst eating sandwiches at lunchtime. In time she would get used to it, she knew. In the meantime money was tight until she was paid. It was beans on toast or bacon and eggs, unless Craig or Carrie turned up with a takeaway or

204

a casserole. At least she would be paid before Christmas, when she would get a week off.

On this particular Monday morning she had returned home, having walked with the children to school, to leave Buster in the house, which he resented, when the phone rang. It was Mr Dawes. His gentle voice was cautious.

'I was hoping to catch you before you went to work. We've found your errant husband, but I think you should be careful. Mr Wilmott got Interpol to investigate the hospital, which was naturally cagey about giving out information, as it would look as though they had made a mistake. Interpol were able to find out the only other Englishman at the hospital was called Michael Brooks. Mr Wilmott then got the fraud squad to find a Michael Brooks in West One, London, and compare him with your husband's photo. They tried to arrest him but he did a bunk. That's why I think you should be careful. Very careful. I'm sure they'll catch up with him very soon. Mr Wilmott asked me to thank you.'

'We'll take care, Mr Dawes.'

'And by the way, I'm still looking into your mother's affairs. I'll be in touch.'

Jem went to work with her mind in turmoil. What could she do to protect Will, Charlie and herself?

On her return home with the children, a phone call gave her more reason for alarm.

'Jem, this is Janet. Sorry I haven't been in touch; how are you?'

'Fine. I'm working now. Mum died last month.'

'Oh, I'm so sorry.'

'How's the tennis club?'

'Much the same, though the snooty ones don't play in the winter. But I wasn't ringing about that. I was in

Clifton Village this morning, shopping, and I'm sure I saw Rupert. He was in the antique market. He didn't see me and he was too far away for me to say anything. Either he has a double, or maybe you have something to tell me.'

'Yes, he is alive. He has sent me several nasty threatening letters from London, but I didn't expect him to be in Bristol. This is frightening. Apparently there was a mix-up at the hospital in Austria and someone else is in Rupert's grave.'

'Is there anything I can do?'

'I don't think so, but it is good to know I have someone to contact. I get scared thinking about the children. Why don't you drop in after school one day and I'll explain it all to you?' and she rang off feeling very frightened. Dreading a threatening phone call or knock at the door. It was getting dark, so Craig might be home. She had to share her fears with someone.

Craig came straight away, having the same fears for the children, but was more concerned about his mother. He suggested they all came to his mum's flat for a meal. Doris had sprained her ankle, couldn't go to bingo and was bored.

'Have you told the police your friend Janet saw Rupert?' he asked.

'No. They wouldn't believe me. They think I threw my mother down the stairs.'

'Then try Mr Wilmott or the solicitor.' But they had both gone home.

So they all went to see Doris and Debbie. Debbie cooked supper and they enjoyed playing cards until the children's bedtime when Craig took them home, saying he had better not stay the night in case the council found out, and his mum might need him as Debbie was working nights. Jem, rather miffed, made sure the two doors were secure once the children were in bed. She had said nothing to them about their father and the fact he was alive, as she did not want to scare them as well. Was this a mistake? Should they be more aware? She was an independent woman and needed to cope on her own, but Craig could have been more protective. There was little sleep that night, the slightest sound waking her in a panic.

On Tuesday Jem contacted Mr Wilmott's office and left a message, but the day passed quietly with the children excited about the Nativity play and carols they would perform at the end of the week. Jem spent the evening turning one of Charlie's old nighties into an angel's robe, then realised they had no tinsel, nor any Christmas decorations. She hadn't thought of packing such things back in February. She could buy these with her hard-earned money next week.

In the dusk of the afternoon on Wednesday as Will and Jem walked home, hand in hand, Charlie running around them with Buster, Will asked, 'Did Gran Felicity drive a light blue BMW?'

'Yes, it was a very smart car.'

'I think I saw it at the end of the road yesterday evening.'

Jem's heart missed a beat. Did her mother-in-law want to get in touch? She would find that difficult after all this time. 'Was Granny in it?'

'I couldn't see. It was getting dark.'

'There must be lots of people who drive blue BMWs.'

'Not round here there ain't.'

Jem wanted to think Will had an overactive imagination. Seeing him every day she had not recognised how much he had grown physically and mentally over the last

207

months. He had coped with many changes well and was more adult than she realised.

Late in the evening Craig turned up with a bottle of wine. He had cooked his mother a meal, cheered her up and was feeling the strain. Jem didn't mention the blue BMW. Craig hadn't seemed concerned yesterday, and there was nothing they could do about it, so what was the point?

After a couple of glasses Jem began to feel mellow and had a feeling the wine might be a bribe. Besides, she wanted to take her mind off the threat of Rupert.

'What do your family usually do at Christmas?' she asked.

'Well, this year Debbie's workin'. Mum's sister Effie and her husband Dud usually come to tea, but they might be goin' to their daughter's, over to Willowdown.'

Jem took a deep breath. 'I've asked my friend Bill, from the council, and his mother to lunch, but you and Doris must come as well. Then Debbie can come back here when she's finished work, and Effie and Dud if they're on their own.'

'That would be great. Mum would love that.'

'Think you might have to provide a few plates, knives and forks. The kitchen will be very squashed. Perhaps we could eat in the front room.'

'I can bring the plastic table and chairs in from the garden,' so they spent the evening planning Christmas.

Craig suggested, 'I'll bring some of my veg from the allotment. I've been storing potatoes, onions and carrots in the shed.'

'Your plot's done well this year.'

'Yes. If you like I'll bring you a cabbage tomorrow.'

'That would make a nice change from baked beans,

208

though Charlie would probably prefer mushy peas.'

'What about bubble and squeak? And sausages. I'm feeling hungry already.'

As he was leaving Jem mentioned, 'Will said he saw my mother-in-law's car yesterday. At the time I wondered if she wanted to get in touch again, but I've been thinking – was Rupert driving the car? If he's in the area, the place he would be staying is with his parents. They would never give him away. Perhaps I should contact Mr Wilmott again.'

'I think so. If he grabbed the kids – I don't know what I'd do. They're such good fun. Must be somethin' to do with their mother,' and he kissed her goodnight.

Jem telephoned Mr Wilmott and told him she thought Rupert might be staying with his parents at the manor, and then she walked to work at the hospital.

Mr Wilmott contacted the police, who sent two policemen in a car to investigate. They wandered round the house, banged on doors, peered through windows, but their quarry had already left, and the garage was empty. Where was Rupert, and what would he do?

PART EIGHT

Rupert spent the morning collecting his money from the
art valuer, then went to the travel agent to collect his ticket
for the Irish ferry. Feeling he had done well, he lunched in
an expensive restaurant overlooking the Suspension
Bridge, then set out to find the boyfriend. He wanted to
hurt this man and had brought his mother's largest kitchen
knife for the purpose. He had at last remembered where
he had seen the boyfriend before. He was the gardener.
This fuelled his fury and resentment even further. How
could she prefer a gardener after the life he, Rupert, had
given her? If his memory served him right the gardener
had come on Thursday to their avenue and dealt with
several gardens. Hopefully his routine was the same.

He cruised around for a time, the familiar houses
fuelling his anger. Condemned. No longer able to live in
his own home. Then he saw the Jones Garden Improvements van. The man was packing away his tools, then he
jumped into his van and drove away.

Rupert, in his mother's fast BMW, could follow with
ease. The two vehicles drove across the grassy Downs,
where Olive had been incarcerated in a home, and along
shop-lined roads until they came to Northfields. The van

turned off along small side roads until they came to a garden allotment site. The van stopped and Rupert held back, waiting to see where the man went. With a spring in his step the gardener walked along small grassy paths to a plot and examined the plants. Rupert was ignorant of such things; they were just green leaves. Then the gardener unlocked a shed on the plot.

Rupert, hiding the knife up his sleeve, slowly and quietly got out of his car and walked up to the plot where his enemy was bending over some plants.

'Did you know you're an adulterer, you bastard? Stealing another man's wife?'

The young man looked up in surprise, then slowly straightened himself, one hand behind his back.

'I do now. You really are a stuffed git. What do you expect after the way you've treated Jem? How many women have you tricked and let down in the last few years? You don't want her, and she doesn't want you. Just go *away*.'

'You've no idea; she's no idea how I've suffered since she tried to kill me. Lost everything. She's ruined my life. It's now her turn to suffer. If I get you – she will.' With that Rupert whipped the knife out so it gleamed in the orange angry wind-swept sky of the setting sun, and advanced towards Jem's lover.

He realised his mistake as the gardener stood steady, his garden fork raised to attack.

'You don't grow up round here without knowing how to defend yourself. Despite never learnin' to play rugby.'

PART NINE

Jem, Will and Charlie were crossing the main road on their way home from school when Craig's van drove past and they all waved.

'There's that BMW again,' said Will.

They stared.

'That looks like Daddy,' announced Charlie.

'Oh no,' gasped Jem. 'Come on, kids, we must run home. We need to get the car and get to Craig's allotment as fast as we can. Craig may be in trouble.'

They dashed to the house, dumped their bags, found the car keys and were off. Buster, excited, decided to jump in the car as well. They roared along the roads, horn blaring, scattering the school children wandering home, until they came to the allotment.

There they saw two men silhouetted on Craig's plot arguing angrily. There was blood on Craig's arm and his thigh. He was thrusting his garden fork towards Rupert, who was dodging.

'Kids, stay here. I'll go and try to talk some sense into them.'

Jem got out of the car but Buster was in front of her. He bounded up to the two men. No one knew whether he wanted to defend Craig or greet his old master, but Rupert gave him a vicious kick and sent him rolling.

'Nobody does that to my dog,' Will muttered angrily to himself. He got out of the car, went to Craig's van and found a spade.

The adults were by now all shouting, Craig keeping Rupert at bay with his fork, so they didn't notice Will in determined mood as he walked up behind his father, raised the spade and brought it down on his head.

Will wasn't strong enough to do damage but brought his father to his knees, dropping the knife, which Jem swiftly retrieved.

Rupert slowly got to his feet, eying his son. 'You always were a little runt. How dare you hit your father?'

'Fathers are supposed to be caring. They don't kick dogs.'

'As your father I'll tell you what you can and can't do,' and he grabbed Will by the neck. Craig tried to lunge at Rupert but his bloodied arm had weakened him and he stumbled. It was Jem saying, 'Buster, kill,' that brought Rupert to his knees again as Buster bit his ankle.

'Right, dead husband of mine,' said Jem, brandishing the kitchen knife. 'Get up and walk into that shed.'

Rupert unsteadily rose to his feet and glared at Will.

'How can you treat me, your father, like this? My family's blood is in your veins. I sent you to a good school. Tried to get some sense into you. Now what does your future hold? Nothing.'

Will, overwhelmed by what had happened, shrugged.

'Craig's my dad now. He likes me.'

'Get in that shed!' shouted Jem. 'Will, can you find the padlock in Craig's pocket? He must be bad. He's fainted.'

Given something to do, Will recovered and, fumbling in

Craig's dungarees, found the padlock. As his father backed into the shed, away from Jem brandishing the knife, Will slammed the door and snapped the padlock shut.

'Right,' commanded Jem, 'we need a phone box. The police and an ambulance. Come on. Come, Buster.' The three of them raced back to the car and a screaming Charlie. In the crisis they had forgotten her. Perhaps, Jem thought, thinking of what they had witnessed, that was for the best.

An elderly resident from the houses opposite came out of his front door.

'Is Craig all right? We could hear shouting.'

'No, he isn't. Have you got a phone?'

'Come in.'

The man showed them in and Jem rang 999 and explained the situation. His wife had the kettle on and was making hot sweet tea for the shock, she said.

'I ought to get back to Craig,' said Jem.

'Off you go, dear. We'll look after the kiddies,' answered the wife.

The old man went with Jem, carrying a torch. He said his name was Daniel and he had the plot next to Craig. They often chatted. He could remember Craig as a nipper. 'A right tearaway he was. Good to see him settling down.'

Craig was moaning in pain. Jem, stroking his sweaty forehead, noticed not only was there a gash on his arm but his thigh had been opened as well. He must have lost a large quantity of blood. No wonder he had fainted. She thought she ought to try and find the van keys in his pocket, which she did, then put her coat over him to keep him warm. Daniel was collecting up the tools and was shocked to see the bloody kitchen knife.

214

'He must be a wrong 'un,' commented Daniel.

'He is indeed,' said Jem. 'I should know. He's my husband. But for not much longer.'

The noise of police sirens came nearer and two sets of flashing blue lights stopped by Craig's van. Paramedics trotted over the allotments and gently placed Craig on a stretcher. Jem gave them details of his injuries, his name and address, and they were soon gone. The police wanted more explanations, but by now Jem was getting cold and tearful. She needed to get home, see to the children and call on Craig's mother, not give a long drawn-out account to the police. Neither did she want to face Rupert. She gave the police the knife and keys to the padlock, then left.

Reaction was setting in with Will and Charlie and they were upset – Charlie crying and Will morose. They drove in silence.

In the warm kitchen the TV was put on automatically and Jem realised it was still children's television. She felt it was midnight. Finding an old packet of fish fingers at the bottom of the deep freeze and a tin of mushy peas, she set to cooking tea. There were tears in her eyes as she remembered Craig's idea of bubble and squeak for tea. She hoped he was OK.

Whilst they were eating she told the children what she expected had happened to their father – the mix-up at the hospital, his different identity, the threatening letters and how he wanted to kidnap them.

'I didn't tell you any of this before because I didn't want to frighten you.'

'But why didn't he come home when he came out of hospital?' asked Will.

'As you both know we had to move because there was no money. Your dad had asked people to invest in a

215

scheme that turned out to be wrong. What the people were investing in, giving their money to, didn't survive, and they lost their money. It is what is called "fraud". That's against the law. The police would have arrested him, so he became someone else. Michael Brooks. Poor Michael Brooks died in an accident the same day your father had his fall, in the same hospital. He is now buried in the churchyard near Granny Felicity and Grandpa's home.'

'Now the police have caught Daddy?' asked Charlie.

'You're safe, darling,' her mother reassured her.

'No, not that. Do we have to go back to the other house?'

'No, we can't. Someone else lives there now.'

'Oh, good. I'd miss Sasha and the Williams boys.'

'And I'd hate to go back to that school. Latin, and no football.'

Jem laughed with relief.

With food and within the security of their home the children were recovering. Jem was surprised at their lack of interest, but then they had seen little of their father apart from holidays, and even then he was usually off with some male friends or a different woman. He was a distant and scary figure in their lives. To Rupert his offspring had been a status symbol, like a trophy wife.

Now she had to cope with the rest of the evening – Doris, hospital, police – but first she would go and see caring and dependable Ruth to see if she could babysit. Ruth invited her into the kitchen where she and Joel were washing up the evening meal. They were both shocked that Craig had been attacked and injured.

'And you were worried about Will and Charlie!' exploded Ruth. 'He really was out to make you suffer, but it's Craig. Poor guy.'

216

Joel was looking baffled by all this, so had to be filled in with the whole story.

'This used to be a quiet street,' he said, 'but at least you can feel the kids are safe now. You've been wrestling with this for six months, but it's over, praise the Lord.'

'Joel, are you in this evening?' asked Ruth. He nodded. 'Then I'll look after the children. Thomas and Martha can come with me. You, Jem, go and see Doris – she must be so worried, and stuck in that flat – then check on Craig.'

Debbie was working nights, so Doris, standing at the door holding two walking sticks, was very pleased to see someone.

'I don't know where Craig has got to. I was getting worried.'

'That's why I've come,' said Jem gently. She got Doris sitting down and related the story again.

'I've got to get to see him. Oh, my poor Craig.'

'I know. I would like to make a suggestion. You can't do much with your ankle. Craig is going to be laid up for a bit, and it's my fault entirely. Debbie can't be here all the time. If you can get down the stairs in the flats, would you like to stay with us until things get better? That is, after we've been to see Craig. You can have Mum's room downstairs. The bed's still there.'

Doris looked thoughtful for a moment, then smiled. 'Yes, that would make life easier. I can see Craig and would enjoy the company. Thanks. Can you pack my bag for me?'

Jem felt Doris, despite her worries over Craig, was enjoying the invalid role.

It was slow progress down the concrete stairs. A cheerful neighbour gave them a hand and carried the bag, interested in the news of Craig's attack. A drama. The news would be spread via the pub in no time. Jem was not in the mood for news. Others hadn't sensed the anger, the hatred, or the blood that had seeped into that meeting on the allotments. Doris and her neighbour were only conscious of the smell of stale food and urine. That was nothing new and they ignored it. It was a matter of space again. Too many people too close together.

Getting into the car, with help, Doris said to Jem, 'You seem a sensible girl. Why did you marry someone like this man who's attacked Craig? Not that I can talk, thinking about Craig and Debbie's father.'

Jem considered this during their drive to the hospital.

'He was handsome, and in the early days considerate, charming and rich. Charm conceals so much – selfishness and greed. I think it was being too successful that ruined him. He thought he could do anything.'

Finding Craig in the hospital proved to be difficult. There seemed to be no central reception desk and it was a mystery where to start, so they went to Accident and Emergency. After a clerk had shuffled files and fiddled with computers they were sent to ward D in a central block. This was a long walk, so Jem found a wheelchair. She pushed Doris down an ill-lit road, then negotiated lifts and corridors before they found the ward.

'Visiting is over,' announced the nurse.

Jem patiently explained the situation and she relented. 'Sorry. People with stab wound injuries have usually been hauled off the streets after a drunken brawl.'

They found Craig sedated, bandaged with a bag of blood being dripped into his body. He was asleep and very pale.

The nurse returned, more sympathetic. 'He'll be all right in the morning. Probably send him home before the weekend. Staff shortages.'

218

'I work here,' said Jem. 'I'll come and see him tomorrow. If he wakes give him our love.' And they left disappointed but relieved.

As they were leaving the ward Doris turned in the wheelchair. 'We've forgotten all about Debbie. She doesn't know. She can't go home to an empty flat. Can you wheel me over to the maternity block and we can see her, or leave a message?'

Luckily Debbie was in reception talking to a young Indian doctor whom she introduced as Rajdeep. They told her what had happened and she was upset, so Rajdeep put his hand on her shoulder.

'I'll go and see him when I come off duty,' she said, 'then I'll pop round to visit you. Thanks, Jem, for looking after Mum.'

'Well, I feel the whole thing is my fault.'

Driving home, Doris said, 'It is so kind of you to ask us for Christmas Day.'

'Now this has happened I'm very glad I did. I feel so free now Rupert has been arrested. Since June and the first threatening letter I received, a great weight has been on my shoulders.' Then she asked, 'Is Rajdeep more than just a doctor? He seemed concerned as well.'

'I think I've heard her mention him.'

'If he's special do tell Debbie to ask him for Christmas as well.'

The two women felt closer today than they had before.

Having installed Doris in the living room with Ruth in control, complete with bedding and all Doris would need, Jem set out for the police station to give her account of 'the incident on the allotments', as the file was entitled. It was the same detective sergeant who had visited her at home.

'Didn't I come to see you a month ago? Someone suggested you pushed your mother down the stairs,' he said superciliously.

'Yes. Now you have in your custody the man who wrote that anonymous letter. As you know he has viciously attacked someone.' She explained the events of the evening and said she would bring in more anonymous letters in the morning. The sergeant showed her out in a more conciliatory manner.

Jem drove the children to school. Would there be news of last night's attack? The 'jeering news network' worked fast around here. The Nativity play was at four o'clock, and Jem promised to be there.

She drove to work so that she could bring Craig home when he was discharged.

'What's happened to you?' asked one of the horrified typists. 'Your coat's covered in blood.'

'Oh, damn. I forgot to shove it in the washing machine.' Then to a delighted audience she told the story yet again. They all agreed she must go to see Craig at coffee time, however much work there was.

Craig was sitting up in bed and his smile as she walked down the ward made him look like his old self, but as he talked she could tell he was still weak and in pain. He said there were twenty-four stitches in his arm and thirty in his thigh.

'The doctor said it was lucky the assailant didn't stab anything more vital, which I think the bastard was trying to do. What's happened to him?'

'He's locked in the police station. I've made a statement.'

'Debbie called in on her way home. She said Mum's staying with you.'

'Yes. So will you be when they let you out. I caused all this, so I'm trying to make amends. When can you leave?'

'I won't be able to do anything.'

'I know. What we must do over the weekend is get your diary. Is it in the van? I've got the keys and Daniel is keeping an eye on it. Then ring round all your clients. I'll look after you and Doris as long as it takes. That is if you don't mind Will and Charlie. They finish school on Tuesday, I finish work on Friday, then I don't start again until next year. If the council complain I'll go and see Bill Edwards.'

She could see Craig relaxing. He had someone to look after him.

'But this afternoon, I can get off at 2.30 if I work through the lunch break, then I'll pick you up and take you home. Oh, shit. I've forgotten to bring you any clothes. You'll never see those dungarees again.'

'Ring Debbie. She'll be awake about lunchtime. Ask her to bring a big T-shirt, boxer shorts and my dressing gown. I couldn't cope with clothes.'

As she left she kissed him lightly. 'Did you hear what Will said before you passed out? He said, "Craig's my dad now. He likes me."'

Craig laughed with pleasure.

So at 2.30 with the other typists' blessing Jem picked up Debbie, helped Craig into a wheelchair, and took them home. Debbie wanted to come with her to the school play, so they left mother and son together. Jem felt she had suddenly become part of a large family. Something she hadn't experienced before.

The Nativity play was a great success for all the wrong

reasons. Mary got stage fright and the teacher had to make a quick substitution. The shepherds started waving to their mums, who waved back, taking attention away from Joseph and his important lines with the innkeeper. This unnerved Joseph, so he punched the innkeeper when he said there was no room for them at the inn, and all hell was let loss with toy lambs being thrown. The baby Jesus doll was lucky to survive and the second Mary left in tears.

The riotous applause from the audience made the children think that this was the way the play should be and they bowed with big grins on their faces, though Charlie in her angel nightie looked puzzled. It hadn't been like that last Christmas, but she remembered what her mother had said about foreign lands and said nothing.

Will and the older children sang carols from all over the world and managed to sing in tune. There were cups of tea for the parents whilst the children changed and tidied up, which gave Jem a chance to introduce Debbie to Ruth, Kim and Charlene, realising Debbie would be coming to the house more often. They were all concerned for her brother. Jem had brought the car, so the children piled in and Debbie, being the only one with any money, bought fish and chips for six, then after the meal went back to work.

There was a dispute about beds that evening as Craig had most claim on the downstairs bed. In the end they managed to steer Doris up the stairs into Jem's small bedroom and Jem had some blankets on the sofa in the living room next to Craig. This meant she could play nursemaid and give him painkillers and antibiotics as needed.

The weekend was a mixture of cooking meals, bought with the Jones family money, and a flurry of activity caused by Debbie and the children. Jem made several casseroles and cakes, enjoying cooking as she had done in her other life. Debbie turned up after her morning sleep and bullied Jem and the kids into buying a Christmas tree and decorations. Whilst they were out they checked Craig's van, where they found his diary and a large pot for the tree. Craig was finding the noisy, excited children difficult as he was in some pain, but with his crutches he managed to climb the stairs and spent much of the day asleep on Jem's bed.

On Monday morning Jem telephoned Mr Dawes and made an appointment for four o'clock that afternoon. She had a hectic day working, checking on her injured guests and collecting the children from school before being seated in Mr Dawes's office.

Mr Dawes was amazed by the news that Rupert had attacked Craig. 'I thought he was after the children.'

'He wanted to cause as much damage to me as he could. Craig was a better target.'

'He won't get bail if he's been violent, so you can feel safe for several years, until he comes out of prison.'

'Will I be asked to appear in court?'

'Not for the fraud case, but yes for the assault on Craig.'

'I never want to see him again. Which is why I'm here. I need a divorce. I want to be free of Rupert Somerville-Thomas.'

The two of them got on to the details of the case, agreeing that adultery would be the easiest cause and that Jem would be able to claim legal aid. Jem went home to her extended family feeling more secure than she had felt since her first visit to Mr Dawes in January, eleven months ago.

Jem had never enjoyed Christmas so much. It really started on Christmas Eve with Will and Charlie putting out their Christmas stockings with a glass of whisky and mince pie for Santa. She filled the stockings that were Craig's largest socks with satsumas, chocolate money, dinky toys and felt pens whilst Doris reminisced about Christmases gone by; when Craig got stuck in the snow on the Cotswolds, and how next-door's dog stole the chicken that was all they could afford. The stories made Jem laugh, though she suddenly felt sad, shed a few tears, realising how much Olive would have enjoyed the evening.

Debbie and Rajdeep called in with presents before they went to work. Rajdeep had brought a long Indian cotton gown called a dhoti for Craig. 'He might find this lighter and more comfortable over his wounds,' he explained. Indeed it was, regal and majestic as it flowed around him. Then the couple went off to work. Jem babysat for the Williams children whilst Ruth and Joel went to the midnight service, then all was peace and quiet until morning, except for the police cars chasing drunk drivers.

She stuffed the turkey listening to excited children upstairs finding their stockings, then with Doris's help peeled potatoes for nine. Would the turkey be big enough? It had cost enough. At least the vegetables were free from Craig's allotment.

Jem was worried about the inexpensive presents she had bought her children, but it was something they would have to get used to. Will was pleased with his football and Charlie with new furniture for her dolls' house.

Later in the morning Will was happily playing football in the cul-de-sac and admiring Tom's new bike. Charlie was showing Kim and Sasha her new dolls' house furniture. Bill Edwards and his mother, Susan, arrived and made a great joke of trying to assemble the garden table to make room for everyone.

Kim and Sasha were just leaving and Doris asked, 'Are you going home to a turkey dinner with your mum and dad?'

Kim looked awkward. 'No. Dad's not there and Mum's got flu.'

'Oh dear!' exclaimed Jem. 'Perhaps you could have lunch here. Let's go and see how your mum is.' She ushered the girls over the road and found Jo curled up on the sofa, coughing. She dissolved into tears when Jem asked how she was.

'Look, let's get you into bed, then we'll look after Kim and Sasha. I'll pop in to see you later and bring some food if you want it. Where's Ted?'

'He's had to go out,' Jo said, then added, 'to see his mum.'

Jem made the sick woman a cup of tea whilst the girls got her into bed. Kim and Sasha practically skipped back to her house.

'Two more for lunch,' Jem called from the front door. 'Better get some chips out of the deep freeze.'

'You know,' mentioned Bill as he opened a bottle of wine, 'I really will have to report this household to the Housing Department. Gross overcrowding and far too many people enjoying themselves.' Those present gave him a cheer.

The meal was very jolly with jokes from the older diners and crackers keeping the children chuckling.

There was a lull when Craig went to rest, Bill and Susan gallantly washed up and Jem made a sandwich and a Cup-a-Soup for Jo left in bed over the road. Debbie and Rajdeep were at the table eating a late lunch when Jem returned, and Effie and Dud had arrived. Doris was putting them at ease amongst so many strange people.

When settled with cups of tea, Dud did conjuring tricks and kept them all amused for an hour. Fuelled with Christmas cake and mince pies Bill introduced charades and, after a few glasses of wine, got them singing rounds. This led to noisy confusion.

Bert came round to complain about the noise, then, seeing the wine, returned with Vera to join in. There were more songs. Jem, having noticed Sasha nodding off, quietly took the girls by the hand and walked them home with a goody bag of cake, mince pies and paracetamol for their mother. She made sure they were all settled for the night and promised to return in the morning. There was no sign of Ted.

Back in her living room the songs had progressed back in time to the forties and fifties. The younger people had retreated to the kitchen to play cards. Debbie was teaching the kids how to play Cheat. There was 'Somewhere Over the Rainbow' coming from the front room and laughter from the kitchen. Jem smiled at the mixed sounds of people enjoying themselves. For a few moments she remembered that this time last year they had been in a smart hotel in Austria, celebrating Christmas more formally in evening dress. She did not regret the passing of those days, though she had enjoyed the skiing. Yes, this was more real, down-to-earth, and lasting.

Boxing Day morning Jem, with a headache, went over to No. 7 to see how Jo was. She was still in bed but looked better and wasn't crying, which was a good sign.

226

'I've got something to tell you,' she announced.

Jem sat down on the bed.

'I was lying yesterday about Ted. I didn't want to spoil everyone's Christmas Day. He's gone. Gone for good. Even taken his clothes. I haven't told the girls yet. He got very angry with me for having flu. As if I could help it! "There's always something wrong with you, you depressing cow," he said. "I know where I can find love with a woman who cares for me." I did care for him. Just couldn't show it.'

The tears had started and Jem held her hand.

'This woman lives in Birmingham. He's been seeing her all the time. So he's gone.'

Jem sighed. 'I'm so sorry if you really loved him. But I think he treated you very badly and neither you nor the children will miss him. I know I didn't miss Rupert when he had his accident. The atmosphere of tension went from the house. It was so peaceful.

'You get over the flu, and then you'll feel better about everything. I must get back to my houseful. Kim and Sasha are welcome to have lunch with us. It's bubble and squeak. Then they can come out with us. We're taking Buster and the football to the Green by the Stream.'

So the holiday spirit continued for another day. They even pushed Craig along to watch the football in Olive's wheelchair, which Jem had forgotten to return to the Red Cross.

The new year brought the family back down to earth. The atmosphere was grey and bleak from the weather to returning to school and work. Doris and Craig stayed for a few days, looking after each other, until his wounds were healed and the stitches were out. The house seemed even greyer without the company. They all looked forward

227

to the weekends when Jem would pick up Craig with his crutches. Will's football matches, burgers at McDonald's, and the cinema kept them cheerful. Craig didn't move in as this might lead to Jem losing her council house, but she missed his company.

Jem tried to keep it to herself but there were problems with the DHSS. She had been summoned to their offices and asked why she had been claiming widow's allowance whilst her husband was still alive. Fortunately she had tried not to collect it from the post office once she had realised Rupert was still alive – she had had the money from making curtains and her carer's and children's allowance, so usually there had been enough to make ends meet – but there were still six months the department demanded. In desperation she went to see Mr Dawes, who was already dealing with her divorce. A formal letter setting out the details of the situation mollified the DHSS and they agreed to Mrs Thomas paying off a reduced amount in weekly payments, but it meant there was less money than she had hoped. Jem felt Rupert had it easy. First six months in a Knightsbridge flat, then prison. Not a thought on how to juggle his finances.

The February school half term was to start next week.

'Do you know,' Jem mentioned to the children, 'we've been here a complete year? It was half term when we moved in.'

'We pretended to be explorers,' said Will as he stirred his Coco Pops to make the milk go chocolate.

'I like going out to play here better,' mused Charlie, 'but the other house was nicer.'

'That's true,' agreed their mother. 'And although it's sad, it is easier without Gran being here. She was a tie.'

228

'D'you remember the time she escaped?' Will asked, with a laugh. 'You went spare.'

'I liked the jigsaws,' added Charlie. 'Can you get another one from the library?'

'Yes, of course.' *Well, if that's their reaction,* Jem thought, *we're doing OK.*

She had been wondering what to do with the children over half term, as she didn't want to use up holiday time from work, preferring to keep it for the summer. Jo, from No. 7, came to her rescue. Jo, as Jem had expected, seemed better now Ted was no longer there. The girls too seemed less subdued. Jo still had depression but no longer spent her days in a dressing gown. She herself suggested she would keep an eye on Will and Charlie. Will wanted to be grown-up like the Williams boys and make sandwiches at lunchtime, but they were to tell Jo where they were and not leave Meadowleaze. This all went well. Jem gave Jo a small amount of money for her trouble, and it was agreed to do the same over the Easter holidays.

It wasn't really Jo's fault this arrangement didn't work out. Will, growing fast and feeling older, having lived through the experience of his father attacking Craig and standing up to his father himself, started going around with Tom's older brother, Luke, now at the comprehensive. Ruth had often said Luke was a wild boy and Will was taken in by his arrogant showing-off. Hanging around the shopping precinct and meeting up in the woods with Luke's mates seemed so grown-up. He was becoming a man of the world. Will told his new so-called friends about Craig's encounter with his father, exaggerating his own part, and the boys were impressed enough to let him tag along. Jem had noticed a change in his behaviour, and Ruth warned the protective mother Luke was becoming a teenager she couldn't order about any more; he couldn't be asked to keep an eye on Will. She too was hoping they would grow out of it.

'Jo isn't making Will stay in the close. He knows he should, but bikes off with the older boys. Jo takes no notice.'

'Jo's a dark horse,' Ruth said. Then she laughed. 'Is that racist? I know she's depressed, but living in the other half of the semi, you hear things. The rows and the language. And there used to be occasional men calling when Ted was away.'

'You're saying that I'm being naïve,' said Jem.

'Yes, but for the best of reasons. You want everyone to be well and happy. You hang on to that man of yours, and be happy yourself.'

'But what about Luke? You must worry.'

'He has been warned. He knows he's mixing with the wrong crowd. I hope he gets a scare and realises these boys are a mistake before they get up to worse things. But Will is much younger. You must worry. We just pray and know God will look after our boy. We include Will in our prayers.'

'Thanks. Perhaps Will has inherited some of his father's more unfortunate genes. He does like showing off, and thinking he is important. It's Good Friday tomorrow, and I'll be home until Tuesday. I think I'll tell Jo I don't need her any more and make different arrangements come the summer.'

They had been sitting in Jem's kitchen and Ruth got up to leave. Will came in looking vague. Was there lager on his breath? He may have been tall, but he was only nine.

Ruth left murmuring, 'Good luck,' and Jem sent Will to his room. Later she heard him being sick in the bathroom

230

as Charlie wandered around, asking what was wrong with her brother.

Next morning Jem walked purposefully over to No. 7 with a gift of hot cross buns. She gently told Jo that Will had been going further than Meadowleaze and she herself would be home for the rest of the holiday.

'You'll need me for the summer, Mrs *Career Woman*,' sneered Jo. 'You'll need *me* to look after your kids.'

'I don't,' said Jem, backing away. 'You haven't been keeping an eye on Will. He's been roaming all over the place. I've paid you, but now the arrangement has come to an end.'

The abuse that followed her out of the front door was amazing. Jem had never heard such language. Ruth was right; she was too naïve. Jo was annoyed because she would lose a little money – but what volatile anger. Would Kim and Sasha no longer be Charlie's friends?

But it made no difference to the girls. They still turned up every day, their mother only eager to be rid of them. The two women, though, kept their distance for a long time.

In the end Jem came across an old story in a book from her childhood she had rescued from her previous life and was reading to Charlie. It was by Tolstoy and told of two girls who had been playing in a muddy pool, and their mothers scolded them for getting their clothes dirty. This turned into an argument between the mothers whilst the children returned to play in the pool. An older woman remarked the children were wiser than their parents.

With an olive branch, in the shape of a bunch of daffodils, Jem did her best to make peace with Jo. The younger woman, no less depressed and having found a

231

morning cleaning job, felt less resentful and they were talking again.

The next hurdle, but this was more of an ordeal, was the court case for assault. Due to the knife attack Rupert had been on remand in prison for five months. The fraud charges had yet to come to court in London and Jem would have no part in that.

Both she and Craig were sent subpoenas in early May. Jem found her funeral suit at the bottom of the wardrobe and, suitably dressed, presented herself with Craig at the court. Mr Dawes, as her lawyer, joined them and showed them the way into the court. Jem noticed, seated beside Rupert's lawyers, Gerald and Felicity. After a year and a half they looked older and their input would add trouble, she thought. What kind of people were they to ignore their only grandchildren? Rupert, having spent five months inside, had a grey pallor that didn't suit his fair looks.

She was called and recounted the tale of her husband's death, bankruptcy, her change of address, and the anonymous letters. She then had to recall seeing the white van followed by her parents-in-law's car, and driving her own car fast to the allotment. She gave her view of the assault, then was cross-examined by the defence lawyer who did his best to destroy her character – Felicity and Gerald had been busy – but she held fast.

Craig's account, stutteringly given, provided a similar picture. As a part of his evidence it came out that he was not just a boyfriend but had the intention of marrying Jem, but as her husband had returned he could not do so at present. An account of Will's part was read out. Then Daniel from the allotments gave his account.

The jury were sent away to consider their verdict. On their return they declared Rupert guilty of grievous bodily harm and the judge sentenced him to nine months. He commended Craig and Will on their behaviour, then, smiling, asked Jem if she had ever before had a proposal of marriage in a court of law. Apart from Rupert and the Somerville-Thomases looking grim, everyone left the court smiling.

Mr Dawes led them down the steps out of the court. He was laughing.

'Given a couple of months I'll have good news for you about the divorce. Well done. Jemima, you did so well in the witness box.'

The couple were left to walk away, hand in hand.

They stopped off for a drink at the Queen's Head, partly to celebrate, and partly to calm down. Some of the locals knew of the court case and asked of the outcome. Craig could have had free pints all evening, but as they sat at a small round table he started fiddling with a beer mat and became serious.

'Rupert's got nine months. He's already been in prison on remand for five months. With good behaviour he could be out in two months. Say, July. What's life going to be like then? He's going to want revenge.'

'But the other case, fraud, surely that will have taken place by then and he'll be in jail for years.'

'I hope you're right.'

'Forget about it for today. Let's get home and tell the children all went well. That should please them.'

Life continued peacefully. Jem took a week off from work at the hospital over half term and the three of them enjoyed their week together. Will was told he wasn't going out with Luke and his mates, and, after his experience with too much lager, accepted this. Jem kept them busy with bike rides, a visit to the museum, and hiring videos for the evening, when the front room seemed to be full of children from the cul-de-sac. Jem felt it was a time for her to re-establish the bond she had with the children after a traumatic year.

True to his word, Mr Dawes contacted Jem in July. The couple went to see him one warm sunny afternoon.

'I'm delighted to tell you that the decree absolute has come through, so, Jemima, you are now divorced and free to marry again. I'll ask my secretary for a celebratory cup of coffee.'

Over the coffee the necessary paperwork was done.

'I need to pay you for all this,' Jem said.

'It was very straightforward. You could have legal aid, but that has to be repaid. Your family has given me much work in the past. Let's make this my wedding present. I'm perhaps one of the few people who understand what you've been through since Rupert's death – I mean accident.'

'Thank you. You've always been a great help. A support in changing times.'

'Now, the other piece of good news – well, at least from your point of view – is that Rupert's trial for fraud will begin at the Old Bailey in a fortnight.'

Craig gave an audible sigh of relief. 'I thought that might be the case. I hope the press don't find out that you were his wife, Jemima. That combined with the assault charge could be newsworthy to the gutter press. Forewarned is forearmed, as they say.'

'I'll keep out of the way, not talk about it and warn the children to do the same.'

'Presumably Rupert will be sent to prison and you and

the children should both be safe for at least four years,'
Mr Dawes said. 'But judging by other similar cases he
may only be in prison for that length of time, taking into
account good behaviour. It's something for you to think
about. The police have ways of giving you a new identity
in a new area, but do you want that, having uprooted
yourself once already?'

'Thank you, Mr Dawes,' said Craig. 'You've been
talking about a situation that's been worrying me as well.'

'That's a long time away,' said Jem. 'Now I'm looking
forward to another holiday at Butlins and a wedding.'

Feeling like old friends they shook hands with the
solicitor and left to begin a new life.

There was a double celebration at home as the school term
had finished and the children were happy to have six
weeks of freedom ahead of them. Jem had given up on
childcare, as it was too expensive. The children asked if
Tina could come and stay, as she would be on vacation,
but, remembering Tina and Craig in the garden shed, Jem
thought this was a bad idea. The children had been
enrolled at a holiday club at the school for two weeks.
They would all have two weeks away together. She just
hoped if she came home at lunchtime but worked later in
the afternoon it would be all right.

Meanwhile a wedding, however small, took some
organising. Booking their slot at the registry office in
Quakers Friars, finding the necessary birth and old
wedding certificates. Jem hadn't realised Craig was two
years younger than her. Finding out when Debbie was free
to come to the ceremony and babysit. This was her
wedding present to them: to look after Will and Charlie
for a weekend so the young couple could have two days to

themselves. Visiting charity shops with bored children so they would look reasonably smart was difficult. Charlie had a tantrum and it dawned on Jem she wanted to be a bridesmaid. 'I want to wear a long dress,' she wailed. Jem revised her plans. Find an outfit for herself, then Charlie's dress.

Carrie insisted on coming with her as she enjoyed shopping, even in charity shops. In the end they decided on a pale blue dress and jacket. 'No hats,' said Jem, remembering the pretentious weddings of the past.

Carrie looked disappointed.

Jem relented and smiled. 'Do what you like.' Whose wedding was it? At least they had found a dress that Charlie liked, and Carrie was happy to take up the hem to suit her small frame.

For the so-called reception they decided on a barbecue in the cul-de-sac. All were asked if they would bring their own food and drink. Ruth and Joel volunteered to do the cooking. If it rained they would all get wet.

The big day arrived. The ceremony was arranged for Friday afternoon as all the Saturdays were booked up. Amidst the shoppers everyone tried to park their cars. Bill Edwards arrived in his best suit straight from his office in the council house. Carrie and Dave were there, Dave having been chosen to give Jem away. 'Give her away from what to what?' he asked.

Craig's mum gave Jem a bunch of freesias because no one had remembered flowers, and the ceremony, in its civil, impersonal way, went ahead. Charlie felt proud to be the bridesmaid and hold her mother's flowers. Jem was now Mrs Craig Jones. There were photos and confetti. It was a random collection of people. Apart from Craig's family, including Effie and Dud, few were related to one another. Mr Dawes was there, along with Bill Edwards and Susan, Vera and Bert, Janet from the tennis club, Carrie and her family, even Tina. A random crowd, but they had all come together because they cared. The cars were found, one with a parking ticket, and they returned to Meadowleaze for the party.

Joel and Ruth had the barbecue going, sausages and onions wafting an inviting smell over the area. Their older sons, Luke and Matthew, were setting up the stereo. Mr and Mrs Jones returned to the music of Dolly Parton's 'I Will Always Love You'. Soon the residents of the cul-de-sac including Jo, Charlene and the children, but missing Darren Sparks out looking after his illegal empire, had spilled out onto the path into the garden, and through the evening they toasted the bride and groom. They danced to U2 and Queen. The young ones found the adults' gyrations embarrassing and escaped to play games on Luke's computer; Luke's parents had given him computer games as it stopped him mixing with the Sparks's gang. Much to the children's amusement a police car arrived with blue lights flashing and asked the wedding party to turn down the noise. The police left after a hot dog apiece and glasses of wine that no one would mention.

In the morning Craig and Jem left in her car for a weekend away. No one knew where, and no one asked what went on.

On Mrs Jones's return she found a note from Mr Dawes. It read, 'This is your mother's inheritance to you. She would be very happy about today and would hope you will use this wisely.'

Good old Mr Dawes, thought Jem, as she looked at the

cheque. He had been like the grandfather she had never had.

She knew what Craig would like to do with the money. Did she want to do the same? Would this buy the land they needed? Before Craig needed to know anything she would ring round the estate agents.

Casually over supper she asked Craig how much land a nursery needed. 'That is, of the plant variety,' she added.

'The one I've been thinking of, about half an acre. You're not pregnant, are you?'

'No. I was just wondering. I don't want any babies just yet. Later. First we've got to get the kids to accept you permanently. Can we get a double bed in that box room, or do we gently turf one of your stepchildren from their haven? There are wicked stepmothers in stories, but are there wicked stepfathers?'

'Of course not. Stepfathers are all good, and I don't want to rock the boat. They've been great so far. Perhaps I can build in a base and we can just buy a mattress.'

There were many things that needed to settle down and be thought about. Babies were the last thing on Jem's list, but not on Craig's.

Three weeks later, after a happy time away at Butlins, the children were back at school and Jem was back at work. One lunchtime she picked up the post and an estate agent had sent through details of several parcels of land. One looked quite reasonable. 'A small field next to a farm on the agricultural levels north of Avonmouth.' The farmer had been letting out the land to horse owners, but now he was retired he needed a larger lump sum to help out with his pension. She would take the children on a drive after school with the excuse of walking Buster and have a look.

The field was flat, but slightly higher than fields nearer the estuary. It was surrounded by a hedge full of colourful autumn berries, and some ash trees on the far border. It met approval from Will and Charlie with 'It's pretty' and 'Buster would like it', so she returned to Northfields wondering what Craig would make of the idea of half an acre.

In the evening Jem asked the children to be very good for an hour. She wanted to take Craig out for a drink.

'You're not taking my new dad away, are you?' Charlie asked warningly.

'No, darling. There's something I want to tell him quietly.'

'It won't be quiet in the pub.'

'But they can talk man to man, or woman to man, without us being in the way. It's serious stuff, but we can take it!' Will was developing a schoolboy's sense of humour and an insight into the world beyond his horizons. 'May have to do with land.'

As they strolled to the pub Jem told Craig of inheriting some money from her mother, of which Rupert had known nothing. It was enough to buy half an acre of agricultural land between Avonmouth and the Severn Bridge.

'Could you, would you like to, make a nursery out of it? It's been used as a horse paddock for many years.'

Craig looked distinctly dazed.

'I'll buy us a double whisky,' suggested Jem as they arrived at the Queen's Head.

It was a mild evening, so they sat outside at one of the trestle tables. A friend of Craig's wandered by. 'Not feeling too good, mate? Sitting outside's bad for your health.'

'Get lost, Barry. I'm thinking.'

239

'What have you done to him, Missis?' asked Barry, laughing.

'Get lost, Barry,' Jem repeated. She could be quite threatening when she wanted.

Craig turned to her. 'You mean this?'

'Yes.'

'Money like that doesn't happen to people like me. Well, if it does, people either try to get a mortgage or buy a car.'

'This could happen if you wanted to start a nursery. You've always said it was your dream. How would you set about it?'

'Where did you say it was?'

'Farmland between Avonmouth and Aust.'

'It would be quite low-lying. Alluvium. Wonder what the drainage is like? Did you say it was a horse paddock? All that manure would be good. Could I go organic? I need to see it.'

'What would you grow?'

'Everything,' he said, throwing his arms wide.

As they wandered home he talked of the plants he might grow, seedlings for garden centres, older and herbaceous plants that would take longer to nurture. A polytunnel. The autumn would be a good time to start. He would have fewer clients and could get the ground prepared.

'I didn't realise you'd been thinking about this for so long.'

'Along with going to New Zealand, it's been a daydream since I started work. In my mind I can imagine it. I can see you doing the sales, handing over polyanthus plants at so much a pot. So come March you can pack in your job in the mending legs department, and work with me on the seedlings and summer flowering plants for pots and hanging baskets.'

240

'Me?' asked Jem.

'Why not? You like gardening.'

'But my job. The hospital. Money.'

'If you want this nursery to work, this would be the best way. Keep on working till March. We can save as much as possible. I'll keep on my most lucrative clients. We'll be OK. I thought you'd like to be a gardener.'

One half of Jem, angry, felt, *The Man has taken over again. Do I want this? It's my own fault for suggesting it. But he's not Rupert. We can do it together.*

'Yes. Now you come to talk about it the idea is appealing.' She took his hands in hers. 'We'll make a go of it together.'

The farmer, Jim Clutterbuck, was pleased to sell his land to a young gardener. 'That's the way cultivating the land is going now. Profitable dairy farming is disappearing. Having my farmhouse next door will deter vandals and thieves. And don't worry about flooding – we're just above the flood plain here. You can see where the land starts to rise towards Almondsbury.'

Craig and Jem spent the winter evenings planning the nursery. The children were content with their stepfather's being there all the time. He took them both to football matches and the cinema and bought them fish and chips, so he was 'ace'. Even Doris's Sunday visits were acceptable with the puddings she brought and the games she played with them. After Gran the children had assumed all elderly people couldn't talk, but Doris, as they knew from Butlins, talked all the time.

During the winter Craig borrowed a rotivator from a mate and between routine jobs started to cultivate his half-acre. He bought a polytunnel and started planting out seeds under cover. His plans were coming together. Jem couldn't get over the change in Craig as he worked so enthusiastically. Charlie, too, was interested, but Will, having got tired of rotivating, was unimpressed. More often he wanted to be off with his friends, some older boys, and Jem was too busy to notice.

By March Jem had given in her notice at the hospital. She was sorry to leave, as she would miss the company of women like herself, children taking up their time, some with problems and entangled partners, but she was eager to start her new life.

Now began the happiest time she could ever remember. Everything was a surprise and different. She had no idea of the depth of Craig's knowledge on gardening.

Craig had kept in touch with Fred Tucker, his mentor, who had often helped him out with a plant problem. Fred was curious to see Craig's nursery and came to visit. Jem, pausing in potting geraniums to shake muddy hands with Craig's old friend, could sense the bond between them and the help Fred would be.

They had erected a small shed by the gate where Craig kept his tools. Beside it he put up a sign saying, 'Jem's Garden Centre', which pleased her. Jem had put in a Calor gas cylinder so they could boil up a kettle, or fry eggs and bacon at weekends when the children sometimes came to help. After Saturday football Will and some mates would grudgingly come along and do some weeding, as the countryside for some of them was a novelty.

Here again Craig seemed wise. 'The kids are fine. It'll do them good. But they are bored and difficult. The comp is looming and they'll soon be trouble.'

Charlie came to the nursery uncertainly until Craig found her an area for her own garden. The child wanted instant prettiness so Jem took her to charity shops looking for shells and fossils, a treasure hunt they both enjoyed. Once the alyssum and lobelia started flowering it was easier.

An unexpected pleasure was going once a week to the local market at the nearest small town. They set up a stall in the marketplace. Jem had the feeling she had gone back to medieval times and should be wearing a long skirt and wimple, selling flowering plants, herbs and young vegetables. There were people to talk to, and cash changing hands. Customers got to know the couple and asked for advice. They became part of the local scene and got to know the gossip in the Market Inn at lunchtime.

Another surprise was living outside in the presence of the natural life of the countryside. Jem had assumed she had learnt all about natural history at school. She knew what a robin looked like, and a rabbit. Yes, that flower was a primrose. But living with nature was different. She had had no idea about the different wild flowers and bought a book to identify them. Craig just regarded them as weeds. Jim Clutterbuck, the farmer, was delighted to tell her about the birds and taught her to recognise them and their calls. The first time she saw a kestrel hover and then dive on a mouse amazed her.

She was outside hoeing in the twilight and a badger lumbered by. Delighted, she told Craig. He was annoyed and installed a low electric fence. 'They'll dig everything up,' he said.

These were three very happy years, but all good things come to an end.

PART TEN

Craig had been warning her of change for twelve months. He remembered his own past and teenage years. He could see in Will's manner the gradual dissolution of ideas and ambitions. Although exams and college were the way to a better future, he just wanted to bum around with his mates imbibing their thoughts, alcohol and drugs. There was nothing in Northfields or the school. The boys he mixed with and the overly made-up girls he occasionally brought home had the same behaviour. The future was bleak and with no exams and no money they were trapped, without the encouragement and vision to find a way out.

Jem tried to understand this way of thinking in terms of her own childhood. She had been used to parents and schools that pushed her in the right direction. Now, having told Will and Charlie to think of themselves as being in a foreign land five years ago, she had more understanding of the words she had said. A foreign world had become home. The different way of life had made them accept the views of their neighbours and friends. They were great people, her neighbours, but she had always expected her children to have the wish to rise to college and university, to live in places they chose to live in, rather than Meadowleaze. Despite the fact she enjoyed living in the district, she expected her children to want more from life, although she herself no longer wanted it.

Craig's nursery was going well but she could tell he wanted change. To sell out and move on to his goal of emigration and New Zealand.

Craig was more aware of Will's problems and his increasingly awkward, irritating ways. Staying out late, rudeness, not working and bunking off school. He remembered his own uncomfortable teenage experience. Even the police, who had been so suspicious when Olive had fallen down the stairs, stopped Jem in the precinct one day and warned her of her son's behaviour. He had been seen throwing bricks at the windows of a derelict building on the other side of the estate.

Craig, thinking back, said, 'I know. Throwing bricks was an outlet. Made you feel powerful. "I'm the king," I used to shout, and I'd sing, "We are the champions, my friends." At the time it was great. It was frustration. I didn't know where I was going. Now I do.'

'It takes time and patience,' mused Jem, 'to sort yourself out. It happens to most teenagers. If you're lucky, parents keep you on the right track, but you resent it.'

'Well, you know where my thoughts are heading.'

'Yes. New Zealand.'

But the first sadness had nothing to do with Will. Buster died. Rupert had given Buster to Jem when they had moved into their smart new home when she was expecting Will. Buster had been Will's companion for his entire life. He died quietly of old age but the family were very sad. Even Ruth gave them some flowers, as he had been a companion to everyone in the road for five years.

*

245

The summer holidays were now upon them. Will was being very difficult and spent little time at home. It was no surprise when the police brought him home one evening saying he had been offensive to other people down in the precinct.

Will stomped off to bed with a challenge: 'Are you going to beat me, like my father?'

'Of course not. Just go to bed.'

A week later he didn't come home all night. Jem was out of her mind with worry. He was only twelve. Who was leading him astray? She had seen him talking to Darren Sparks's cousin at the end of the road. She should have been home more frequently, to keep an eye on him, but she had been busy in the nursery garden. Craig drove around the entire estate looking for him. The police brought him home at five in the morning.

The policewoman sat down in the kitchen without being asked. 'This is a final warning. Your son was found in the woods smoking cannabis. He's only twelve and is under the influence of older boys who use him as a drug runner. He has little idea of his mates' ideas, but wants to be "big and strong" in the eyes of the bad boys pretending to be his friends. I hope you can keep him under control. Otherwise he will end up with a criminal record. He's been acting as their messenger, taking drugs to other people, without realising what he is doing. As a reward he's been given a smoke to get him addicted. I think he should have a better future than the Sparks family. It's up to you.'

Craig had taken Will upstairs. He needed a shower and a clean start. Charlie was so pleased to see him it made the homecoming easier. There could be no harsh words.

Craig came downstairs, wound up. 'We've done everything we can for Will.'

'I could have done more. Been here more often.'

'I know. It wouldn't have made any difference. We need a new beginning. Your first husband will be out of prison next year. I don't want to confront him again. He'll be angry, bitter, want revenge and take it out on the kids. How about it? Sell up and go to New Zealand? A new life for us all. You know it's what I've always wanted.'

Jem burst into tears. 'I like it here. The people. They've become my friends. Proper friends. Charlie likes it here too. But Will! Would a new place make a difference?'

'What if his dad got in touch with him? He's obviously vulnerable to persuasion if the Sparks family have got to him. I don't know. Let's sleep on it. That's what my mother would say.'

Doris might have slept on it, but Jem couldn't. In the few hours left until it was time to arise again to another day Jem just lay there. What did she want? What was most important? Craig and the children. Nothing else mattered. She needed to find out more about New Zealand, and what the children thought about emigration. She hadn't realised Craig had been finding out much more from his cousin in New Zealand and the Embassy about market gardening in the North Island and there was a promising future.

The police had frightened Will enough about the future awaiting him, if he kept the same company, to keep him home for some time. But he was equally scared of the Sparks's gang, and their influence, if he left their company. He had seen the bullying inflicted on older boys. He bunked off school and spent hours playing on Luke's PlayStation, unbeknown to either parent.

After weeks of soul searching and looking through information from the New Zealand Embassy, and talking to the

247

children as adults who could understand, Craig and Jem made the decision to emigrate.

'Do you remember how we became explorers when we moved here, learning to live in a different house with different people? We adjusted and enjoyed the company round here. We've become more tolerant – putting up with Bert's drunken singing and Jo's bad temper.'

The children looked wary.

'Now we're going to be explorers again in a new continent,' enthused Jem. 'A new climate, different countryside – mountains, sulphur springs, snow in the south, more sunshine. New races of people and ways of life. We've done it once. We can do it again.'

'I don't want to,' shouted Charlie. 'I like it here. I like playing with my friends. I don't want to go!'

'I do,' exclaimed Will. 'I hate it here, and the thought of meeting Dad again. There will be blue sea. I could take up surfing.'

Charlie, aware of the police and tension around the home, grudgingly agreed. Not knowing what the future held.

Jem had no family to leave, but Craig's mother was upset.

'I've known you've wanted this for many years. I've seen the way Will is too. I know it will be best for you, but I will miss you. Butlins and Christmases. But Debbie's here with Rajdeep. Fancy a daughter of mine being married to a doctor. And the baby is due in five months. I'm looking forward to that and perhaps looking after a grandson or daughter when Debbie goes back to work.'

The nursery garden was put on the market. Jim, the farmer, said he would be sorry to see them go, but Fred Tucker, Craig's past mentor, was more than happy to add it to his growing chain of nurseries. As Jim had said, this was the way things were going. People watched too many television gardening programmes and bought plants, whether they understood them or not.

At last, after much form-filling, legal negotiation and packing they were prepared to leave. A container was parked outside the semi and their meagre possessions packed inside, except for Will's bike, which he gave to Tom, and Charlie's dolls' house, which she gave to Martha. The container would arrive in Auckland in two months. Before that they would live in rented accommodation whilst they found some land. Jem had her typing qualifications and a good reference from the hospital, so her chances of finding work were good.

There were tearful goodbyes from Ruth, Joel and their family. Vera and Bert too were sorry to see them go. Charlene and Jo said they would also miss them. But, of course, the worst goodbye was from Craig's mum and Debbie.

At last they were on the plane out of Heathrow. The children were at one minute excited, and the next missing Northfields. Will seemed relieved to be away from the Sparks's gang, but Charlie was sad on leaving her friends. Her mother reassured her there would be new friends, and warm sea for swimming and surfing.

Jem was doubly happy, now certain a baby was on the way. When they were finally in the air heading towards the southern hemisphere, she told Craig, who was delighted.

'That's marvellous. A new beginning, new life and a new family. You're great. You and those disreputable children. I'm so glad I came to look after your garden all those years ago.'

A couple of hours later Jem was flicking through an in-flight magazine about New Zealand and its attractions.

'I didn't realise there was skiing in the South Island. I wonder if Will and Charlie remember what they learnt. I'm sure they would love to ski again. And I could teach you. It was pretty exciting – high snowy mountains and the peace.'

Craig took her hand. 'It wouldn't be good for the baby. No, you're not going skiing.'

'Why not?'

'Rupert. The North Col – you shouldn't talk in your sleep.' Rubbing his thigh, which still pained him, he added, 'Pity you didn't do the job properly. It would have caused us far less trouble.'

Jem thought back to the snow-clad mountains so many years ago. How life had changed. No more comfortable wealth, but by exploring a different world she had gained more understanding of people, and realised that often the least of people were the most important.